MY MOTHER'S SHOES

MY MOTHER'S SHOES

ELIZABETH JEAN ALLEN

YELLOWBACK MYSTERIES
JAMES A. ROCK & COMPANY, PUBLISHERS
ROCKVILLE • MARYLAND

My Mother's Shoes by Elizabeth Jean Allen

is an imprint of JAMES A. ROCK & CO., PUBLISHERS

My Mother's Shoes copyright ©2008 by Elizabeth Jean Allen

Special contents of this edition copyright ©2008
by James A. Rock & Co., Publishers

Address comments and inquiries to:

YELLOWBACK MYSTERIES
James A. Rock & Company, Publishers
900 South Irby Street, #900, Florence, SC 29501

E-mail:
jrock@rockpublishing.com   lrock@rockpublishing.com
Internet URL: www.rockpublishing.com

Trade Paper EAN: 978-1-59663-586-9

Library of Congress Control Number: 2007932047

Printed in the United States of America

First Edition: 2008

For my husband,

Chris,

whose love
and support
I cannot live without.
Thank you.

CHAPTER ONE

Once upon a time, life was simple for the everyday princess. Oh sure, she had to deal with fire-breathing dragons, vicious stepmothers, and poisoned apples, but the problems were temporary. She would eventually be rescued by Prince Charming and *live happily ever after.*

I picked up the tray, groaning under its weight, and started weaving my way through the crowd to the table of men in the corner. I'd known most of them since kindergarten. Not one of them qualified as Prince Charming.

Prince Charming exists. I grew up under the shadow of Lynette O'Reilly Natali Matthews Sheridan Pruitt LeBlanc. To survive that, you had to believe in fairy tales. *Prince Charming is out there hiding in a room full of toads. Kiss enough toads and you'll find your Prince Charming.*

Right. So you find your Prince Charming, what then?

The storybooks end with *and they lived happily ever after.* They don't tell you that Prince Charming morphs back into a toad after a year or so. Instead of charming his wife, he's happily clipping his toenails at the kitchen table and belching over beer with his buddies on Saturday night.

I set the tray down and started distributing the drinks. My mother married five times, had numerous affairs, and never found a Prince Charming. What are the odds of my finding one on the first try?

Thousand-to-one? No, living in the city the odds may be a thousand-to-one, but here in Small Town, USA, the odds are higher. There just aren't enough Prince Charmings to go around. So I married a toad and called him a prince. What else could I do?

My name is Annie Natali—actually it's Rosetti until the divorce is finalized. Getting married is easy. All it takes is $25, a couple of promises, and a signature on the dotted line.

I did it. I signed my name and committed my life to a toad. That was two years, two weeks, and three days ago. I understand why the judge insisted that I sign the document in pen. I can't erase my name and pretend it never happened.

My mother married five times and ended up in divorce court four times. The fifth time around she didn't bother with the lawyer. She wrote her husband a note, rolled it up, secured it with her wedding ring, and disappeared into the night.

I glanced around at the men sitting at the table. "Do you want anything from the grill tonight?"

A chair scraped back and another man dropped down at the table. I glanced up and my smile faltered. I sucked in a breath and bared my teeth in what I hoped passed for a smile. It was the best I could do under the circumstances. "Good evening Jay, what can I get for you?"

"Does Mark know you're slinging drinks in this dive?"

First off, the Mountain isn't a dive. Well, it was a dive when my daddy bought it, but the glasses are washed between uses now, the liquor's not watered down, and there hasn't been a fight in over a week.

Secondly, I don't sling drinks, though pouring one over the top of my brother-in-law's head did have a certain appeal. Unfortunately I had already handed out the beers, so Jay's natty little sweater and silk shirt were safe.

I don't like him. I tried, honest to God I tried, but Jay acts like he's a direct descendent of Zeus, the supreme ruler of the gods and lord of the skies. He's not. He's a toad.

"Do you want something from the bar or not?" I needed the tips more than I needed to wipe the smirk of Jay's face. I drove to Raleigh last week and talked to three different lawyers. They all insisted on money up front. I work for Harry Pruitt's building and construction firm, and since leaving Mark, I'm back to helping my dad out a couple of nights a week as well.

I make enough money working for Harry to live, but that's it. I saved my tips for over six years to come up with the money to buy my car, and then I had to keep working to pay the insurance. In another six years I might have the money to file for divorce.

"I want to know why you're here instead of at home where you belong." Jay snapped me out of my reverie and back to attention.

"If you're not ready to order, I'll come back." I glanced around as I started backing away. Jay has one of those deep, gravely voices that can be heard across a football stadium even when he whispers. A hundred pairs of eyes were riveted on us.

Jay grabbed my arm stopping my retreat. "Why did you walk out on Mark?"

"Stay out of it, Jay." I couldn't tell him. Not here. Not with half the town listening in. The vultures would swoop down and attack. The gory details would be spread from one end of town to the other. There would be no living with the stink.

"Amy said Mark was better off without you. She's right, but he wants you back." Jay shrugged as if he didn't understand it but was willing to go along with it for his brother's sake.

Shut up! Shut up! Shut up! Don't make me say it. Please Lord, strike him mute.

"If you come home, he's willing to forgive and forget." Jay's lips peeled back into a sneer. "I'm not surprised. I told Mark to get off his knees, but he wouldn't do it. You've been leading him around by the nose since before you guys were married."

What! My Irish temper and the need for justice just trumped the desire for a quiet, amicable divorce. I'm the wounded party here, not Mark. "Do you know why I left Mark?" My words were quiet, belying the anger behind them.

The men at the table shifted back out of the line of fire.

Jay shrugged then held his hands out, palms up. "I know what you accused him of, but it's not true. You're just like your mother, looking for an excuse to leave a good man."

"I'm not my mother!"

"Right."

"I walked in on Mark bonking his secretary on the floor of his office. They were both bare-ass naked and panting like a couple of mad dogs—and he wants *me* to apologize! Why? Was it because I forgot to knock?"

"That's bullshit! Mark wouldn't … not in the office … not with …" Jay's denials tumbled out before my words truly registered, and then his words stumbled to a halt.

My smile was as thin as the cutting edge of a knife. Dignity be damned. I was going for the throat. "Amy set me up. She called and told me Mark had some papers he wanted me to sign and could I stop by on my lunch break. Now do you think he would have been rolling around on the floor with his secretary if he knew his wife was stopping by?"

Jay's mouth opened and closed, but no sound came out. Recovering, he shoved away from the table knocking his chair over in the process. His eyes were hot and his face florid. "You're lying!"

I scrambled back. Would I ever learn the meaning of the word prudence?

Doug Matthews pushed away from the table and grabbed Jay's arm jerking him back. "Cool off before you do something stupid."

"Let go of me!"

Doug tightened his grip. "Think! You touch her and her father will take you apart."

"I don't care!"

"Maybe you don't, but I can't let you beat on the kid just because she had the guts to tell you the truth."

Jay stumbled back. The quiet words packed a powerful punch. He didn't want to believe it, but he did. I could see it in his eyes.

"Mark and Amy." It wasn't a question, just a bald statement of fact.

"Yes."

Jay eased his arm free of Doug's grip. He glanced at me then back at Doug. Grabbing his jacket off the back of the chair, he elbowed his way through the crowd and out the door.

I wanted to cry. Good intentions didn't mean much when they

could be underscored by a few callous words from a jerk. Mark was the guilty party, but I'm Lynette O'Reilly's daughter. As long as the gossips didn't know why I left Mark, all they could do was speculate. Now with a few facts to twist, the story would grow and mutate, taking on a life of its own. Before you know it, it will be as deadly as the creature from the Black Lagoon.

"Annie."

I glanced up at Doug. He wasn't Prince Charming, but he was a friend, and for a few short years he was my stepbrother. "Thanks for coming to my rescue. I knew better than to goad him."

"You didn't. He was goading you."

"So? It won't make a difference."

"Annie, you're not your mother."

"How can I be sure? My marriage only lasted two years. Lynette's usually lasted three years. She even made it to her fourth anniversary once."

"Annie, don't."

"Father Nolan is going to damn me to hell for all of eternity." Or tell me to go home. He's always telling us forgiveness is a virtue. In time, I could probably forgive Mark, but a good marriage requires trust. The only way I could trust Mark to keep his tallywacker in his pants would be to cut it off and put it in his pocket, and then what good would it do me?

"Father Nolan won't damn you to hell. This mess is Mark's fault, not yours. Now, what is Mark's cell phone number?"

"Why?"

"Jay's liable to kill him."

Hmmm, a funeral instead of a divorce. It was a thought.

Forget it. You'd have to wear black for a year.

"Annie, give me the number."

Sighing heavily, I rattled off the number before turning away. A new wardrobe would be nice, but I've never cared for the Goth look. Besides, if I thought Father Nolan would damn me to hell for considering divorce, what would he say to murder?

It isn't Mark so much as the gossips that keep me looking for a way out of this mess. I'm so tired of being compared to my mother. I inherited her stature, her love of shoes, and her curly red hair. That's were the similarities end. Too bad no one believes me.

I kept my eyes averted as I made my way back to the bar. It wouldn't make a difference. Fresh fodder was fresh fodder. I could almost see Edna Telley rubbing her hands together and cackling before reaching for the phone.

The old witch. How would she like it if everyone knew her daughter shared more than just a drink with Ralph McPearson the last time they traveled to Charlotte on business?

"Annie."

I glanced up and felt some of the tension ease when I saw my best friend standing by the bar. Tabby is the absolute best friend in the world. If I need a shoulder to cry on, I can count on her to pull out a box of tissues and help me mop up the tears. She isn't a sucker for a sob story though. I turned to her for sympathy more than once and ended up with a swift kick in the ass.

"Hey. What can I get for you?"

Tabby slid onto one of the stools near the end of the bar and grinned. "I thought Tony only had live entertainment on Friday and Saturday nights.

I felt my face heat up until it matched my hair.

Tabby laughed at my discomfiture. "I need to drop another 20 in the pool before the odds change."

"What! People are betting on me?"

"Sure. Most of the guys figure Mark's bank account will lure you back, but the women figure it's the fit of his jeans." Tabby fanned her face with her hand. "Either way, odds are leaning toward reconciliation. Most figure you'll be back with Mark by Memorial Day." Tabby's grin widened. "Why are you surprised? Money changed hands every time your mother said I do."

"I'm not my mother!" I knew the town's people bet on the longevity of my mother's marriages. Most people like to gamble and they like to win. Lynette's marriages were predictable, making the odds better than the average scratch-off lottery ticket. I went into my marriage believing in Mark, in us. Finding out his love was an illusion cut to the bone.

Tabby sobered. "What are you doing here anyway? It's a weeknight."

I shrugged rather than answer. I wasn't willing to think about the dismal state of my finances let alone talk about it.

"Annie ..."

I cut her off. Once Tabby latched onto a subject, she would beat it to death and then dissect it. If I liked dissecting things, I would have taken biology in high school. I don't, so I didn't. I took astronomy and earth science. My choices were prophetic. I shot for the moon, missed, and ended up burying my head in the sand.

I grabbed another set of mugs and started filling them. "What can I get for you?"

"Billy will get your order." A big burly hand wrapped around my arm and yanked me back. Luckily I already set the mugs down or there would have been beer everywhere. "I need to talk to the kid."

The Irish are known for their tempers, but an angry Italian can match it shout for shout. If the grip on my arm was any indication, my father was fighting back a rage that rivaled the eruption of Mount Vesuvius when it buried the city of Pompeii. At a guess I'd say he now knew why I left Mark. "Dad, relax."

He gave me a shove sending me through the swinging doors into the kitchen and on to his office in the back. Apparently his anger wasn't directed just at Mark. He stepped ahead of me and grabbed my arm again. He was pulling me now instead of pushing. Twenty-seven years old and he was dragging me along like a petulant child.

"Daddy ..."

He yanked the door of his office open and pulled me through it. With a quick shove, I landed in a chair with a thump.

"Why didn't you tell me?"

"Daddy ..."

"Why?" He loomed over me. It wasn't the first time he'd used his size to intimidate me into confessing all.

I put my hand on his arm and stared up at him beseechingly. "I love you Daddy." I couldn't out shout him and I couldn't intimidate him, so there was no point in trying. There was only one thing left to do. The tears welled up.

"You're not getting around me that way. Now answer the damn question!"

I slumped back in the chair. So much for the poor-pitiful-me routine. "I told you."

"You told me you left Mark. You didn't tell me why."

"I didn't think you wanted to know. When I told you, you just shook your head and went back to serving drinks."

"I thought you left him for …" His words trailed off.

I abruptly sat up and nudged him back so I could stand. He didn't nudge worth a damn, but I kept pushing until he took a step back. "You thought I left Mark for another man."

"What was I supposed to think?"

"You might have asked me. You might have a little faith in me."

"I do."

"Right." I didn't even try to keep the skepticism or the hurt out of my voice.

"Annie …"

"I'm short and I have Lynette's curly red hair. We share the same preference in shoes and we both think of heaven in terms of charge cards with no credit limits and free access to the mall. And we both have lousy luck with men. That's where the similarities end. I'm not my mother!" I pushed past him, grabbed the doorknob intent on escape, and then I was airborne.

My butt landed back in the chair again. "Damn it Annie! I was wrong. The least you could do is give me a chance to apologize."

"Why should I?"

"Because I'm your old man. You know I'm stupid, but you love me anyway. Give me a chance to make it up to you."

"Gee, you sound like Mark." I sniffed. "He said the same thing to me. Do you want me to forgive him too?"

Daddy's eyes glittered. "Don't even think about it."

I crossed my arms over my chest, anger coming to the rescue. "Don't worry. When Lynette left, she left. She never gave men, *or me*, a second chance. As I'm my mother's daughter ..."

"Damn it Annie, I didn't mean that!" He raked his hand through his hair. It was a familiar gesture. He was frustrated, not really sure how the conversation turned on him.

"You probably have customers six deep by now, and you left Billy out there alone." Reminding him of his responsibility to his customers and to his business was the only way I could think of to end the argument. Accepting his apology was out of the question. He spoke without thinking, which meant he spoke the truth. He would always see me as my mother's daughter. No matter how hard I tried, so would everyone else in town. Small town living. You gotta love it.

He glanced over his shoulder obviously recognizing the truth in my words. Seeing that, I pressed my advantage. "Go. You know the customer always comes first."

Dad swung back around. "Is that what you think of me? Was I that bad of a father?"

"No."

He glanced over his shoulder again. "I need to get back out there."

"Go."

"Annie." I didn't respond to the quiet demand in his voice so he grabbed my chin and tilted my face up until our eyes met. "You're not your mother."

Right.

I needed a couple of minutes to regroup before heading back out front. Even if I didn't need the money, I had to go back out there. If I didn't, the gossipmongers would add another chapter to tonight's saga. It wouldn't stop the talk any more than a wedding ring stopped my mother from sleeping around, but I had to try.

Why?

Maybe I should take my mother's lead, pack up, and disappear into the night. Start somewhere new where family histories and preconceived ideas didn't damn me to hell before I said a single word.

That takes money.

Right. I fished the tips out of my pocket and threw the apron aside before heading back out front. My career as a barmaid wasn't over, but I was through for the night.

I snatched a Corona out of the cooler and a slice of lime from the prep area and then stepped around to the other side of the bar. "Sorry about that." I said quietly as I slid onto the stool next to Tabby.

Tabby nodded her head toward my father. He was serving drinks at the far end of the bar. "So, I guess Mark gets to live."

I sighed heavily. I couldn't help it. Tabby's my best friend, but she's a product of her environment. Growing up, she spent more time in her mother's beauty parlor, The Curly Do, than she did at home. There's something about the pungent smell of permanent solution, shampoo, and bleach that triggers the gossip gene. It's sort of like Pavlov's dogs responding to light stimuli.

I glanced over at Tabby. She raised her eyebrow inquiringly. I sighed again. As a hairdresser, Tabby's talents are wasted. The CIA could put her to good use. Instead of interrogating suspects, offer them a perm. Truth serum and bamboo shoots would be a thing of the past.

"Dad's afraid I'll go back to him."

"That's not going to happen is it?"

"No …"

"Jesus Annie."

"What?"

"You hesitated."

"No I didn't."

"Yes you did, and if you go back to that bastard you can find a new best friend."

"What makes you think you're my best friend?"

"Humph! Did you tell anyone else about the time you spied on Luke through the hole in the wall between your bedroom and …"

"Fine, fine! You're my best friend. Now shut up."

Tabby grinned. "I didn't expect to see you here tonight. It's a week-night and you have to work tomorrow."

"So? It's early yet."

"Come on Annie, give."

"I didn't want to be home alone tonight." Realizing what I was giving away, I changed tactics. Tabby's gossip antenna was finely tuned, but hope springs eternal. I didn't want to answer any more questions tonight. "Dad was short handed so I pitched in. Besides, I could use the money."

"Why?"

"Lawyers are expensive."

"No, why didn't you want to be home alone?"

"Oh, did I say that?"

"Yes."

I chewed on my lip. I didn't want to put my thoughts to words. Thinking about it was bad enough. Saying it out loud would seal my fate. Mark wanted me back. Jay called that one right. *Forgive and forget.* He was making it hard not to. "Mark's turned up the heat."

"What did he do?"

"He sent me a pair of shoes."

CHAPTER TWO

I poured my fourth cup of coffee and wearily sat down at my desk. I stayed at the bar later than intended and drank more than was wise. Not a good thing to do when you have to work the next day.

Work? If you went back to Mark you wouldn't have to work. You could stay home, raise babies, and spend your free time shopping.

I shut off that line of thought with a groan. I wasn't giving in. Mark said he was a leg man, but he's not. He likes boobs, big bodacious 36-double-D's. As a 34-B with room to spare, I can't compete with the Amy's of the world. Every time a woman with big boobs smiled at him I would wonder. Will he break his vows again?

There's a shoe sale at Belk this weekend.

I closed my eyes and prayed for strength. I wanted to go shopping. Shopping always made me feel better. If Mark waved a Visa Card with no credit limit in front of my nose, I'm not sure what I would do. I would liked to think I would say no, but I'm not willing to bankroll my future on it. There were sacrifices and then there were *sacrifices*.

I rolled my chair back and stared at my shoes. They were nice shoes, Italian leather, comfortable … but I've worn them every day for two solid weeks. *The Southern Woman's Book of Etiquette* clearly states that a lady never wears the same shoes two days in a row. If Miss Clara, the reigning queen of etiquette and decorum, knew I wore my black leather flats every day for the last 14 days, it would take a bucket full of smelling salts to revive her.

In my defense, I haven't had a whole lot of choice. After walking in on Mark and Amy two weeks ago, I headed straight for the house. Maybe

I should have started by packing up my clothes, but I didn't. It took three trips in my little Mazda to haul all of my plants, my two cats, Palmer and Mascara, and Grammy's collection of Schwan's ice cream tins to Tabby's. When I came back for my clothes, Mark was standing in the doorway like an avenging angel.

He was pissed.

Sometimes men are so clueless. He actually thought an apology and a few flowers from the grocery store would do the trick. It was insulting. He was screwing his secretary instead of eating the tuna on rye I made for his lunch. Mark said he *loved* tuna on rye. A truck full of flowers wouldn't change the fact that he lied to me.

In any event, if I wasn't staying, and I wasn't, he wouldn't let me in the house. I had a couple pairs of jeans at dad's, and I could use some of Tabby's blouses, but damn it, I need my shoes.

A woman can't have too many pairs of shoes. It's the one and only thing my mother and I agreed upon. Can you imagine playing basketball in running shoes? It's just not done. No, to play basketball you need high tops.

Hiking boots, snow boots, flip-flops in assorted colors, slides, Crocs, leather walking shoes in black, brown and suede, platforms, black velvet pumps, penny loafers … I need my shoes more than I need my bras and panties.

You forgot to mention the stilettos.

Okay, so I have more stilettos than boots. At five-two, I need the extra height.

Why do you need the stilettos? You swore off men.

I wear stilettos because *I* like them.

Why do you really wear stilettos? It's not for the comfort, that's for damn sure. No, you wear stilettos because they're sexy. Men look at you in a pair of stilettos and they can't help but wonder what you'd look like wearing nothing but the shoes. Your mother wore stilettos. She knew, and so do you.

I jumped out of my chair and stomped around the office giving my conscience a swift kick in the ass with an imaginary stiletto while I was at it. "I'm not my mother!"

Hah! You walked out on your husband and you're considering divorce.

I wasn't unfaithful! Mark was.

So? Mark wouldn't wander if he had what he wanted at home.

And what's that?

Boobs. Your mother got implants and she went from gorgeous to stunning.

God no!

R-i-i-i-ng!

I was losing an argument with myself. I didn't want 36-inch-double-D's. I would be so top heavy, I wouldn't dare wear stilettos. I would fall flat on my face.

There's always a man around ready and willing to hold you up.

I closed my eyes and an image of my mother sprang to the forefront. She was walking out of a bar clinging to a man's arm as if her life depended on it. At least I think it was Lynette. I wanted it to be Lynette. It *couldn't* be me.

You talk the talk, but you don't walk the walk. Give up the stilettos and then we'll talk.

I bonked my head on the desk. I can stand on my own!

Not as long as you're wearing stilettos.

R-i-i-i-ng!

My choice in shoes has nothing to do with the men in my life.

What men? Are you going back to Mark or are you lusting after someone new?

I snatched up the phone. "Pruitt Building and Construction, may I help you?" The cheerful tone and the corresponding smile were forced. The call was a means to an end, a way to end an argument I couldn't win.

I never used to question my judgment. Since leaving Mark, I can't even decide between liverwurst and corn beef on rye. What difference does it make? It's not a life and death decision. Hesitating before choosing chili with beans I can understand, but liverwurst? Liverwurst doesn't even cause gas.

"Hi, babe."

My smile dropped and was replaced with a scowl. Mark always seems to know when I'm at my lowest. "What do you want Mark?"

"I just wanted to hear your voice. I miss you."

"Right." I was aiming for flippant, but it fell short of the mark. Mark was hard to resist when he turned on the charm. Back in the Garden of Eden, Eve knew the snake was charming her. She knew he was lying even as she reached for the forbidden fruit. Charmers have that kind of power. They make it impossible to say no. Mark was no exception.

He's lying, he's lying, he's lying …

"I'm serious Annie. I made a mistake. I don't like admitting it, but I am. Come home and I'll make it up to you."

"What about Amy?"

"I fired her this morning."

"Why?"

"She set me up. Annie, you're my wife. I wouldn't deliberately hurt you like that."

"Oh, it's okay to screw around as long as I don't know about it."

"That's not what I meant and you know it. I want you to come home. I'm tired of sleeping alone."

"It's only been a couple of weeks."

"It feels like a lifetime."

"You want me to forgive you?"

"Yes."

"What about Jay? Is he willing to forgive and forget?"

Mark huffed out a breath. "There's nothing to forgive. Amy only went out with Jay once. I wasn't encroaching on his territory."

"Oh. Well, was Amy encroaching on my territory? For that matter, how do you determine who was encroaching on who? Was she screwing you or were you screwing her?"

"Don't be crude!"

"Yes, it was crude, crude and disgusting."

"Annie, it was an impulse, a spur of the moment thing. It's not like we were having an affair. It was the first and only time I ever cheated on you."

"You expect me to believe that?"

"Why not? It's the truth."

"Okay, why would a faithful husband whose wife is on the pill need to carry a condom in his wallet, and keep a box for emergencies tucked in the drawer of his desk?"

"When did you go through my desk?"

"I didn't." I responded with smug satisfaction.

"Why do I put up with this?" Mark hissed quietly, more to himself than to me. "Annie, I haven't carried a condom in my wallet since high school, and I don't have a box stashed in my desk."

"Oh, well you were wearing a condom. As far as I could tell, that's all you were wearing. If you had to run over to Bradley's Drug Store before lunch, I don't think your little tryst qualifies as an impulse."

"Annie! Enough! You made your point."

"Good, so you're not going to fight the divorce."

"I said you made your point. I didn't say anything about a divorce. Come home."

"I can't. You changed the locks."

"That was to keep you from doing something stupid. Once you're back where you belong, I'll give you a key."

"Moving out was the right thing to do. Mark, I need my clothes."

He was quiet for a minute. I don't know if it was because he was seriously considering my request or using the time to reign in his temper. Mark's not a patient man. Butt that against my stubborn streak and any situation could turn explosive.

He sighed heavily. "You're right."

Finally!

"You need something to wear Saturday night."

"Saturday night?" I asked faintly. There was something and I knew it was important, but I couldn't remember what it was.

"You forgot." Disgust, resignation, and frustration were all evident in Mark's voice. It could have been feigned or it could have been real. It's hard to tell with him.

"Mark …"

"Grandma adores you. If she knew you forgot her birthday, she'd be hurt."

Oh shit.

Sarah Rosette is Mark's paternal grandmother. She was thrilled when Mark and I started dating. She said Mark needed a strong willed woman to keep him in line. Come to think of it, maybe I should have taken that as a warning instead of a blessing. "Mark, I can't."

"Annie, she's 82 and she adores you. Skipping her birthday party would break her heart."

"Blackmail's not going to work. I'll call Sarah and explain. She'll understand. Your father was a philanderer and so was your grandfather. It's a character flaw passed from one generation to the next. Those were her words, not mine."

"I said I was sorry. What more do you want?"

I didn't know how to respond to that.

"So, when are you coming home?"

A leopard can't change his spots, teenagers can't resist breaking curfew, and philanderers can't keep their peckers in their pants. That's just the way it is. "I am home."

"Fine! How bad do want your clothes?"

"Mark!"

"Come to the party with me, and I'll let you collect your clothes."

Sometimes I think Mark knows me better than I know myself. I hate wearing the same clothes day-after-day, and I'm tired of washing my panties out every night.

"Well?"

"I'm thinking."

"Come with me Annie. What's the harm in maintaining an old woman's illusions?" Mark cajoled softly.

I bit my lip. I wanted my clothes and I would love to attend the party, but not with Mark. "We drive separate cars and you let me collect my clothes tomorrow."

"I'll pick you up at seven and you can come over to the house Sunday afternoon to pick up your clothes." Mark countered.

"No. I don't trust you. Besides, I need something to wear to the party."

"Okay, I'll be over at six-thirty, and I'll bring a party dress along."

"Compromise. If you have a dictionary handy, you might want to look up the word."

"Fine. You can come by tomorrow afternoon and pick up your clothes. We'll head to the party from the house."

What? Does he think I'm crazy? "Forget it."

"Okay, I'll pick you up for the party and you can collect your clothes on Sunday."

"Okay. Get a pen and write this down. I want my blue dress, the off the shoulder one, my blue sandals, a pair of panty hose, my sapphire earrings and matching bracelet, and my little black beaded evening bag. Oh, and I need my makeup too."

"Do you want panties or a thong?"

"Stay out of my underwear drawer!"

Mark chuckled. "What's the matter Annie? Is pawing through your panties worse than dreaming about you? I keep the coconut massage oil next to the bed. When I have trouble sleeping, I rub it on my chest and go to sleep dreaming of you. It's not same, but since you left me, it's all I've got. I miss you."

I felt my resolve melting away. I had to get off the phone before I said something really stupid like telling him I missed him too. "I'll see you tomorrow."

"Later, babe."

I dropped the phone back into the cradle, pushed away from the desk, crossed over to the window, and gazed out into the empty parking lot. Going to the party with Mark was a mistake. The minute I agreed, the back of my neck started tingling. It didn't matter how much I wiggled my shoulders, it just wouldn't go away.

Genetics is a funny thing. The Irish are known for their luck, their flaming red hair, and their tempers. The Italians are known for their incredible food, their romantic cities, and yes, they tend to fly off the handle too. I'm half Irish and half Italian. Considering the mix, I should be able to play the stock market with reasonable confidence, whip up an incredible pasta primavera, and write prose that touches the heart. Nope. My Irish luck was diluted down to nonexistent; I overcook pasta, consider romance novels sappy, and my temper was multiplied by ten.

My Grammy was full-blooded Irish. I don't know how lucky she was considering her husband died right after my mother was born, but she knew things. She even knew Salvador Sanchez was going to choke to death on his dentures days before it happened. Grammy said it was *The Sight*. It was a gift, a part of her Celtic heritage.

Having *The Sight* had to be frustrating. Suppose you needed a new pair of shoes for a night out on the town, but you only have your lunch hour to shop. Unfortunately you know there's going to be an accident at the intersection of Lexington Avenue and Fifth Street. If you avoid that intersection, you'll never make it back to work on time. What do you do, forget the shoes?

I didn't inherit *The Sight* and I'm immensely thankful for that, but I inherited something. It's sort of like a heightening of the senses. I think of it as women's intuition times ten. In any event, it was tingling now.

Trouble was brewing. Going to the party with Mark wasn't the half of it.

"Annie!"

I scrambled back to my desk nearly knocking over my dieffenbachia plant in the process. All thought of Mark and the party disappeared. When Harry bellowed, he was looking for an excuse to fire someone. It wasn't personal, just his way of relieving stress. He's a big lumbering hulk of a man who likes to throw his weight around, figuratively speaking anyway. His management skills lean toward intimidation and veiled threats. For the most part, it works.

Pruitt Building and Construction is an equal opportunity employer. At least it says so on the stationary. In truth, I'm the only employee that has to sit down to pee. Harry has very narrow views on a woman's place in the world. The workplace isn't one of them.

"Yes sir." I don't like kowtowing to the attitude, but I need my job. I'm not giving him a reason to fire me. In a town this size, employment opportunities are limited and I don't want to move.

You may not have a choice.

I am pretty good at ignoring problems, at least until I figure out how to handle them. I've been ignoring this one for two solid weeks and I still haven't figured out what to do.

It's Mark's fault. When it comes to originality, he scored a big, fat zero. Everyone knows that an affair with your secretary is so cliché. It's been done to death. Someone with a little flair would have chosen a supermodel or a rock star. Barring that, he could have turned to his best friend's wife. Nope. Mark goes for his secretary who just happens to be *my* boss's daughter.

Maybe I'm creating something out of nothing. Harry hired me. I didn't think he would, but he did. He was my mother's fourth husband. Their marriage fell apart less then six months after they said I do. It didn't matter how many times Lynette stepped up to the alter; she never understood that fidelity was part of the deal. It's been years, but Harry still hasn't forgiven her.

I remind Harry of Lynette. I don't know why. Sure, we both have red curly hair, green eyes and smattering of freckles, but Lynette's only five-foot-two and I'm five-foot-two-and-a-half. She's thinner than I am and she has bigger feet. Lynette wears a seven and I only wear a six-and-a-half. We're nothing alike.

Well anyway, Harry needed a secretary and wanted a whipping post. I fit the bill. I scrub the toilets, make the coffee, process the invoices, do the payroll, and put up with his snide remarks and sexual innuendoes.

I've worked for him for nine years now. I'm pretty good at tuning him out when he starts spouting smut, and he's pretty good at tuning me out when I ask for a raise. Over all we have a fairly good working relationship.

I'm not sure how Harry will react when he gets wind of Mark and Amy's affair. He may fire me, but Harry's a shrewd businessman. Firing me would not be cost effective. He'd have to hire a secretary, a cleaning service, and put one of those 900 numbers on speed dial. I don't think he'll do it.

"Annie!"

I snapped back to attention. "Sorry. What can I do for you?"

"Take a break. Go shopping or something."

"What?" I stared at him with my jaw hanging down to my knees. Time off, as in paid time off? It wasn't possible. Harry was too tight fisted for that. Raises were doled out under duress and overtime … Harry considered overtime the curse of the lazy man. If you couldn't get your work done during regular hours, you were slacking off. Slackers dropped off the payroll with frightening regularity.

"You heard me Red, go shopping." He glanced down at my shoes and a lurid grin spread across his face. "Buy a new pair of shoes and some sexy underwear, and maybe I'll give you that raise you've been asking for."

Jerk! I'll bare my ass to the Pope before I let Harry see my panties! "You want me to buy sexy underwear?"

Harry shoved his hands in his front pockets, rocked back on his heels, and grinned. "Don't forget the shoes. You used to wear sexy shoes and now all I ever see you in is those ugly black things."

I cocked my head sideways as if considering the suggestion before reaching for the phone. I wanted to shove my *ugly black shoe* up his ass, but I need my job. Better to delegate the honor. "Marsha likes to shop. Maybe she can meet me at the mall and help me decide between French high cuts and a thong."

Harry's a big man. A lumbering hulk is a fairly apt description, but the man can move when motivated. The receiver was knocked out of my hand before I pressed the first number. "Are you nuts?"

I grinned up at him. Harry owned Pruitt Building and Construction, but Marsha owned Harry. They married a little over five years ago. He thought he was getting a trophy wife and ended up with a ball and chain. Marsha is two years younger than I am. In high school she was the captain of the cheerleading squad, but she went to the University of

North Carolina on an academic scholarship. When she came back to town five years ago and then married Harry three weeks later, even the gossipmongers were speechless.

Marsha doesn't love him. No one even considered that a possibility. No, Marsha married Harry for his money. She saw it as an investment. Harry chain smokes, drinks like a fish, and is a hundred pounds overweight. Odds are he'll be dead in another ten years.

Harry turned away from me and stared out the window. "Get out of here before I change my mind."

A shiver danced up my spine and settled down on my shoulders. "Are you firing me?"

"No, be back by one."

"Harry, what's going on?"

"Better yet, take the whole day." He turned and disappeared into his office.

I stared at Harry's retreating back for a moment and then glanced out the window. The place was empty. Harry and I were the only ones here. Everyone else was out at the new construction site.

He wants me gone.

Maybe he has a load of hot tools or high-jacked lumber coming in. With the crew out on the site, you would be the only potential witness.

I pulled the bottom desk drawer open, grabbed my purse, and slammed it shut before bolting for the door. What I didn't know couldn't hurt me.

CHAPTER THREE

Damn, damn, damn. I might as well dye my hair black and call myself Italian. Whoever coined the phrase "The luck of the Irish" had to be three sheets to the wind.

Good luck, like sweets, are doled out by the ounce. Any dieter knows that if you eat two ounces of candy, you'll gain three pounds. I had my bit of good luck. Harry gave me the day off. I knew there would be a price to pay.

I glanced down at the gas gauge. I needed gas. The plan was to stop by Hess Express on my way home from work, well after Edna Telley's shift. I would rather stick a needle in my eye than be in the same room with that old bitty. If we were in Salem, Massachusetts in the 1500's, Edna would have been the first one tied to the stake. Her forked tongue has destroyed marriages, ruined reputations, and sent stable businesses into a decline. The house next to hers has been bought and sold eight times in the last ten years.

I can make it to Speedway.

No you can't!

I glanced down again. The fuel light came on days ago and now it was blinking franticly. *Give me gas! Give me gas! Give me gas*! Swearing, I swung the wheel and pulled into the Hess Express. I wound my way around to the pumps in the back. There was a black Dodge Ram pickup parked by one of the pumps out front. I knew that truck. It was Miguel Manning's. I haven't seen Miguel in months and haven't talked to him in years. He was a part of my past, a closed door.

Be honest.

Okay, at 15, he was the center of my universe. I thought he was Prince Charming, but as luck would have it, he turned into a toad when I wasn't looking.

He's gorgeous, I can't deny that. His build was a gift from his father, broad shoulders and lean hips with every thing in between. His eyes, hair, and skin tone reflect his mother's Latino heritage. It's a heady combination.

He's still a toad. Kiss him and you'll end up with a face full of warts.

As we hadn't said ten words to each other in over 12 years, kissing is out.

You're thinking about it.

No, I'm not thinking about kissing Miguel. I'm just not thinking about walking into the Lion's den without a whip. I eased up to the pump and killed the engine. They were pay-at-the-pump pumps, but I gave up shopping for Lent. I gave all my charge cards to Mark three weeks ago. I don't think he'll give them back to me after Easter.

I stepped out of the car and girded my loins. I can do this. I walked quietly up to the building and pulled the glass door open. Half way through the door I froze.

"... Doug nearly beat that poor boy to death before Carl and Reggie managed to pull him back. It was Annie's fault. She stirs up a ruckus every time she's in the Mountain. Personally, I don't see why Tony puts up with it."

My fingers tightened on the metal frame of the door until they turned white. I was stuck somewhere between mortification and anger, not really sure which way to turn.

"Annie's working there again."

When Fate sets me up, she gives it her all. Here I was worried about what Edna would say and practicing my blank stare. The blank stare was for Miguel's benefit. I wanted to make sure he knew I hadn't forgiven him.

Well anyway, if I hadn't been so focused on that, I would have realized the time. Luke Sheridan stops in every morning to buy a cup of coffee and chat with Edna. Women aren't the only ones who like to gossip.

Luke's a detective for the Sheriff's Department now. I almost had a heart attack when the sheriff hired him. He threatened to kill me, and now he carries a gun! I have a better chance of surviving a confrontation with the Chicago Slasher or Mad Jack Calruza than Lucas Sheridan.

I heard the gurgle of the coffee machine and shifted my eyes to the left. Miguel snapped the lid on his coffee, glanced over at me, and winked. I was so flummoxed by the wink that I completely forgot about the blank stare.

"Hah! She says she's working, but she's not. That's just an excuse to hang out at the bar. That girl's so much like her mother, it's scary. She'll either latch onto a new man or rob the bank, probably both."

"Now Edna, you know Lynette was wanted for questioning, not …"

"She took off! If that isn't an admission of guilt, I don't know what is. She better not come in here and try to rob me. That's all I've got to say."

"Who are you talking about, Annie or Lynette?"

Edna shrugged. "Doesn't matter."

Luke's radio came to life. He reached down and turned up the volume. "Possible Code 27," the dispatcher's voice crackled through the speaker. "Pruitt construction site."

"Ten-four."

"Code 27? I thought a Code 27 was a homicide." Edna sucked in a breath. "Oh my God! Do you think Annie killed Mark? It would be just like her to take advantage of the situation and pin the blame on Jay."

The blood drained from my face.

Luke shook his head, but didn't respond as he pushed away from the counter and turned. He spotted me and pulled up short. His eyebrows disappeared beneath the lock of black hair drooping over his forehead.

By their own volition, my eyes shifted to the gun riding over his right kidney. I swallowed hard. It was huge. I backed up a step. "Mark's not dead! I talked to him this morning. Don't shoot me!"

"Annie!"

I didn't wait to hear what he had to say. I spun on my heels and darted for the relative safety of my car. I slammed the locks into place, fumbled with my keys, and cursed when I dropped them.

I reached down and snatched the keys off the floor. My head bopped back up in time to see Luke spin out of the parking lot. I drew in a breath, held it, and then released it slowly. The panic receded enough for me to admit I panicked. Mark's not dead. At least I didn't kill him, and I don't think Luke wants to kill me either. If he did, I would already be dead.

I crossed my fingers and reached for the ignition. Going back into the Hess Express was out of the question. Edna thought I was a murderer and she keeps a sawed off shotgun under the counter. She would shoot first and ask questions later. I eased out onto the road and headed across town.

I think I can. I think I can. I think I can. It worked for The Little Engine that Could. Why not me? *I know I can. I know I can. I know I can . . .*

I turned off Leeds Avenue into the Speedway gas station and collapsed back in the seat. I was exhausted. I drove across town on fumes and the power of positive thinking. Don't let anyone tell you it can't be done, because it can. I just proved it.

I climbed out of the car and headed in. The kid manning the register barely acknowledged me when I handed him the money. Gossip didn't interest him. Nothing interested him but the music blaring through his headphones and the porno magazine he was paging through.

He had the right idea, not the porn, but the attitude. He didn't care. Lynette didn't care. She hopped from one bed to the next faster than a kid could hopscotch down a sidewalk. It didn't matter if she was married, or if the man was married, who knew, or who was hurt.

Lynette cared. She even joined Nymphomaniacs Anonymous.

I rolled my eyes. What my mother did or didn't do doesn't matter anymore. She packed up and disappeared ten years ago. The gossips were in mourning for close to a year, and then they turned to me. They wanted *me* to fill her shoes. Even if I wanted to, I can't. Her shoes are too big.

That won't stop Edna and her cronies from trying.

Let them. I have enough real problems to worry about without adding 20 versions of last night's incident to the list. I need money. Mark, the dirty rotten scoundrel, blocked access to our joint savings and checking accounts.

Is that legal?

Probably not, but until I talk to a lawyer, there's little I can do about it. Why didn't I heed Lynette's advice and keep a little on the side?

You didn't want to jinx your marriage. Lynette kept more than money on the side.

I twisted the gas cap back into place and slammed the little door shut. I should be thankful rather than bemoaning my losses. I have a roof over my head, a job to support myself, and a car that's totally paid for.

You're broke, sleeping alone, and tied to an ass-hole.

So much for looking on the bright side.

I signaled and slipped back into traffic. My eyes shifted to the rearview mirror then back to the road in front of me, and then back to the mirror. Frowning, I watched a pickup weaving in and out of traffic. Half the men in town drive pickups. It wasn't necessarily Miguel's. Even if it was Miguel, why would he follow me? We aren't even friends.

You used to be.

So?

Forgive and forget. It wasn't his fault.

So? It doesn't matter if you are a 15-year-old girl with stars in her eyes or a 27-year-old woman. Betrayal cuts to the bone and leaves you bleeding.

I made a sharp right into the Bi-Lo parking lot shoving the morose thoughts aside. The day off was a boon and it was slipping away from me. I grabbed a cart and headed into the store mentally reviewing my shopping list.

I moved out of Tabby's and into my Grammy's old apartment last weekend. The apartment building is really a house that has been converted into four apartments. Grammy did it years ago. When she died, she left the house to my mother and me. Lynette wanted to sell it, but Grammy stipulated in her will that it couldn't be sold until I turned 21. Lynette couldn't sell it, but that didn't stop her from refinancing it. The rent from the four apartments barely covers the mortgage now.

Grammy's apartment was 1-A, and the tenants moved out two months ago. It needs new appliances, new carpet, and some other work, but Mark wanted it rented out "as is." I didn't want to argue with him, but I wasn't willing to rent it out until the work was done. I let it ride. I figured I would have a better chance talking him into the repairs after our income tax refund came in.

For once Mark's stubborn streak worked to my advantage. The apartment's a mess, but it's a roof over my head and it's cheap.

I headed to the produce department and started dumping salad fixings into the cart. I followed up with cereal and milk, a dozen eggs, buns, lunchmeat, a box of chocolate donuts, a bag of Hershey's Kisses, and chocolate pudding. My life's a mess right now. Chocolate helps.

I wheeled the cart around and headed for the cleaning supplies. I can live with worn carpet and temperamental appliances, but the grunge the renters left in the bathroom had to go.

I crouched down to study two different brands of toilet bowl cleaner.

A tingle slid across the back of my neck.

Ignore it!

I wiggled my shoulders around until the tingling dissipated. I picked up another bottle of cleaner. The tingle slid across my neck again. I scrunched my shoulders up and rolled them again.

You might as well look. The problem's not going away.

I raised my head slowly and met Amy's gaze. *Oh shit!* There was a spiteful gleam in her eye and her lips curled back into a snarl. I set the bottle of toilet bowl cleaner down and stood. *Lord, get me out of this.* "Good morning Amy."

Ears perked up as the silence settled over the store. The daring eased down the aisle so as to not miss a single word of the exchange.

"You cost me my job!" Amy's hand came up and her fingernail drilled into my chest.

Don't make a scene! Don't make a scene!

My hands landed on my hips. I'm the wounded party here. Amy was screwing *my* husband. He may be a no good dirty rotten scoundrel, but he's my no good dirty rotten scoundrel. "You cost me my marriage. I would say we're even."

"Marriage! You didn't have a marriage. You can't blame a man for looking elsewhere when he can't get it at home."

"What?" I stared at her aghast.

"Mark told me what it was like. You're sexually dysfunctional. You're scared to death of sex. Mark's a virile man. What did you expect him to do?"

"Sexually dysfunctional!"

"He wants a divorce, but he's afraid it will push you over the edge and you'll end up in the loony bin."

I held my temper. It wasn't easy, but Amy is bigger than I am, and she knows how to throw a mean right hook. "You are right about one thing. Mark is a virile man. He wanted it every night. When we were first married, we had to start setting the alarm for five so we wouldn't be late for work. Saturdays, Mark rarely let me out of bed before noon, and then he usually followed me into the shower."

"No! That's not true! Mark wouldn't lie to me!"

"Believe it. Mark's Italian. He wanted it morning, noon, and night. Do you really think he'd be content with an occasional tumble with you?"

"No!"

"Face it Amy. Mark kept you around because you were easy. He probably would have fired you years ago if you hadn't shoved your silicone-enhanced boobs in his face."

Amy's open hand snaked out and she slapped me across the face. "Mark loves *me*. You're the diversion."

I stumbled back, slamming against the shelves of cleaning products. A bottle of Windex teetered back and forth finally losing its battle with gravity. It hit the floor and the top popped off. The blue solution splattered everywhere.

I raised my hand to my cheek, shocked to the very core of my being, and then I saw red. I pushed off the shelves and slammed both my palms into Amy's chest shoving her back a step. "He lied! You were easy and he couldn't resist. He's sorry for it now."

"You're wrong!" Amy lunged. Her foot slipped on the wet floor and she stumbled forward slamming into me.

I screamed, at least I think I screamed. I'm not really sure. In any event, there was no stopping the momentum. We were going down. I hit the floor with Amy sprawled on top of me.

I tried to roll out from under her, but Amy is four inches taller than I am and at least 30 pounds heavier. The added weight and the fact that she landed on top gave her the advantage.

Her fist connected with my jaw snapping my head back. Stars erupted in front of my eyes when my head bounced on the floor. "You lying bitch! Mark loves me!"

With a manic giggle, Amy rose up on her knees then dropped down on my chest. The air whooshed out of my lungs. Her knees slid forward pinning my arms down. My head connected with the floor again.

Do something before she kills you!

Pain, rage, and a healthy dose of adrenaline spurred me into action. I'm not ready to die. Mascara and Palmer would be orphans and Mark would claim my car. He's not getting *my* car. I bucked, and then rolled counting on Amy's weight to do the job. "Get off me you stupid bitch!"

It worked. Amy rolled off of me with an enraged cry. I grabbed on letting the momentum of the roll pull me out from under and up on top. I scrambled for purchase with Amy's screams ringing in my ears.

An eye for an eye. I pulled my arm back, clenched my fist …

What happened?

One moment I was aiming for Amy's jaw and the next I was hanging like a rag doll a foot off the floor, my arms swinging wildly, and my feet peddling air. No! It wasn't fair! I finally got the upper hand and someone breaks up the fight.

"Are you nuts?" the whispered hiss was accompanied by a bone jarring shake.

"She started it!" I kicked at the air. "Put me down!" I grabbed the front of my shirt and pulled on the neckline. The material was stretched taut making it hard to breathe.

Miguel lowered me to the floor. Not so I could stand flat footed, but he held me up on my tiptoes.

I snarled as I watched Clyde McDuffy help Amy to her feet. Ever the lady, she tugged her skirt back into place and smiled at her rescuer. My blood boiled. Amy started it, but the blame would fall squarely on my shoulders, *again*.

I pulled down my skirt then let my arms go lax. If I demonstrated a measure of control, maybe Miguel would let me go. I wanted to beat the snot out of the bitch, but Miguel didn't need to know that. If I was going to be charged with assault, I might as well do the deed. "Miguel, let go."

"Forget it. I'm not turning the Tasmanian Devil loose on innocent bystanders. You've caused enough trouble today."

The adrenaline leaked away. If Miguel didn't have a grip on the back of my shirt, I would have been on the floor whimpering like a baby. It hurt to breathe, my cheek burned like hell's fire, and little black dots were doing the tango in front of my eyes. I put my palms on either side of my head and squeezed. It was the only way I could keep it from exploding.

I felt the grip on the back of my shirt loosen until I was standing flat footed, but the hand didn't drop away. If I so much as twitched, I would be jerked back up again. Miguel didn't trust me. Hell, he didn't even like me. If Amy hadn't lost the advantage, it's doubtful he would have stepped in to break it up.

I lowered my hands slowly. The black dot tango had slowed to a waltz. As long as I didn't move too fast, I could see around the dancers. I shrugged the hand off. There was a time when I would have turned to Miguel for comfort and support, but those times were gone. We coexist in a town of less than 10,000 people now. I don't even nod a greeting if we pass on the street. I don't think I'll get away with ignoring him this time.

Self-righteous ass-hole!

Who gave him the right to stand in judgment over me? It was self-defense, not that I care what he thinks. I stepped away. I already took a beating. I wasn't going to wait around for a verbal bashing to go with it.

"What were you thinking?" Miguel grabbed my arm and spun me around. "You can't beat up on your husband's secretary even if she deserves it."

Adrenaline is an amazing thing. It can give a little old lady superhuman strength and spur a lazy man into running a mile-a-minute, but when it's gone, you're as weak as a noodle and every bodily injury is magnified by ten. I closed my eyes for a moment willing the pounding in my head to subside. I could whimper, cry, and rail against the fates after I got rid of Miguel. I didn't want him to know how much I hurt. I didn't need a surly Knight in Shining Armor hovering over me.

Miguel's eyes narrowed. "You're hurt."

I jerked my arm away. "I'll live." I spun away from him but had to grab the edge of the shelf for support. I straightened slowly, stepped away, and reached for my cart.

Miguel's hand came down on the cart holding it in place. "Come on. I'll take you to the emergency room."

"No! Why do you care anyway? You assumed I started it. Consider the beating punishment for my sins." I wrestled for control of the cart.

"Did you start it?"

"What difference does it make? I'll take the blame. I always do." Hurt and humiliated, I didn't even try to stop the tears. I backed up a step and turned away. "Keep the cart. I'll get a new one."

CHAPTER FOUR

R-i-i-i-ng.

Vexed, I glared at my purse. I didn't want to talk to anyone.

What if it's Ed McMahon calling to tell you that you won a million dollars from the Publishers Clearing House Sweepstakes?

I turned back to the sink, rinsed the washcloth with cold water, and reapplied it to my face. It's not Ed McMahon. He doesn't have the number. Two days after I left Mark, I changed my cell phone number. I had to. He wouldn't quit calling me. Tabby and my father are the only ones that have the new number. Dad closes the Mountain every night at one, and then spends an hour cleaning up. Odds are he isn't even out of bed yet. It has to be Tabby. She undoubtedly heard about my bitch slapping session with Amy and wants a play-by-play. I'm not up to it.

The purse stopped ringing then promptly started ringing again. "Damn it all to hell!" Sometimes Tabby's worse than Edna Telley and that's saying a lot.

R-i-i-i-ng!

I grabbed my purse and yanked my phone out. "What?"

"Are you all right?" Tabby asked softly.

My anger dissipated like a puff of smoke. "Yes, the only thing I hurt was my dignity, and I don't think that's fatal."

I wasn't lying. I managed to drive home without killing myself, and as long as I didn't breathe, my ribs didn't hurt. So the headache lingered, but at least the black dots were gone. A few hours of sleep and I would be right as rain.

Yeah, and the big bad wolf's a vegetarian.

Okay, so I felt like death warmed over. I would live.

"Why aren't you at work? Oh, God! Harry found out and he fired you!"

"Bite your tongue. Harry gave me the day off."

"Paid?" Tabby asked incredulously. "I don't believe it."

"Believe it."

"Why?" Harry's frugality was a well-known fact. He didn't give employees days off with pay. Harry had an ulterior motive. Tabby knew it and so did I.

"I don't know."

"Do you think he knows about Mark and Amy?"

"I don't know. I don't think so."

"Do you think he was meeting someone and didn't want you to know?"

"Tabby! I don't know why he gave me the day off. He just did."

"Okay, so why was Amy in Bi-Lo? Did Mark send her out to buy another box of condoms? Why didn't she just go to Bradley's Drug Store?"

"Tabby!"

"Why wasn't she at work? Was she following you?"

I rubbed my temples. I wasn't averse to discussing and dissecting the situation, but not now. Once the questions started, Tabby wouldn't stop until she had all the details. The last time that happened, she left Myrtle Lambert sitting in the chair with permanent solution on her hair. The poor woman left The Curly Do with an afro. "Tabby, I don't know why Amy was in Bi-Lo and I don't care. Drop it."

"Okay, okay, but that's not why I called. Carla Anderson told Angie Greenburg, who told Margie, in strictest confidence that ..."

"Tabby, please."

"Shut up and listen. It's important."

I dropped the washcloth in the sink and straightened. Tabby's voice wasn't conspiratorial. It was worried. After years of listening to her, I can tell the difference. "What?"

"The bank's going to repossess your car!"

"They can't do that! I paid cash for it."

"According to Carla, Mark used the title for collateral on another loan."

"He can't do that."

"Well he did, and he's behind on the payments. If the loan isn't up to date by the fifteenth you'll lose your car."

"Mark's a dead man."

"Kill him later. Right now you need to get your hands on some money."

"How?"

"What about your mother's safety deposit box?"

"Do you actually think she left town without emptying it?"

"You do. If you didn't you would have checked the box years ago. Every year when the bill comes, you say you're going to close it, but you don't. What's in the box, Annie?"

I sighed heavily. Tabby was right. I knew what was in the box, as least I did. My mother went through four messy, mud-slinging divorces. As most of Lynette's marriages only lasted a few years, and the wounded party usually had proof of her extracurricular activities, she rarely got more than a token settlement.

Men think of a person's financial worth in terms of property values, stocks and bonds, and cash. Adding in the value of jewelry rarely occurs to them. Lynette knew that and capitalized on it. She usually walked away from a marriage with barely enough money to survive until she hooked up with a new man, and a truck full of jewelry.

When she left one man and started dating another, all the jewelry given to her up to that point went into a safety deposit box. I thought of it as Lynette's retirement fund.

The safety deposit box was Lynette's little secret. It was in Raleigh rather than a local bank. When I turned 15, she added my name to the box. I like to think she trusted me with her biggest secret but in truth, she just needed a courier. I kept my mouth shut and did as I was told.

"She used to keep her jewelry in there."

"Jewelry?"

"Yeah. It was packed to the hilt."

"It's early yet. You can make it to Raleigh before the bank closes."

"It's my mother's jewelry, not mine."

"Annie, Mark's fighting dirty. You need money. Pawn some of the jewelry and hire a lawyer before you lose everything."

"My mother would never understand."

"What else can you do?"

Kill Mark.

I shut off that line of thought in a hurry. I didn't want to kill him, but he would pay for putting my car in jeopardy. "I'm going to Raleigh."

I tried not to think as I drove across town. When Lynette finds out I *borrowed* from her retirement fund, there's no telling what she'll do. She trusted me. If I pawn the jewelry, there would be no getting it back.

Whatever the consequences, I have to do it. Mark put my car at risk. The car is mine. It took six solid years of working weekends at the Mountain to save the money to buy it. On Friday and Saturday nights the Mountain is usually packed belly to butt. Carrying trays full of drinks, I had to elbow my way through the horde over and over again. In every crowd there were at least a dozen toads ready and willing to take advantage of the situation. They would pat my tush or cop a feel … I can't tell you how many times I've been propositioned. Lynette will just have to understand. I earned that car.

One problem. The key to Lynette's safety deposit box is back at the house. I may have lived there for the last two years, but the house is Mark's. The only thing I can lay claim to are my shoes, my clothes, and the box of tampons stashed under the sink in the master bathroom.

Mark's house is in New Hope, a new subdivision out on the east side of town. The city's in the process of annexing it, but as of yet it still falls outside the city limits. That puts it in the Sheriff Department's jurisdiction.

I eased off the gas. I didn't want to do this.

Chicken.

Damn straight. If I'm caught, Mark will have me thrown in the clink, and he'll give the key to Luke for safekeeping. I wouldn't see the light of day until I was ready for bifocals and orthopedic shoes.

How many times did Carl Sweeney try to put a tip down your bra before you convinced him you would break his fingers if he tried it again?

Carl got the message … eventually.

Okay, remember that New Year's Eve party when Andy Tisdale tried to give you a tonsillectomy with his tongue? You broke two of his toes. He couldn't wear a shoe for six weeks.

I stepped on the gas again. The no-good dirty, rotten, scoundrel wasn't going to win. I'm not breaking and entering. Well I am, but I'm not. I'm entering, but I don't plan on breaking anything. I'll go in, get the key, and get the hell out of there.

What about your shoes?

I had to think about that.

The community of New Hope is made up of predominantly young, childless couples. There are a few children, but they are packed off to the daycare most days. Status comes with a price tag. Mama *had* to work to help pay the mortgage.

I pulled into the driveway as if I had every right to be there, pulled the garage door opener out of the glove compartment, pointed it at the garage, and pressed the button. The garage door started grinding its way up. I shot through the opening barely missing the bottom of the garage door before hitting the button again.

"I'm in." I whispered into an imaginary walky-talky. I was the inside man. It was my job to go in and bring out the loot. I wasn't alone. My cohorts were guarding the entrances and exits. Only a fool would go in without backup.

Okay, so I'm a fool, but I've come this far. I might as well go for the gold, or in this case, the key.

I dropped the garage door opener into my purse and eased out of the car. The car door closed with a quiet click. The silence was unnerving. I hesitated on the steps leading from the garage to the kitchen, made a sign of the cross, and promised God I would say a hundred Hail Mary's. I wasn't doing anything wrong. I was retrieving *my* property, but it wouldn't hurt to have a few Hail Mary's in the bank. You never know when you'll accidentally step over the line.

Mark wasn't home. I was 99.9 percent sure of that. It was that 0.1 percent that had the adrenaline pumping. I really don't like being this nervous. It's bad for the complexion. My face gets all blotchy and then I break out in hives.

I eased the door open and stepped inside the kitchen. I crept through the kitchen listening for tell-tale sounds of an intruder.

Scratch that. I'm the intruder.

I crossed the kitchen unscathed and snuggled up to the door between the kitchen and the living room. I peaked around the doorjamb. My eyes went wide. All thought of slinking evaporated. Stepping into the living room, my hands landed on my hips. For the first time since leaving Mark, his actions made sense. He didn't want me back in his bed. He just didn't want to pay for maid service.

The place was a pig's sty. There were beer cans and abandoned Styrofoam cups, empty Subway bags, Kentucky Fried Chicken boxes, pizza boxes, and spent packets of Taco Bell hot sauce, soy sauce, used napkins, and plastic utensils everywhere. I couldn't even see the coffee table for the trash piled on top of it.

I had to tuck my hands in my pockets before making my way around the mess. I wanted to rescue the sofa pillows. It took two months of diligent shopping to find sofa pillows to match that burgundy couch. I didn't touch them, but felt like I was abandoning friends in their hour of need.

I took the steps two at a time. The clock was ticking. I had to get out of there. Averting my eyes and holding my breath, I cut through the bedroom and into the bathroom. If Mark was sleeping with Amy in our bed, I didn't want to know about it.

The bathroom wasn't much better than the living room. I ignored the mess and made a bee-line for my ginger jar. The ginger jar is decorative as well as useful. It sits on the back of the toilet all prim and proper with a supply of tampons in ready reach.

Lynette entrusted the key to me. I didn't want to lose it. I couldn't put it in my jewelry box. When a burglar goes to all the trouble of breaking in, rifling the jewelry box is a guarantee. I've never heard of a B and E guy going for a bunch of tampons.

I tipped the jar up and slid the tampons out. The key was taped to the inside bottom. It just took a moment to peel it free. I replaced the tampons and set the ginger jar back in its place. The key went into my right front pocket.

Retracing my steps, I headed back downstairs. I wanted to check on my shoes, but I had to count on God and Fate standing watch over them for another day or two. I cut through the living room and into the kitchen and nearly jumped out of my skin when the phone shrilled.

It was either habit or an ingrained sense of duty that had me automatically reaching for it. My fingers jerked to a stop mere inches from the receiver. I'm a redhead, not a blond. I knew better than to answer the phone.

I needed to get out of there, but I waited for the answering machine to kick in. I felt like a voyeur, but I did it anyway. I already had to go to confession. Adding one more sin to the list wouldn't make much difference.

It's time to turn up the heat. You know what to do.

I scowled at the phone. Eavesdropping is no fun when you don't understand the message.

* * *

I have the key. It's a small victory, but after the day I've had, I felt good about it. I guess Fate knows me pretty well. I can stand up to adversity as long as she throws me a bone every now and then. In spite of all the things that have gone wrong in the last two weeks, I have plenty to be thankful for. As long as I don't pay the electric bill and the water bill at the same time, I have money to eat. I have a roof over my head and a bed to sleep in at night. Okay, so the bed's just a sleeping bag on the floor; it's better than a cardboard box in the alley.

If my luck holds, I might even be able to slip out of town unnoticed.

I pulled into the alley between Lexington and Fifth Avenue. Tabby rents an apartment over the antiques store, Hidden Treasures. She has to move her truck out of the alley on garbage pickup day, but other than that, it's a pretty sweet deal.

Tabby offered the use of her truck, but now I was eying it with trepidation. My Mazda is a four on the floor. Tabby's pickup is a three-speed and hard as hell to steer. I can drive it, theoretically, but I've never actually put it into practice.

There's no help for it. I'm tired of having my movements monitored by every gossip in town. I locked up the Mazda and climbed into the pickup. "I can do this."

Fine, you can do it, but what good will it do? Your hair will give you away.

I rolled my eyes upward. A lock of red hair fell down across my face mocking me.

"Fine!"

I slid out of the truck, went back to the Mazda, and rooted around in the trunk until I unearthed a baseball cap. I slammed the trunk and marched back over to the pickup.

I gathered up my hair and shoved it under the hat then perched my sunglasses on my nose. I glanced in the mirror and smiled grimly. Mentally crossing my fingers, I shoved the key in the ignition.

CHAPTER FIVE

I signed my name, handed the key over to Ashley, the pert little bank teller, and then started rubbing my temples again. My headache was back. The flashes of light and black dots were dancing again. The rhythmic pounding between my temples mimicked an Indian war dance. Stress can do that. It has nothing to do with the number of times Amy managed to slam my head against the floor.

I waited for the girl to find the box, insert the keys, and open it up. Maybe I could curl up on the floor and take a quick nap while I waited. I doubt the tiles are any harder than the floor of my apartment.

"Here it is." Ashley flipped the door back and pulled the long thin box out of its resting place. "Ouch, this thing is heavy. What do you have in there anyway?"

"Bricks."

Ashley grinned. "Sorry, I know I'm not supposed to ask."

"It's just old coins and jewelry. My grandmother is asking for the broach that Grandpa gave to her for their 25th wedding anniversary. It's not in her jewelry box. I'm hoping it's in here." The lie slid off my tongue like a burnt offering sliding off Teflon. It scared me. I thought I was a good cook, but a lousy liar. If I'm a good liar, does that mean I'm a lousy cook?

"Good luck." Ashley waved as she headed back to her station. "Let me know when you're done."

I held the box for a moment letting the relief wash over me. The sucker was heavy. Lynette didn't stop by the bank on her way out of town.

Why would she? The jewelry is her retirement fund. She won't need it for another twenty years. When she finds out you stole from her, she'll come after you.

I took the box around to the other side of the partition and set it down with a thump. Sometimes a conscience can be a real pain in the ass. Right or wrong, I don't have much choice. I needed money. Blocking my conscience, I started unloading the box.

Ten minutes later I had most of the jewelry separated into groups, rings in one pile, bracelets in another, a collection of pendants, and two broaches. It was an impressive collection. The men in Lynette's life had good taste in jewelry.

I glanced back into the safety deposit box to make sure I had it all. My heart did a little flip and my stomach rolled. With the care reserved for a hand grenade, I reached in and pulled out the two manila envelopes. They were bound to be just as explosive and by opening the box, I had already pulled the pin.

Both envelopes were fat. I set one down and lifted the flap on the other one. Newspaper clippings, pictures, and little scraps of paper tumbled out. I didn't know what to expect, but it wasn't that. I picked up one of the articles and perused it. I never understood my mother, so how could I possibly understand the importance of an obituary for some old lady who lived in Ashville 20 years ago?

I didn't want to open the second envelope. The tingling on the back of my neck already told me what was in it. The question was, how much? My fingers inched forward. Borrowing my mother's emergency fund would be easier than pawning the jewelry.

I snatched up the envelope and opened it. The air clogged back in my lungs and the little black dots in front of my eyes grew into great big blobs. I grabbed the counter for support. There had to be a 100 hundred-dollar bills in there.

That would be … I stumbled over the math. It was better not to know how much money was there.

Ignoring the problem won't make it go away.

My mother worked as a bank teller. She handled a lot of money, but she didn't make much. She never would have been able to save that much money on her salary. So where did it come from?

She embezzled $250,000 from the bank and cleaned out John LeBlanc's safe before she skipped town.

No. I don't believe that. Mama was a lot of things, but she wasn't a thief. Besides, my mother would never risk prison. The orange jumpsuits would clash with her hair.

Okay, maybe she made it?

I pulled out one of the bills and studied it. I haven't seen too many hundred-dollar bills, but it looked real enough. Pulling out several, I checked the serial numbers. The FBI always checks the serial numbers. I don't know why, but they do. The numbers weren't even close. I guess that's a good thing.

I counted out 20 hundred-dollar bills then shoved the rest back into the envelope. Where's the guilt? I should feel guilty. I was stealing from my mother. It would take a lot of Hail Mary's to get out from under this. It probably ranks up there with walking out on adulterous husbands.

I settled for feeling guilty about not feeling guilty and tucked the bills into the pocket of my purse. Hesitating, I pulled them out again and tucked them into my bra. Fate has it out for me. If I leave the money in my purse, I'll be mugged on the way out of the bank. I've racked up enough bruises for the day.

I studied the jewelry spread out on the counter. With the cash, I didn't need to sell any of it now.

What are you wearing to work on Monday? Amy ruined your skirt, your slacks are at the cleaners, and you look like a fool wearing those shoes with jeans.

Annoyed, I snatched up three rings, a bracelet, a pendant, and a broach. I dropped them in my purse before I could think better of it. I'm not buying a new wardrobe or any new shoes, well a pair of sneakers would be nice. Actually, I need something to sit on. I need a sofa. On impulse I grabbed two more rings and a choker. If I'm going to buy a sofa, I might as well buy a chair to match.

Hurrying so as not to give myself time to change my mind, I piled the rest of the jewelry back into the box. I snapped the lid back down, stepped around the partition, and signaled for Ashley. The back of my neck started doing that tingling thing again. I swung around to grab the safety deposit box off the counter and froze. The manila envelopes were still lying there.

"Find what you were looking for?" Ashley asked cheerfully as she replaced the box and handed the key back to me.

"I found a little more than I bargained for. Sorry I took so long." I gave her a smile as I tried to shove the envelopes further down in my purse.

* * *

The first three pawn shops were a learning experience. By time I pulled into the forth, I had it down to a science.

"Two-hundred. I can't give you any more than that without clearing it with the manager."

My hands came up to my temples and I slowly massaged them. The Tylenol took the edge off the headache so massaging my temples wasn't really necessary, but it brought the man's attention back to my battered face.

"Okay, two-hundred and twenty-five and that's my final offer."

Shame on you.

I'll do penance on Sunday, but in all honesty the broach is worth a whole lot more than two-hundred and twenty-five dollars. "Thank you." I whispered quietly. I kept my gaze down not willing to let the man see the triumph in my eyes. He thought I was hocking my jewelry to escape an abusive husband. Who was I to tell him otherwise?

"It will take a couple of minutes to write this up. I'll be right back." The man disappeared into the back room.

I didn't dare pawn the jewelry all in one place. This shop was okay, but I liked the third one best. They had the most jewelry. I even saw a pendant that reminded me of one my mother used to wear. I think John LeBlanc, my mother's fifth and final husband, gave it to her as a wedding present. I'm not really sure.

"All I need is your signature to seal the deal."

I picked up the pen and signed Betsy Ross. I pawned my engagement ring at the first pawnshop and I signed my real name. After that … if they really cared, they would have asked for identification.

I had to pawn my engagement ring. It was the only way I could think of to explain my newfound wealth. I have to get my car out of hock, and when Mark finds out he'll start asking questions.

Your engagement ring was a family heirloom.

I limped out to the truck. Okay, so I pawned the ring to piss off Mark. He shouldn't have used my car for collateral. *That* pissed me off.

I have some pieces of jewelry left, but I've run out of pawnshops. The rest of the jewelry can wait. I want to go home, curl up in a corner, and sleep off the effects of my altercation with Amy, but I have Tabby's truck. Tomorrow I would be back to driving the Mazda, working until five every day, and working at the Mountain every weekend. The idea of furniture, something besides clothes and shoes that I could call my own, appealed to me. The only furniture in my apartment is a rickety old table and two chairs left behind by the last tenants.

I needed a boost. I gave up shopping for Lent, but I was thinking shoes and sundresses when I made that promise, not a sofa. Buying for the apartment is not the same as buying for *me*. God will understand.

Settling into the truck, I fished around in my purse for my bottle of Tylenol. The headache was coming back and my knee throbbed in time with my heartbeat. Maybe I should pick up some groceries and go home. Thanks to Miguel and Amy, I left Bi-Lo empty handed. I can always borrow the truck again next week.

R-i-i-i-ng!

I swallowed the tablets and guzzled a half a bottle of water.

R-i-i-i-ng!

I retrieved my phone and flipped it open. "Tabby, have I ever told you you're nosy?"

"I'm not nosy!" Tabby responded indignant.

"Good." I waited a beat.

She puffed out a breath. "Okay, I'm nosy. Did you find what you were looking for?"

"It was all there."

"Good. Problem solved."

If only it were that easy.

"Now you can hire a lawyer and tell Mark to go to hell. So, when are you coming home?"

"Later. I want to do some shopping while I'm here."

"That's fine, but …"

"What?"

"I need to talk to you and I would rather not do it over the phone."

"Why, what's wrong?"

"Just come home. Don't go back to your apartment. Come here. We can order a pizza."

"What is it?"

"Annie …"

"Something's wrong. I can hear it in your voice. Did Amy press charges? She started it, but I don't think that will make a difference."

"It's not that."

"What?" I knew Fate was setting me up. What little good luck I have always comes with a price tag.

Tabby hesitated. "Luke is looking for you."

"Luke!" I squeaked. "He wants to kill me."

"Annie! He was 16. Sixteen-year-olds threaten to kill their little sisters all the time. Nothing ever comes of it."

"Tabby, you didn't see the look in his eyes. He meant it."

"Well, what do you expect? You embarrassed him."

"And that justifies murder?" Luke was the son of Lynette's third husband, Bryce Sheridan. Once Lynette and Bryce married, Luke became my stepbrother. I had to exorcize the dreams and the fantasies. Even at 16, Luke was a hunk. I didn't want to do it, but he was my brother then and daydreaming about him was wrong.

My intentions were good and I might have succeeded, but Luke was at an age where looking at a girl, even a skinny 13-year-old, was better than nothing. He drilled a hole in the wall between his bedroom and mine. He didn't consider the fact that if he could watch me, I could watch him.

It was late one night, I don't remember how late, but I was in bed. I heard Luke come in. I was already having trouble sleeping so listening to Luke move around in his room really annoyed me. I was ready to go complain, but I stopped to peek through the hole first.

I never did get around to filing a complaint. I didn't realize his intent when he shucked his jeans. Seeing him in the all-together was an eye opening experience. He pulled a magazine from under his mattress and flopped down on the bed. Luke stared playing with his penis and then …

"Maybe I should move to Charlotte."

"Annie, you need to talk to him. It's important."

"No. I'm not talking to Luke, not now, not ever." I know I'm over reacting, but I can't help it. Luke scares me. It's not because I think he's going to pull out his gun and put a bullet between my eyes, but because he still manages to slip into my daydreams. Luke was a hunk at 16. He's improved with age.

"Annie …"

"No!"

"Annie, you don't have a choice. They found your mother's purse, and one of her shoes up by Harry's new construction site."

My stomach clenched. "So? She lost her purse. Big deal. It doesn't mean anything."

"How can you say that? They stopped work and are searching the whole area looking for a body. They think your mother's dead."

"I'm surprised they even care."

"Annie!"

"Tabby, my mother's not dead."

"Are you sure?"

"Yes."

"Oh. Well, you might want to let Luke know that."

"Luke can go suck an egg. I'll talk to you later." I closed the phone and switched it over to voice mail. I knew my good fortune wouldn't last. When Fate kicks me in the ass, she puts some muscle behind it. I stretched out my leg and rubbed my knee. *What now?*

CHAPTER SIX

I pulled up to the curb in front of Grammy's and killed the engine. There was only room for two cars in the driveway. I usually leave those spots for Ralph and Sam. Ralph walks with a cane and Sam is a 100 if he is a day. A few extra steps won't kill me. I'm not so sure about them.

The third apartment is rented out to Angie Rehnquist. She's an elementary school teacher and is engaged to one of the guys on Harry's crew. She will be moving out the end of June.

Stiff, sore, and immeasurably tired, I just sat there staring at the darkened building. I needed to go in, put the groceries away, then crawl in bed, and die. I stayed in Raleigh far longer than anticipated. Part of it was blatant stubbornness. Lynette isn't dead. She's in Las Vegas playing blackjack and slamming shots.

I leaned against the door and pulled the handle. I tumbled out of the pickup and landed on the ground with a thump, adding insult to injury. I straightened my legs slowly before rolling into a sitting position. Maybe I should have stopped at the rest stop and stretched, but I know ax murderers and serial rapists stay one step ahead of the law by moving around. With my luck, The Chicago Slasher would pull in for a pit stop right behind me.

Groaning just a little, I rolled over onto my hands and knees.

"Damn it Annie!"

I let out a surprised yelp. If I hadn't recognized the voice, I would have had a heart attack right there on the spot. Now that would give the gossips something to talk about.

Annie Natali died of fright late Friday night. She was pronounced dead at the scene. According to eyewitness accounts, Lynette O'Reilly's ghost was seen hovering over the body. She was digging through Annie's pockets and screaming about money and jewelry ...

I'm losing my mind.

Miguel reached down, slid his hands under my armpits, and lifted me to my feet. "You've always been stubborn, but I didn't think you were stupid!"

I twisted away from him. "Did you have to scare ten years off my life? Jeez!"

"You fell out of the truck." Miguel glared at me, his voice accusing. "What the hell were you thinking? You're stiff and sore and probably have a concussion. Instead of staying home and resting, you go gallivanting across the country."

"I wasn't gallivanting! I had some errands to run so I ran them. What are you doing here anyway?"

"I've lived on this street all my life. It dead ends a couple of blocks down. Traffic is practically nonexistent. That's one of the reasons I opted to say here." Miguel took my arm and tugged me toward the house. "Not today. There was more traffic on this road then there is on Main Street at high noon."

"Wait! I need my groceries."

"Get inside, Annie. Luke Sheridan's been sitting over by the trees all evening. He took off a few minutes ago, but he'll be back. You'll have to talk to him eventually. Do you want it to be tonight?"

"No." I whispered.

"Go. I'll get your stuff."

I opened the outer door and limped down the hallway to my apartment. The apartments run from front to back giving each one a view of the front yard and the back. I turned on the foyer light then made my way back to the kitchen flipping on lights as I went. Miguel was right behind me flipping them back off again. I dumped my purse on the counter, turned, and faced him. "The lights won't make a difference. He'll see the truck on the street."

Miguel dumped the bags of groceries on the table then took my chin in his hand and studied my face. His scrutiny was unnerving, but I held his gaze. We're no longer friends, but he has a streak of chivalry. If he sees me as a Damsel in Distress, I'll never get rid of him.

"You did a pretty good job of hiding the bruises, but the makeup's coming off. What are you hiding under the jeans and long sleeved shirt?"

"Just some bruises."

"And …" Miguel still had a firm hold on my chin, but it was his eyes that held me immobile. Miguel always knew when I was lying. He didn't tolerate it when we were kids, and he wouldn't tolerate it now. If I didn't confess all, he'd strip me down and find out the truth for himself.

"I sort of wrenched my knee too."

"Headache?"

I dropped my gaze. "Just because I have a headache, doesn't mean I have a concussion. You always said I was hard headed."

Miguel dropped my chin and stepped back. "Give me the keys to the truck."

"Why?" I asked as I fished them out.

"I'll put it in my garage for the night. That'll buy you some time."

"Thanks, but I need it first thing in the morning."

"Don't thank me. You are avoiding Sheridan's questions for the night, but not mine. I'll be back as soon as I stash the truck."

"Miguel …"

"Shut up." He snatched the keys out of my hand and stomped out of the apartment.

I put the groceries away, fed Palmer and Mascara, and gazed longingly at the bedroom door. My bed was just a sleeping bag on the floor, but it was calling me. Miguel was pissed at me. I don't know why. I haven't done anything to deserve his wrath.

So?

So it didn't matter. Mascara wove around my feet then looked up at me all sad and serious. I scooped her up and settled down in the chair to await my fate.

I heard the quiet knock on the patio door. I let Mascara slide to the floor and rose. I crossed over to the patio door, pulled back the vertical blinds, and lifted the broom handle out of the track. I slid the glass door open, but didn't step back to let Miguel in. "If I promise to sit quietly and look appropriately contrite, would you consider postponing the lecture until tomorrow?"

Miguel nudged me back. "The lock's broken."

"I know. Doug promised to come by and fix it this weekend."

"Good. Have him install a deadbolt on the front door while he's at it." Miguel walked over to the stove and flipped on the light above it. "Turn off the light."

I slapped my hand down on the switch. "Are you trying to scare me?"

"Maybe." He turned and studied me in the muted light. "When's the last time you've eaten?"

I waved his concern away with a disgruntled snort, yanked a chair out, and dropped down on it. "Cut it out. I'm not a kid anymore."

"You're not eating. You're losing weight."

"Summer's coming. I want to look good in a bikini." My chin jutted out, daring him to argue with me.

"Men want curves, not a bag of bones."

"Back off, Miguel."

Miguel pulled open the refrigerator and studied the contents before pulling out a package of ham and some cheese. He grabbed the mustard and dropped it all on the counter, then went back for the lettuce. "I'm hungry even if you're not. Now, where's the bread?" He spotted the bag of rolls and grabbed them.

"Miguel, I'm tired, so if you want to yell at me, get it over with so I can go to bed."

"Why do you always assume I'm going to yell at you?"

"Tradition. You always yell at me, and you always assume I'm at fault. Just for the record, Amy approached me, she initiated the conversation, and she threw the first punch. Flipping her off me was just dumb luck. Thirty seconds before you pulled me off, she was on top of me beating the snot out of me. If the witnesses say otherwise, they're damned to hell for lying."

"Dumb luck?" He set a napkin with a fat sandwich on it in front of me before going back to the refrigerator and pulling out the pitcher of iced tea.

"Yeah, dumb luck. It's the only kind I have. If it wasn't for the red hair, I would never believe I was Irish."

He set the glass of tea next to the sandwich. "Eat." He picked up his and sat down across from me.

I poked at the sandwich. "I told you, I'm not hungry."

"Annie, you're dropping weight, weight you can't afford to lose. Now eat."

I picked up the sandwich and nibbled at it before setting it back down again. "I haven't lost weight."

"Right." Miguel nudged the sandwich toward me. "Take a real bite this time."

"Bully."

Miguel gave me a smile that was all lips and teeth. "Damn straight. I have a reputation to maintain."

I took a big bite then talked around it. "There, are you satisfied."

"No, but it will do for now." Miguel mumbled under his breath then drew in another breath and released it. "Annie, do you know why Luke is looking for you?"

I nodded as I hastily swallowed the second bite. "Tabby told me they found Lynette's purse when they started digging the foundation for the new mall."

"You don't seem overly concerned."

"Luke thinks Mama's dead, but she's not."

"How can you be so sure?"

I rolled my eyes as I licked the mustard off my fingers. "I got a birthday card from her a few years ago."

"So you know where your mother is living."

I rolled my eyes again. "No. She didn't put a return address on it."

"Are you sure it was from your mother?"

"Who else? I hadn't heard from her in seven years, and she didn't even bother to write a letter. Lynette's the only one I know who can turn a thoughtful gesture into an insult."

"Did you recognize the handwriting?"

I guess I was tired. I didn't realize where Miguel's questions were going until he got there. I abruptly pushed away from the table. "Mama's not dead!"

"Annie!" He grabbed my shoulders from behind when I tried to flee the kitchen. "Calm down!"

"Let go of me!"

Miguel ignored my pleas and pulled me back against his chest and wrapped his arms around me. "Annie! I had to ask."

The fight went out of me, and I turned and burrowed into his chest. "Tell me she's not dead!"

"I can't do that." He rocked me back and forth giving the comfort he used to give me when I was a child. "I don't know what the Sheriff's Department turned up, but it's enough to arouse suspicion."

"Suspicion," I sniffled as I rested my forehead against his chest. "That's not proof."

"Luke will be by tomorrow morning. I'm sure he can fill in the details."

I stepped back and glared up at him. "I'm not talking to Lucas Sheridan. If the sheriff wants to send another deputy, fine, but I'm not talking to Luke." I wrapped my arms around myself and paced back and forth. "I don't trust him."

"Do you trust me?"

I grimaced. "I shouldn't. Probably not."

"Do you trust Doug Matthews?"

"Of course. He's my brother."

"Ask Doug to sit in on the interrogation."

"Interrogation!"

"Sorry, bad choice of words. Luke needs to talk to you and I don't think he'll take no for an answer. Think of it as an interview. That might make it a little easier to handle."

"No. I'm not talking to Luke, and unless he arrests me, he can't force me to."

"Annie, you're over reacting."

"Go away. I'm tired."

"Denial's not going to work this time."

"I don't know what you're talking about."

Miguel stared at me for a moment before shaking his head. "Did you lock the front door?"

I nodded.

"Good." He stepped over to the counter, stuck his hand into my purse, and pulled out my cell phone.

"Hey!"

He flipped it open and read the number before dropping it back into the void. "Relax Annie. It's just a safety precaution. Now lock up behind me and go to bed."

"Good idea."

I locked up behind Miguel, downed a couple of sleeping pills, and crawled into my sleeping bag. I wasn't taking any chances. I didn't want to spend the night chasing phantoms and fears around my apartment instead of sleeping.

Asleep, I wouldn't have to think about my mother dancing until dawn in Tahiti while I tried to straighten out the mess she left behind. I wouldn't have to think about my money problems, I didn't have to think about Miguel sleeping in the house next door, and I wouldn't have to worry about the inevitable confrontation with Luke.

✳ ✳ ✳

The persistent ring of the telephone pulled me from my drug-induced sleep. I glanced at the clock, rolled over and drifted back to sleep.

The phone rang again. Swearing, I rolled over to reach the phone. "What?"

"Annie! Open the door. I need to talk to you."

"Daddy?"

"Damn it, Annie! Open the door!"

"Okay. Okay." I unzipped my sleeping bag and crawled to my feet.

I stumbled out of the bedroom and headed for the door. It only took a moment to pull the chair out from under the doorknob and open it. "Why didn't you knock?"

"I did." Dad nudged me back as he stepped through the door. He closed it firmly and flipped the lock. "Are you awake?"

I brushed the hair out of my face and scowled up him. "It's the middle of the night. Why should I be awake?"

"It's almost seven." He glanced down at me, his smile dropped, and his face flushed with temper.

"What?" I stepped back, startled.

"Who beat you?" He growled menacingly.

"Oh that," I yawned. "That's old news. If you listened to gossip you would already know." I leaned against the wall. My eyes drifted shut and I slowly started sliding to the floor.

"Annie! Wake up!"

"I'm awake! I'm awake!" I straightened and glared at him. I wanted to go back to bed. Whatever dad wanted to talk to me about could wait until morning.

With a muffled curse he walked past me into the kitchen. He flipped the light on and started searching the cabinets. "Where did you stash the coffee?"

"There's a jar of instant in the first cupboard."

"Instant?" He made it sound like I was offering him poison.

I shrugged. "No coffee pot."

"Fine. Go wash your face and wake up."

I just leaned on the doorjamb and yawned. "I'm awake."

"Go!"

"You show up in the middle of the night fussing and cussing, but you won't tell me why you're here. With another yawn, I turned and headed back toward my bedroom. "I'm going back to bed."

I heard a hiss behind me, but didn't pay any attention to it. I should have. Dad has about as much patience as a New York cab driver during rush hour. Before I realized his intent, he had me by the shoulders and was propelling me into the bathroom.

"You need to wake up." With a flick of his wrist the water streamed out in full force. He shoved my face down.

I sputtered a curse as handfuls of icy water drenched my face. "Daddy! Stop!"

"Are you awake?"

"Yes!"

He released his grip and turned off the water. "Good."

"Why did you do that?"

"I want to talk to you." With that, he turned and stomped out of the bathroom.

I grabbed a towel and dried my face as I followed my father into the kitchen. "You better have a good reason for waking me up at … it's not even seven. Why are *you* up? Didn't you close the bar last night?"

"I haven't gone to bed yet. I needed to talk to you and I didn't know what your plans were." He poured the water into my only cup and dumped a teaspoon of instant coffee into it. "Sit."

I took the mug of coffee warily.

"What happened? Why do you look like the lone survivor in a three-day brawl?"

"Oh, well," I pleated the bottom of my pajama top with my fingers. I didn't meet his gaze.

"Answer me!"

"I sort of had a little to-do with Amy in Bi-Lo."

"Amy?"

I nodded.

He sighed heavily. "I'm not surprised. Mark and Amy were together for a long time. They were even talking marriage."

"I know what people think, but it's not true." Indignation added heat to my voice. "Mark and Amy broke up long before Mark and I started dating, and we've been married for over two years. How can you say I came between them?"

"Annie."

"I'm not my mother!"

"No you're not, but …"

"But what?"

"Nothing."

"Right. I know what you're thinking, you and everyone else in town. But Daddy, if Mark regrets marrying me, why did he fire Amy, and why is he trying to win me back?"

"I don't know."

"I don't know what to do."

"A few lessons in self-defense wouldn't hurt. You look like hell."

"Thanks Dad." I responded dryly.

"Does Amy look as bad as you?"

My shoulders drooped. "Sorry. I managed to flip her off me, but then Miguel stepped in and broke it up."

"Figures. I'm just glad the bruises weren't Mark's doing. I would hate to spend the rest of my natural life sitting on death row."

I fidgeted in my seat. "Why are you here Daddy?"

Drip ...

He turned away from me and stared out the window.

Drip ...

I pushed away from the table, grabbed the washcloth off the counter, and lobbed it into the sink. *Drip* ... silence.

The silence lengthened. When it comes to gossip, my father has selective hearing. Obviously the gossip regarding my mother made it through his filter system, but he didn't know how to say what needed to be said. "Daddy, the Sheriff's Department is wrong. Lynette's not dead."

He turned around and met my gaze, relief shining in his eyes. "Are you sure?"

"Yes."

"Good. Good."

"Why do you care? You hated her."

"True, but she's your mother, and I don't want to see you hurt by her again. Losing her that way ... well it wouldn't be good."

The knock on the door startled me. *Luke!* I didn't want him to see me like this. I was still in my borrowed pajamas. I don't like pajamas. I prefer nightshirts for everyday and silk negligees for special occasions. I have some awesome silk negligees ...

What are you thinking? It's Luke, not Prince Charming at the door. You don't need a negligee. You need body armor. He wants to kill you, not sleep with you.

You see why I avoid him. I'm a levelheaded woman, but when it comes to Luke, I keep getting my wires crossed. That scares me more than the death threat.

"Can you get that?"

Dad nodded.

"Thanks. If its Lucas Sheridan, tell him I moved and didn't leave a forwarding address." I scampered out of the kitchen and disappeared into the bedroom.

CHAPTER 7

Miguel dropped the tailgate and eyed my new loveseat and chair skeptically. "What did you do? Stop by the dump on your way home last night?"

I wrinkled my nose at him. "They fit the bill."

"What bill?"

"They were cheap."

Dad grabbed the side of the chair and helped Miguel hoist it out of the truck. They angled it around the corners and through the doors finally dropping it in the middle of my living room. "Miguel's right. It's ugly. Why didn't you take some of the furniture when you moved out?"

I shrugged. I didn't think telling dad that Mark changed the locks and wouldn't let me in the house to get my clothes let alone furniture would be wise. They hauled in the loveseat while I shifted from foot-to-foot resisting the urge to hurry them along.

"Thanks for the help." I held out my hand for the keys the minute they dropped the loveseat. "I really appreciate it."

Miguel ignored my outstretched hand, just turned and headed out the door again. I scrambled after him. "Miguel, give me the keys."

He pulled a couple of bags out of the back of the truck and started in again. I grabbed the last of the bags and followed him in, mumbling under my breath. I dumped the bags on the loveseat and turned with my hand outstretched. "Thanks again."

He just stood there staring at me with those dark, unreadable eyes of his. My hand dropped to my side. "What?"

"You don't need to be driving that truck. The clutch is shot and the brakes are soft."

"What!"

"Tell Tabby that I'm taking it over to Andy's. He'll take a look at it and see if it's worth fixing."

"I drove it all day yesterday. The truck's fine." I needed the truck. The rules of trade are pretty straight forward, a dress for a dress and a vehicle for a vehicle. As long as Tabby's truck was in the shop, I couldn't collect my Mazda.

Miguel shook his head. I saw a hint of a smile playing at the corners of his mouth. "Forget it."

"Give me the keys!" I kicked at his booted feet. He made me so mad sometimes.

"Annie cut it out. A temper tantrum may work on Mark, but not on me."

My temper climbed up another notch. "Give me the keys you big jerk!" I put my hands on his chest and tried to shove him back. I would have better luck trying to push in a cinderblock building. He didn't budge.

"Annie." Dad grabbed my arm and pulled me back. I could hear the humor in his voice too. Are all men jerks? "I'll give you a ride over to Tabby's."

"I can't pick up my car until I bring back her truck." I wailed. "Daddy, make him give me the keys."

"Sorry kid."

Miguel gave us a quick salute then sauntered out the door.

Vexed, I turned my ire on my father. In an effort to stem the incoming tide, he threw up his hands and backed up a step. "You can use my truck."

That took the wind right out of my sails, but I wasn't letting him off the hook that easily. He sided with Miguel. I told him the truck was fine. Does he listen to me? No. Why should he? According to dad, women don't know beans about trucks. It's the same with politics and fishing. "Thanks Dad. Once Tabby's truck is out of the shop, I'll drop your truck off."

"You can use my truck *today*."

I grabbed my purse and followed him out the door. I don't know why I try. I never get the last word.

✳ ✳ ✳

I didn't *need* the truck today. Yes, I had some errands to run. I still had to buy some things for the apartment. I had my dad's truck but what I really needed was a vehicle to swap for my Mazda. Tabby has plans for the night. As long as I can't return her truck, she's keeping the Mazda. It foiled *my* plans. Sarah's birthday party is tonight. Without my own transportation, I'll have to accept a ride from Mark.

If you accept a ride from Mark, you'll be sleeping in his bed tonight.

I'm not going home with Mark.

Hah! A few drinks and you'll be hot to trot. Bail on the party before it's too late.

I don't like going back on my word.

Humph! Maybe Mark's not the only one looking for a liaison this evening.

That's not true!

Liar!

Okay, so maybe I'm having second thoughts. Lynette married and divorced with the speed of the lead car at the Indy 500. First sign of trouble and she headed for the door. I didn't want to get caught in the same vicious cycle.

I'm not giving in to Mark's demands, but I'm not quite ready to talk to a lawyer either. Father Nolan offers marriage counseling. If we could repair the rent, rebuild the trust, our marriage might be worth saving.

Get your head out of the sand, girl. Mark won't talk to Father Nolan and he won't quit screwing Amy. Go back to Mark and you're the one who's screwed.

I grabbed a cart and headed into Lowes. I didn't have a comeback for that. Deep down I was afraid it was true. Rather than analyze my feelings and Mark's motives, I threw the problem aside. I'll figure it out later. Right now I wanted to shop. Locks were first on the list. I swung the cart around the corner and looked down the long aisle of locks and bolts. I couldn't stifle the groan.

Whatever happened to simple problems and easy solutions? It wasn't like I was picking out a pair of shoes, where color, style of the heel, open-toed vs. close-toed, and straps vs. buckles had to be considered. Picking out locks should be easy. Locks were locks and doorknobs were doorknobs.

I studied all of the locks. As far as I could tell, the only significant difference was the price. They all came with two keys. There where gold ones, silver, bronze, and antique finish.

I picked up one package then set it down again. I wanted to buy the cheapest one, but I knew that wasn't the thing to do. Just because I couldn't tell the difference between the 20-dollar lock and the 50-dollar one didn't mean no one else could. Buying the cheapest one would be like buying a faux leather jacket thinking nobody would notice. It wasn't worth the risk.

I dropped a doorknob and deadbolt set into the cart and headed toward the paint department. I can't afford to replace the appliances and the carpet, but I can afford to paint. It's a start.

I spotted Edna Tilley while I was waiting for the paint to be mixed. Instinct had me ducking my head and turning the other way.

She spotted you!

Why fight it? I could run, but I couldn't hide. Edna and her cronies would find me. They would corner me, pluck my feathers like a hapless chicken, and then throw me into a sizzling cauldron of insidious gossip and serve me up for lunch.

Fine. I turned and met the challenge head on. There was room in the pot for more than one chicken. No point in frying alone.

"Good morning Edna. How are you?"

"I'm surprised to see you out and about today. You've had a rough week."

I rolled my eyes. "Tell me about it."

Edna waited a beat, but I closed my mouth and looked at her expectantly. "Well, I heard you beat up Amy."

With a wink and a grin, I responded. "Really? That's not quite what happened, but the truth really doesn't matter. If you can't elaborate on a story, what fun would it be?"

"Oh, well," Edna shuffled her feet. "You were supposed to be at work."

"Funny, that's the same thing Mark said when I walked in on them." I picked up the paint cans and lowered them into my cart. "I really need to get going. I have a lot to do today. It was nice talking to you."

"Annie, wait!" Edna grabbed my sleeve to stop me. "What about your mother? The Sheriff's Department is looking for her body out at the construction site! Aren't you upset?"

I smiled again. "Oh, I'm sure Mama will get a big kick out of it. She always enjoyed stirring up trouble."

"But …" Edna stared at me as if I had just sprouted two heads. "She's dead, murdered. Doesn't that bother you?"

"Mama's not dead. I got a letter from her not long ago."

"What! Where is she?"

"I'm not sure. She moves around a bit, but she misses this place. She's always reminiscing about one incident or another when she writes to me. Just last month she carried on about the time she found you locked in the bathroom, bare …"

"Tell her hi next time you talk to her." Edna cut in as she spun around and took off down the aisle.

Grinning, I wheeled my cart around and headed for the checkout aisle. Miracles do happen. I scored one on Edna Tilley.

* * *

I made it home without further incident. Lynette's money was burning a hole in my pocket, but I managed to resist temptation.

Dad stopped by earlier this afternoon. He had Billy drop him off so he could pick up the truck. He knew I was planning on forgetting to return it. A girl can't get away with anything these days.

I cleaned out the kitchen cabinets and put in new shelf paper, washed and waxed the floor, and scrubbed out the bathtub. It would take hours to scrub out the toilet, so I left it for another day. As long as I hover at least six inches above the seat, I won't get any cooties.

I showered, did my hair, and tried to hide the bruises on my face. I've always kept an emergency kit in my desk drawer at work. I had makeup, clear fingernail polish and emery boards, Tylenol, and tampons.

Scrubbed clean and made up, I climbed back into my dirty clothes. The ball was in Mark's court. If he didn't bring something appropriate for me to wear, I wasn't going.

I had an hour yet. I spent the time cleaning out and reorganizing my purse. I still had the envelope of money in my purse. I don't like carrying that much cash around, especially when it's not mine, but until the locks are changed, I can't leave it in the apartment. I glanced at the clock again.

I grabbed my keys and slipped out of the apartment. I walked down the hallway, climbed the stairs, and traversed the hallway between the two upstairs apartments. I stopped under the pull down stairs leading to the attic and gave the cord a yank.

I haven't been in the attic since John LeBlanc told me to clear my mother's stuff out of his house. I didn't know what else to do with it, so I shoved it up in the attic. What better place to stash the money?

Back in my apartment, I finished emptying my purse. I flipped it upside down over the box I was currently using for a trashcan and gave it a good shake. Dust, lint, and tiny bits of paper floated down. I caught a rogue pen before it hit the bottom of the box. Satisfied, I started reassembling the contents: wallet, pens, brush, comb, green scrunchie, barrettes, compact, lipstick, emery board, cell phone, my journal, and two EpiPens.

The journal's a habit I picked up from my mother. I used to keep it in the nightstand beside my bed, but I caught Mark reading it once. After that I kept it in my purse.

I've carried the EpiPens for as long as I can remember. Some people are allergic to bee stings. I'm not that lucky. I'm allergic to peanuts. It doesn't take much to trigger an allergic reaction. My throat starts closing up and I can't breathe. The EpiPen contains a dose of epinephrine and it's spring-loaded. It's saved my life more than once.

I don't like to eat out. I hate asking how every dish is prepared or if they use peanut oil or corn oil. It annoys the waitresses and embarrasses the people I'm with. Fortunately Sarah's birthday party is at Giovanni's. I've eaten there hundreds of times. I know what's safe and what's not.

I heard the knock at the door and dropped the EpiPens into my purse. If Mark remembered to bring my evening bag, my wallet, cell phone, and the EpiPens would be transferred to it. There wouldn't be room for much else.

I opened the door blocking the entrance with my body. If Mark wasn't toting clothes, I wasn't letting him in.

His hands were empty.

"Where are my clothes?"

Mark smiled innocently. "I'll bring them in later."

"Go get them."

"There's time." He started to nudge me back.

I gave the door a quick shove. It caught Mark's toes and he jumped back with a curse. I slammed the door shut and flipped the lock.

I told you so. I told you so. I told you so.

There's nothing worse than a conscience that likes to gloat. Mark's early. Was he counting on a quickie before we headed over to the restaurant? I slipped the chair under the doorknob for added protection. Why didn't I call Doug and ask him to install the new locks this afternoon?

"Annie!" Mark pounded on the door.

"Go away! Why did I think I could trust you? You're nothing but a liar and a cheat."

"Open the door!"

"No!"

"Fine! I'll go get your damn clothes."

I stood by the door listening and grinned when I heard the outside door slam. I think Mark's a little annoyed with me. If he wants a tumble, he'll have to track down Amy. As he fired her yesterday, I don't think she'll be in the mood either.

I peeked through the peephole. Mark was back with a small overnight bag and my dress draped over his arm. "Open the door Annie."

"Set the stuff down and go back out to the car and wait."

"Jesus Annie! You're my wife. I've seen you dress before."

"True, but you lost that right two weeks ago. Drop the clothes and go back out to the car and wait, or the deal is off."

For close to a minute, Mark didn't move. He looked angry. It didn't bode well for a pleasant evening. With deliberate care, he set the overnight bag down and dropped the dress. He backed away from the door.

I sighed in relief. Why did I think we could work things through?

I waited until the outside door opened and closed before easing the chair from under the doorknob. I flipped the lock and unlatched the door.

Watch out!

I barely had time to register the thought before a big hand slammed against the door. The door caught me in the chest and I stumbled back tripping over my own feet. I landed on the floor and skidded to a stop.

Mark grabbed my dress and the overnight bag and heaved them in my direction. He stepped through the opening and stopped, feet spread, hands on his hips, and glowered at me. "Don't *ever* tell me what to do."

I slowly slid the overnight bag off my stomach and sat up. I didn't think about the rug burn on my forearm or the additions to my repertoire of bruises. Mark's voice was quiet, menacingly so.

Mark has a temper and he always yells when he gets mad. I'm used to that. It's when his voice drops to a whisper that I get nervous. At that point the anger has turned to rage, and rage shuts off the conscience. I started whispering quiet prayers as I tried to figure out a way to diffuse the situation. Mark was beyond reason.

There was another knock at the door. "Am I interrupting something?"

Thank you Jesus.

Mark's head whipped around. "What the hell are you doing here?"

Luke didn't answer him. He stepped through the door and surveyed the scene. His eyes narrowed and his mouth thinned. He looked back at Mark and then back at me. "What's going on?"

I scrambled up off the floor gamely swallowing the groan. I dusted the lint and the dust off my jeans before meeting his gaze. "Good evening Luke. What can I do for you?"

"I need to talk to you. I drove by and saw your light on, thought I would take a chance and stop in."

"She can't talk to you now. We're heading over to my grandmother's birthday party shortly." Mark had that innocent smile plastered on his face again.

"Annie?"

"He's right, but it's a dinner and not a party. Mark's dropping me off at the Mountain around nine. We can talk then if that's okay."

Mark's head swiveled back toward me. His eyes were hot. "Annie, I'm sure the deputy has better things to do on a Saturday night. You can talk to him on Monday."

What? Does he think I'm stupid? "Luke?" I asked quietly. *Please!* Maybe he's a mind reader or better yet, maybe he has *The Sight*. He's full-blooded Irish so there's a chance. Mark was mad. Retribution was a guarantee.

Luke stepped back with a nod. "Nine o'clock. I'll see you then."

Mark closed the door quietly behind Luke. I don't think his anger had cooled any, but he was doing a pretty good job of hiding it. He moved over to the front window and stood there, watching and waiting.

I didn't move.

The hiss was quiet, almost inaudible. "Annie, get dressed. We don't want to be late."

I glanced out the window before picking up my dress and the overnight bag. Luke's Explorer was still sitting behind Mark's Porsche.

CHAPTER EIGHT

"Did you remember my evening bag?" I asked after exiting the bedroom dressed and ready to go. I'm going to the party. I want to wish Sarah a happy birthday, and Mark's not going to cheat me out of that, but this is the last official outing as husband and wife. Mark won't change. It's time to face that.

Mark grimaced. "No, sorry."

I picked up my purse and slung it over my shoulder. It would have to do.

Mark shook out my wrap and draped it around me. "Ready?"

I glanced up at Mark suspiciously. He was deferential and attentive. It was as if the argument never happened.

He tried to strike up a conversation as we drove to Giovanni's but finally lapsed into silence. He slid into a parking spot and came around to open my door. I reached down to get my purse. "That purse doesn't match your shoes. Why don't you leave it in the car?"

I hesitated for a moment, but ultimately let the straps slide off my wrist. Mark was right. My sandals were royal blue and my purse was a brown leather satchel. Both were fashionable in their own right, but gauche together. He took my hand as I stepped out of the car.

Giovanni's is the only fancy restaurant in town. Their pizza is to die for, but that's nothing compared to their penne rigate and their Sole Marsala. The dinner started out formally, but with each course, and more wine, the mood shifted and lifted. By the time the entrée was removed and dessert ordered, cheeks were flushed and the mood jolly.

I wasn't drinking. I was caught off guard once tonight and once was enough. I wasn't taking any chances. The tyrant was lurking in the shadows. I didn't want to give him an excuse to surface again.

Sarah emptied another glass of wine before turning to me. "I didn't think you would be here tonight."

"It's your birthday."

"So it's true, you moved out."

"Grandma," Mark patted Sarah's hand. "We're having some problems right now, but we're working through them."

"Mark …"

Mark squeezed my leg. It could have been interpreted as an intimate signal or a warning. I took it as a warning and let my words trail off. It didn't matter anymore.

Sarah's eyes shifted from Mark to me and then back to Mark again. His arm was draped across my shoulders. I shrugged it away a couple of times, but it kept coming back. I finally gave up and let it be. It hinted of an intimacy between us that no longer existed.

"Well don't take too long. I would like to see some great-grandbabies before I die." Sarah's blunt declaration cut into my reverie.

Mark laughed. "Don't worry Grandma. By this time next year, there will be a little Rosetti to cuddle and spoil."

Sarah sat back, satisfied. "Good."

I glanced up at Mark through the corner of my eye. What game was he playing now?

The waiter set a double fudge chocolate brownie and ice cream topped with chocolate and pralines in front of me. I glanced up at him frowning. It was decadent and my taste buds were standing at attention, but I didn't order dessert. "You made a mistake. That's not mine."

"I ordered it." Mark blew softly in my ear. "I was hoping you would share it with me."

"Mark, don't." The food, the attention, talk of babies … Mark wanted me to know what I was giving up. I'm standing firm on my principles, but it was getting harder and harder to do. What happened to my conscience? Did she take the night off and leave me floundering on my own? Talk about falling down on the job!

"Open wide."

I opened my mouth to object, but Mark was too quick. A spoonful of pralines and chocolate slid past my lips and danced across my tongue. I swallowed as my taste buds cried out in ecstasy, but then they started gagging and so did I.

Peanuts!

My heart rate jumped as the adrenaline surged through my veins.

Three minutes and counting …

Panicking, I felt around for my purse. I could feel my throat start to swell and close.

"Annie?"

"Peanuts! I need my purse!" My tongue thickened making it hard to talk. The words came out garbled and confusing.

"What?" Mark frowned at me. His cheeks were flushed and his eyes glassy. He matched his grandmother glass for glass. There would be no help on that front.

Your purse is still in the Porsche!

I groped Mark's leg trying to get my fingers into his pocket. I needed the keys. Mark grabbed my hands stilling their frantic search. "Later, baby." He kept a grip on my fingers and grinned at me.

No! I jerked my hands free and shoved away from the table.

I was wheezing, sucking in air as fast as I could. I needed my EpiPens before my throat closed up like a fortress under siege. Where was my purse? I don't go anywhere without my purse. Details and facts were blending and twisting. It was hard to think.

"Annie, what's wrong?"

The car! Your purse is in the car!

I don't have the keys!

So?

I bumped into a waiter carrying a tray full of wine glasses as I shoved my way through the crowd. The sound of glass hitting tile added a tinkling surreal quality to the den. My vision was shifting in and out of focus. I spotted a brass flowerpot with a fake rubber plant in it. It was sitting next to the screen that separated the bar from the restaurant. I snatched it up and stumbled toward the door.

Unseen hands grabbed at me. I wrenched free of their grip and pushed through the double doors. I tripped on the curb. Stumbling, I tucked the flowerpot under my arm like a football, and ran. I spotted the Porsche and lurched in that direction. I opened my mouth to draw in another breath ...

Nothing.

The clock stopped. I was out of time. Lifting the flowerpot over my head, I heaved it toward the driver's side window and dove in after it. I felt around for my purse.

Darkness was crashing over me and then receding like a big wall of water. I was drowning. My hand closed around the EpiPen. Fumbling, I pulled the top off and jammed it against my leg. Another wave crashed over me. I let it pull me down into the warm, comforting darkness.

* * *

I swam close to the surface once, but I didn't like what I saw. I was stretched out under a street light in the parking lot. I know the cement's hard and gravely. It wouldn't be comfortable. There were blue and red strobe lights all over the place and lots of people milling about. The noise level was probably unbearable.

That was enough to make me hesitate, but it was the big oaf of an EMT tech with his fingers in my mouth that sealed the deal. He was shoving a hard plastic tube down my throat. Been there, done that. I didn't like it the first time and I knew I wouldn't like it now. I dove back down into the darkness.

I surfaced again. Nothing good ever lasts forever. I kept my eyes closed and drifted, half in and half out of consciousness. I knew the minute I opened my eyes, the break would be over and all my nerve endings would head back to work.

"Annie, come on now. Open your eyes."

Do I have to? I don't like to hurt, it hurts.

I tried to tell them to leave me alone, but I couldn't move my tongue. The trachea tube was still in place.

Damn.

"Annie, I know you can hear me." Dr. Cantrell's voice was soft, but insistent. "You're scaring your dad. Open your eyes so I can tell him you're all right."

Daddy?

I opened my eyes. As predicted, every nerve ending jumped to attention. I groaned and nearly went under again. Every ache, every pain, was vying for my attention. I couldn't separate one from the other.

"I thought that would do the trick." I turned my eyes toward Dr. Cantrell and glared at her. Her eyes twinkled in response. Doctors heal, but sometimes I think they take immense delight in torturing their patients. They wield needles and scalpels, and dump stingy stuff all over open wounds. I like Dr. Cantrell and she's good, but right now she ranks right up there with the executioners in the 1500's. They liked to torture their prisoners before executing them.

"Are you ready to get that tube out?"

I nodded. I was rarely aware of them putting it in, but the sadistic bastards insisted on waiting until I was awake and aware before pulling it out. It's horrible. You want to gag, but you can't, and for a brief second, you can't breathe. The incident that led to the trachea tube in the first place is still pretty fresh in your mind at that point. Cut off your air and panic sets in. Knowing it's only for a second doesn't make a wit of difference.

It didn't take long before I was breathing on my own again. Drawing air through my bruised and battered trachea hurt, but I was breathing and I was alive. I've had close calls before, but I think this incident ranks right up there at the top. It was too close.

My throat hurt and I knew the combination of drugs floating through my system would have me swelling up like a balloon. The resulting rash would itch and annoy me for at least a week. I've been through it before so I knew what to expect. What I didn't understand was why my arm hurt.

"Can I go home now?" It was more of a croak than a question.

"Keep your shorts on. I'm not done with you yet." Dr. Cantrell snapped on a pair of gloves. "I need to put some finishing touches on my handiwork. I thought I would be done before you woke up. Hold your breath."

"What ..." The question ended on a strangled cry.

"Next time you decide to dive through a broken window, you might want to knock the glass out first."

I leaned over and glanced at my arm. "Ouch. How many?"

"You have more stitches than a hundred-year-old Raggedy Ann doll." Dr. Cantrell rarely minced her words. I usually like that trait in her. Not today. A nice, heartfelt lie would have gone a long way in smoothing my battered ego.

"Scars?"

"There will be some. The cuts on your legs are superficial. There's a small gash on your left arm, but your right arm took the brunt of it. They'll fade in time."

Sure, I believe that.

"Annie, you could have died tonight."

"I know."

"Why did you leave your purse in the car?"

Mark told me to. "I didn't think it would be a problem."

"Well, you were wrong." Dr Cantrell tied the last knot and set her tools of torture down. "Don't let it happen again." She pulled off her gloves and threw them in the trash before disappearing through the curtain with a swish.

I rose gingerly and glanced around for my clothes. The nurse shook her head. Resigned, I slipped into a clean hospital gown. I have a whole collection of them at home. It's not the first time I had the honor of walking out of the emergency room with my butt swinging in the wind. At least the gown matched the putrid yellow and green bruises on my face. I didn't need to look in the mirror to know my makeup was history.

My right arm was wrapped in stark white gauze from bicep to wrist.

There was another bandage on my left arm and about 50 little Band-Aids on my calves. To top that off, I could feel the steroids and antihistamines bloating my face. I would emerge from the cubicle looking like an extra from a 1950's horror movie. Compared to me, Frankenstein was a babe.

I wanted to go home. I would never get there if I didn't stop cowering behind door number three. I drew in a breath and headed for the waiting room. Mark spotted me and then stared at me in open-mouth horror. My chin wobbled. I was trying really hard to be optimistic. I'm up and moving, not on a slab in the morgue. I *was* thankful.

Luke and dad were standing by the double doors, talking. They both straightened when they spotted me. Luke's gaze was assessing, but he managed to keep the horror hidden. They learn lots of useful skills in cop school. That must be one of them.

"Are you all right?" Mark reached out intent on taking my hand, but jerked his back again. Mark would have flunked out of cop school. He couldn't even touch me. My already sagging spirits plummeted to the basement.

I turned on my heel and nearly went down when the stupid little paper slippers on my feet lost their traction. It was the final straw. I broke into tears.

"You'll be all right, baby." Daddy wrapped his arms around me and kissed my forehead. "Let me take you home."

"Annie?"

I turned in dad's arms and silently met Mark's gaze.

Mark's lips thinned. "You're a mess and so is the Porsche. There's blood all over the seats."

I glared in response. The Porsche was Mark's first love. I'm not really sure where I fall on his list, but after deliberately breaking the window on his beloved car, I'm probably close to the bottom, along with Brussels sprouts and cabbage.

Mark's mood did an abrupt about face. "Don't worry about it. The glass can be replaced tomorrow and I'll have it detailed on Monday."

"I need my purse."

"I've got it." He shifted a plastic bag so I could see what was in it. My purse was a bloody mess. I could well imagine what the front seat of the Porsche looked like.

I know Mark expected me to apologize, but I just couldn't do it. Leaving my purse in the car was his idea.

Mark held out his hand. "Come on. Let's go home."

I ignored the outstretched hand and snuggled closer to my father. "I'm going home with Daddy."

Mark's eyes narrowed. He started to say something but must have changed his mind. He dropped the bloody bag at my feet, turned on his heel, and walked out.

CHAPTER NINE

I slept most of Sunday and called off from work through Wednesday. There wasn't much Harry could do about it as I had a doctor's note. Tabby came by Monday evening and helped me wash my hair all the while filling me in on the latest gossip.

The story generated from the incident Saturday night hadn't changed anymore than expected. As the story goes, I ordered the dessert knowing full well it was covered with peanuts and not pralines. I was already depressed due to the state of my marriage. The purse and the shoe unearthed by Harry's crew and the subsequent investigation pushed me right over the edge. I couldn't take it anymore. Suicide was a way out. I started having second thoughts *after* I swallowed the peanuts. In typical O'Reilly fashion, I made a production out of saving myself.

"Seriously Tabby, there has to be a hundred easier ways to kill myself."

"Oh?"

"I'm not going to swallow a handful of peanuts. Suffocating has to be the absolute worst way to die. It only takes a few minutes, but those minutes feel like a lifetime. Trust me, I know. A bullet through the roof of your mouth is supposed to be fast, but I don't have a gun. If you do it right, slitting your wrists is just as fast, but it's messy. Nope. If I wanted to kill myself I would swallow a handful of sleeping pills and drift my way into eternity."

I glanced up at Tabby and my grin faltered. She was wide eyed and as pale as a ghost. "Relax Tabby. I'm scared to death of guns, faint at the sight of blood, and can't stomach anything stronger than Tylenol. I'll be around for awhile yet."

"How can you joke about it? You almost died."

"I didn't. Besides, it was Mark's dessert, not mine." I shifted around to face her. "So, how much money did you lose Saturday night?" It was a blatant attempt to change the subject.

Tabby hesitated, but ultimately went along with it. "I had a blast, but …"

I grinned at her. "How much did you lose?" One of Tabby's suppliers gave her two free passes for a casino boat trip for Christmas. They were expiring soon. She tried to talk me into going with her, but I know my luck. I wasn't about to set foot on that boat. Tabby and her cousin Ashley headed down Saturday afternoon, spent the evening gambling, and came back Sunday.

Tabby grinned in response. "I took your advice and left my debit card in the car. Thank God I did. It's too easy to get caught up."

"You had a good time. That's what's important."

"Yeah I did, but I spent too much money. I'll be eating Hamburger Helper and tuna casserole until I get paid again."

"Face it. You're a closet gambler."

"Not me, but Johnny LeBlanc is."

"Johnny!" Johnny's another one of my stepbrothers. Out of Lynette's five marriages, I ended up with six stepbrothers. Luke, Johnny, and Dave are the only ones still living in the area. I still think of Dave as a brother, but I severed the branch of the family tree that Luke sits on, and used the LeBlanc branch for kindling.

"Johnny started out on the craps table then moved to Baccarat half way through the evening. It wasn't the nickel and dime tables either. He was dropping *hundreds*."

"Johnny? Are you sure?"

"He seemed to know all the dealers. I think the Carolina Casino is one of his regular hangouts."

"Can he afford to do that?"

Tabby shrugged. "I don't care if Johnny gambles away his inheritance and ends up living in a cardboard box, but I care about you. Why were you with Mark Saturday night?

"Does it matter?"

"Yes. If he sweet talks you into going back to him, I'm going to add a few bruises to your cache."

"I wanted to go to Sarah's party, and Mark said he would let me collect my clothes if I went with him."

"Annie, Mark won't give you your clothes. He'll keep making things as inconvenient at possible until you give in and go home. Once he has you back where he wants you, he'll make you pay for embarrassing him."

My shoulders drooped. "I know."

"What were you thinking?"

"Mark's a no good dirty rotten scoundrel, but …"

"Do you still love him?"

"No." I don't know.

* * *

Tabby left me with a lot to think about. Do I still love Mark? No, he doesn't deserve my love, but sometimes the heart overrules logic. Dieters can go months on end without a single piece of candy or dish of ice cream. Then one day, their control snaps. Need and greed overrides logic, and they go on a three-day binge. Just like the dieter, the love Mark and I once shared is bound to trip me up now and again.

Replace him. That's how your mother did it.

God no!

Why not? It would be easier to resist Mark if you weren't so twitchy. You haven't had any in three weeks. Lynette would have been going into withdrawal by now.

I'm not my mother!

You're twitchy.

So? That doesn't mean I'm going to jump the first man I see. I'm not a nymphomaniac.

Luke had a fine package at 16 and he's grown since then.

I rolled off the sofa and stomped around the apartment. Luke! Come on! I would rather swallow a handful of peanuts than sleep with Luke.

I doubt you would spend much time sleeping.

I kicked the ottoman.

Okay, how about Miguel? Your mother said he had the stamina of a race horse.

I grabbed my cell phone when it rang. I didn't care who it was as long as it diverted my thoughts from race horses and well endowed packages.

"Hi babe, how are you feeling?"

I would have given myself a swift kick in the ass, but I'm not a contortionist. Why didn't I check the caller ID? "How did you get this number?"

"I got it from Harry. I didn't know what else to do. You haven't been returning my calls."

Dad was screening my calls. I don't know why it surprised me. He was really pissed when he found out I was with Mark Saturday night.

"How are you feeling? Are you ready to come home?"

"No."

"Why not? You said you loved me. Was it a lie?"

"No, but ..."

"But what? Come home, Annie."

"I can't. I have issues, or are they your issues? It's your behavior, but it's my problem. Does that make it your issue or mine?"

"What the hell are you talking about?"

"Your temper."

"My temper! I thought you left me because of Amy. I fixed that problem."

"Did you, really?"

"Yes."

If you believe that, I've got a pair of Via Spiga hiking boots you can have for ten bucks.

I know he's lying. I'm not that gullible. Besides, Rita Johanson told Carla McDuffy, who told Tabby in strictest confidence, that she saw Amy sneaking out of Mark's house Monday morning and again yesterday.

"What about your temper?"

"I don't have a temper."

"Mark, do you remember the time you threw my antique butter churn through the living room window?"

"That, my dear, was justified anger, not temper. That stupid thing cost a hundred bucks."

"True, but it cost over $500 to fix the window."

"The only true issue is your spending."

I rolled my eyes. I'm a careful shopper. I compare prices and I weigh the satisfaction against the cost before I plunk down my money. Maybe the antique butter churn was a little pricy, but it reminded me of the one Grammy used to have. That made it priceless and therefore an incredible deal. "You're missing the point."

"Annie, I'll tell you what the point is. I want you home. I'll be over in an hour to pick you up."

"No. Would you consider counseling? Father Nolan offers ..."

"Don't be stupid! We don't need marriage counseling."

"I won't go back to the way things were. If you're not willing to go to marriage counseling, then you really don't care about our marriage."

"You know better. Why else would I be begging you to come home?"

"You're not begging, you're demanding."

I heard Mark's teeth grind. He was losing patience. "Annie, come home."

"No."

"Fine."

"What?" I asked with some trepidation. Mark was up to something. I could hear it in his voice.

"If you're not back where you belong by Friday, I'll start sacrificing your shoes."

"You're holding my shoes hostage!"

Mark chuckled. "Yeah, it should be fun. I'll break off the heel first, then I'll strip the leather off, and last but not least, I'll break its sole."

"No!"

"Don't worry, I'll just butcher one. I'll send its mate to you so you know what your continued defiance is costing you."

"No Mark, please." My voice cracked making it sound more like a plea than a statement. He was playing me. Intellectually I knew that, but it didn't seem to make a difference.

"You are my wife. I've given you enough time to work off your mad. Come home." I could hear the smug satisfaction in his voice. He knew my weaknesses. I'll give him that, but I'll be damned if I would give into him. Mark threatened my shoes. If he really loved me, he wouldn't stab me in the heart like that.

"I am home." I'm not giving in, not even for my open-toed, alligator skin high heeled boots.

"Annie, you're starting to make me mad. Don't make me …"

I cut him off. I knew he was getting mad. I just didn't want to know how mad. That way I could pretend he was just annoyed. Mad's scary. "Mark, I'm not going to listen to this anymore."

"Fine. Say goodbye to your hiking boots."

"You wouldn't."

"Try me."

✶ ✶ ✶

"Thanks for the ride Dad."

"Are you sure you want to work today? Dr. Cantrell will write another note if you need it."

"I'm not pushing my luck. Harry's already pissed." He's not the most understanding of bosses and, with or without a doctor's note, if I miss any more work, he will fire me. The Sheriff's Department cleared the construction site yesterday so work resumed today. That should help, but they lost three-and-a-half days because of my mother. *I'll* be paying for that.

"How are you getting home?"

"Tabby's picking me up. Miguel told her the truck would be ready today."

Dad grinned. "Are you still mad about that?"

"Yes. You sided with Miguel."

"Miguel was right. Andy's been working on the truck for three days."

"That's beside the point."

Dad's grin widened. "Right."

"Okay, okay. The truck needed a little work. The least he could have done was let me swap it back before confiscating it."

"Why? Picking on you has always been one of his favorite pastimes."

My smile dropped.

We both lapsed into silence until he turned onto County Road 10. Pruitt Building and Construction is close to town, but outside the city limits. Harry has a great big Quonset for tools and supplies, and a huge fenced-in area for large equipment. The office is built in the right front corner of the building. It's a good set up. Outside the city limits there are fewer codes, less inspections, and fewer taxes.

"Has the Sheriff's Department finished digging around the construction site?"

"Yes. Doug said they were going back to work today."

"Good."

Silence settled between us again.

"Do you know what they found?"

"I know they found Lynette's purse and a shoe. If they found anything else, they're keeping it under wraps."

"Are you sure she's not dead?"

"Lynette's not dead!"

"I wish I could believe that."

"Daddy!"

"Tell me, why did you stop calling Lynette 'Mom' and start calling her Lynette? Did she ask you to?"

Mollified, I went along with the change of subject. Lynette wasn't dead. I was hanging onto that belief until the Sheriff's Department *proves* otherwise.

"No. I just decided that it took more than a biological act to turn a woman into a mother. Lynette didn't have a maternal bone in her body. It just took me that long to figure it out." Daddy thinks I look at the world, and my mother, through the proverbial rose colored glasses. I don't. I can see better than most.

"She loved you."

"No Daddy, she didn't. She might have when I was a baby or even a little girl, but when I reached puberty, she saw me as competition."

"That makes sense. When scoping out men, Lynette made a point of teaming up with the ugliest woman in the bar so she would compare favorably." He glanced over at me and grinned. "You're not ugly."

I laughed in response. No matter how bad things were when I was growing up, dad always managed to make me laugh. "Was that supposed to be a compliment?"

"Of course." He pulled into the parking lot next to Pruitt Building and Construction.

"Tabby's picking you up, right?"

"Yes. Miguel said the truck would be ready, and the asshole jerk better not be lying."

"Annie!"

"Well he is a jerk."

"You two used to be close."

"Not any more." I responded quietly.

"What happened? I didn't think anything would break you two apart."

"Miguel found the charms of an older, more experienced woman more alluring than me."

Daddy jerked upright. "Jesus Annie!"

"I stopped blaming him years ago. It wasn't his fault. I saw men far more experienced than him crumble when Lynette smiled at them."

"Did he tell you?"

"No. I walked in on them. It was worse than walking in on Mark and Amy."

Dad raked his fingers through his hair, a clear sign of his agitation. "She's your mother and I know you love her, but ..." He shook his head, obviously deciding to keep his thoughts to himself. It didn't matter. I knew what he was thinking.

"I better get in there."

"Be careful, baby. Call me if you need anything."

"Thanks for the ride Dad."

CHAPTER TEN

I stood by the door and watched my father pull out of the parking lot and turn onto the road before pushing the door open and going in. I had a ton of work piled up on my desk. Time off always came with a price.

I dropped my new purse into the drawer and turned on the computer. Tabby bought the purse for me. She called it a get well/birthday present combo. I had to throw my old purse away. It was covered with blood. I salvaged my wallet, cell phone, the garage door opener, and my makeup bag. That was it. I even had to throw away my journal and start a new one. I wasn't happy about that.

"What the hell are you doing here?" Harry bellowed from the door of his office 30 seconds later. It looked like he'd already been out to the construction site. His shirt was dusty and dirty, and his jeans torn. Not a good sign. Harry preferred to run his business from the air conditioned comfort of his office.

"I work here."

"Since when? I don't keep slackers on the payroll."

"Harry, I told you I would be back today. I have a doctor's note and you know it." I picked up the stack of invoices and set them next to the computer. I wasn't going to let him intimidate me today.

Brave words. My heart was beating a mile-a-minute. I'm not a poker player. I'm no good at bluffing. I didn't want to lose my job. The pay sucks and the boss is a tyrant, but I'm a good secretary and a passable accountant. Besides, working for Harry beats scrubbing toilets and making beds over at the motel.

Harry's voice went from a bellow to menacingly soft. "You're fired."

"What!"

"Go home. Better yet, go shopping. Pick up some fancy underwear and a see-through nightie."

It wasn't the days off or even the delay up at the worksite. I might have been able to swallow that, but this? It wasn't fair. Amy can have Mark! I'll tie a bow around his tallywacker and hand him over on a silver platter. I don't care as long as they stop screwing up my life. "Harry, please. I need my job. Don't do this to me."

"If you put some effort into your marriage, maybe your husband wouldn't be preying on innocent girls."

Innocent! My panic did an abrupt about face. Anger surged through my veins. Compared to Amy, my mother was the Virgin Mary. Amy gave up her innocence at the ripe old age of 12. She graduated from high school with honors by knowing whose itch to scratch.

Harry stepped into his office and came back out with a box and tossed it my direction. "You've got ten minutes to clean out your desk."

"Good morning, Daddy. I'm sorry I'm ..." Amy's words trailed off when she spotted me. She turned and glared at Harry. "Daddy, you said you would take care of her."

Harry shoved his hands in his pockets and shuffled his feet. "Don't worry. She's history."

I opened the bottom drawer of my desk and grabbed my purse. I slid the straps up on my shoulder. I was fighting back the tears and the panic. Amy was the one caught with her panties around her ankles, but I was the one getting screwed.

Amy had moved away from the door and was watching me the way a mongoose watches a snake.

I looked up at Harry. "You'll regret it." Amy wasn't a bookkeeper. She was a secretary and a pitiful one at that. She knew how to take messages and file her nails. Oh, and she knew how to provide a good lunch.

"Get out of here."

I straightened, shoved the drawer shut with my foot, and met Amy's glare with one of my own. "You want my job, fine, you can have it. You want my husband? Well, you can have him too. Just remember, Mark prefers French high cuts to a thong, and he prefers to be on the bottom. That way you get to do all the work. Oh, and if he pulls out the hand-cuffs, you might want to run. When it comes to the bondage games, he's a little rough."

"Bitch!"

"Annie! Stop it!" Harry grabbed onto Amy's arm to keep her from lunging at me.

"Harry, I don't deserve this."

"Get out of here."

I grabbed the dieffenbachia plant off the top of my desk and walked out. I let the door slam behind me. Why does Fate have it out for me? I'm Irish. Surely that should count for something.

Fate?

Who else?

Mark.

Mark! Why? What would be the point?

He wants you back. Losing your job reduces your options to one and you know it.

I'm not going back to Mark. He keeps saying he wants me back, but it's not true.

He's a lousy housekeeper. Maybe he's just looking for a maid.

Maybe that's it, but hiring Molly Maids would be cheaper than keeping a wife *and* a mistress. The whole situation makes absolutely no sense.

I crossed the parking lot and turned right. I would call for a ride eventually, but for now I wanted to walk. If I called Tabby, I would be stuck answering questions. I'll call her once I figure out the answers.

You'll be in Tennessee by then.

Okay, it's time to look at the situation logically. Mark says he wants me back. When he couldn't sweet talk me into coming back, he tried coercion. When that didn't work, he put the screws to me financially.

You're right. He wants you back. Now tell me why.

That's the problem. I don't know why. He hasn't stopped seeing Amy so he's not repentant.

Money?

I don't think so. I don't have any financial claim on his business or the house. He had both long before we were married. Mark likes sex and he wanted it all the time, but he doesn't need me for that either. Amy is more than willing to warm my side of the bed.

Why did he marry you? Two hundred years ago men married according to their station and then kept a mistress. Amy is Harry's only daughter. Mark should have married her and furnished you with an apartment.

I kicked a stone and kept on walking. Logic wasn't working.

A few minutes later I heard the low rumble of a car coming up behind me. I didn't turn around and look. I didn't need to. The sound of Mark's Porsche was distinct. How did he know I was out here and on foot?

The Porsche slowed when it came up along side of me. The window slid down. "Annie, get in the car."

"Go away Mark."

The Porsche shot ahead of me and screeched to a halt. My steps faltered when Mark climbed out of the car and slammed the door. He stopped ten feet in front of me and stared at me with a glare that chilled to the bone. "Get in the car."

I backed up a step. This wasn't the man I married. The man standing before me had to be his evil twin. He escaped the dungeon and now my loving husband was chained to the wall, and I was chained to a monster.

"Now!"

"No!" I spat the word at him, turned, and ran back the way I came. I hadn't taken three steps when a hand clamped down on my arm jerking me to a stop.

"I said get in the car!" Mark's fingers bit into my arm. I could feel the sutures struggling to hold the torn skin together in spite of the pull caused by his grip. The dieffenbachia slid from my fingers.

Mark yelped when the flowerpot landed on his toes. He kicked it aside before swinging me around. He grabbed my left arm. Skin to skin, his grip tightened and twisted.

"No!" The adrenaline surged through me. Desperation spurred me on. I kicked him and twisted in his grip. It wasn't a fair fight. Mark was a foot taller than I was and he outweighed me by at least a hundred pounds, but I wasn't going down without a fight. My fingernails dug into his arm. He hissed again.

Changing tactics, Mark jerked me up, wrapped his muscular arms around me and squeezed, cutting off my air. My thoughts shifted from escaping to breathing. He spun around and started dragging me toward the car. "Just wait until I get you home."

"No!" My protest was more of a strangled cry than anything. I couldn't breathe. It was Saturday night all over again. I thought I heard a car, but I knew it was just imagination born of desperation. There would be no hero riding to the rescue today. I was on my own.

"Let go of her!"

I felt Mark's steps falter then stop. I recognized the voice. Luke wasn't a Knight in Shining Armor, but he'd do in a pinch. "Help …"

Mark tightened his grip cutting of my words as he swung around putting me between him and Luke. "Annie's distraught. I'm taking her home."

"Release her!" Luke came to a halt six feet in front of us. His feet were spread and his hands at the ready. His eyes locked on Mark.

"Annie needs rest and quiet. I'll make sure she gets it."

"Set her down and step away." Luke's voice was quiet, almost soothing. I wanted to tell him that that tactic wouldn't work on Mark, but I was too busy trying to pry Mark's arm loose and praying. I understand why God ignored me when I asked for the winning LOTTO numbers last week, but one deep breath wasn't an unreasonable request. Surely he would grant me that.

"Annie," Mark gave me a little shake. "Tell the deputy that everything is fine and that you would like to go home." The grip around my chest eased.

Thank you Lord! I sucked in a breath too intent on breathing to bother with talking. I coughed and gagged.

"Put her down and we can talk about this."

Mark's grip tightened again. "No. I'm taking her home. Dr. Ramsey's worried about her and so am I."

"What ..." The air whooshed out of my lungs again. Damn it! How was I supposed to know God would take me literally?

"Annie knew there were peanuts in that dessert, but she ate it anyway. I'm not going to stand by and let her kill herself, not with peanuts, and not with sleeping pills. I'm taking her home so I can take care of her."

Luke's right hand slid down and released the snap on the strap holding the gun in his holster. "Let go of her."

Mark abruptly released me and took a hasty step back.

My knees buckled. Luke grabbed my arm and yanked me back out of Mark's reach. "Step away from him, Annie."

"You've got it all wrong. Annie's depressed, maybe even suicidal. Dr. Ramsey doesn't want her left alone." Mark stepped forward again. "Let me take her home."

I scrambled back with a cry. God's busy right now. I had to depend on Luke to protect me.

"Back off!" Luke stepped between us again.

Mark threw up his hands, frustrated. "Call Dr. Ramsey if you don't believe me!"

"You were dragging her to the car."

"What did you expect me to do? I found her wandering around out here in the middle of nowhere. She was incoherent and babbling like an idiot. I had to do something."

My head snapped up. My eyes were tearing, my nose running, hair hung in my face, and thanks to Mark, my clothes were dirty and torn, but I wasn't babbling.

I saw Luke's gaze travel from Mark to me and then back to Mark. Mark was a consummate actor. He was projecting the image of a concerned husband now. None of the earlier anger and rage was coming through. If Luke turned me back over to Mark, I was doomed. "Annie?"

I grabbed onto Luke's arm. "No! Please."

"Annie can't take care of herself, not like this."

"I'm sure she appreciates your concern, but she doesn't want to go with you."

"Annie doesn't know what she wants. She's distraught."

The patrol car turning down the road caught my attention. The men didn't notice. They were focused on each other. Apparently my status had dropped to *the spoils of war.* I understand the poor damsel's distress now. Her opinion didn't count either.

Mark's head shot up. His eyes narrowed as he watched the patrol car complete the turn and step on the gas. I know what he was thinking. A second officer shifted the odds.

Luke used Mark's momentary distraction to nudge me back another step.

"Have it your way, but if anything happens to her, it will be on your head." With that, Mark turned on his heel and stomped over to the Porsche. Pebbles spit from under his tires as he spun out and took off down the road.

I wasn't sure if my legs would hold me up, but I wasn't gasping any more. That was a good sign.

The patrol car slowed to a stop and the window slid down. "Luke?"

"I've got it. Thanks."

Carl Ingerson nodded. His attention shifted to the cloud of dust flying down the road. "He's pissed."

"You might say that."

"He's gotta' be going 70."

"Closer to 75, if you ask me."

A grin lit up Carl's face. "You're right." He hit the lights and shot down the road in hot pursuit.

All things considered, a ticket wasn't much of a payback, but it was better than nothing.

Mark was gone and I thank the good Lord for that, but I wasn't out of the woods yet. I eased my grip on Luke's arm. I didn't like being indebted to him, but I was. Luke saved my life, twice. Etiquette demanded a thank you. I can do that. In some cultures I would have to follow him around until I had a chance to return the favor. Once I saved his life I would be free to go about my business. In light of that, a thank you was easy.

"Thank you." With that said I stepped around him and headed toward town again. Once my hands stop shaking, I'll give Tabby a call. I don't need to walk anymore. I already saw the light.

"Annie, let me give you a ride into town."

"I would rather walk."

"Annie, we need to talk." My steps faltered. I turned around slowly and faced him. "No we don't."

"Annie, I know what I saw. Even if Mark felt his actions were justified, I can't let this ride. He was hurting you."

I spun on my heel and started walking down the road again.

Luke grabbed my arm and pulled me to a stop. "Annie, get in the truck."

"No questions."

"Annie ..."

"I'm not answering any questions!"

"Fine. The questions can wait." Luke tugged on my arm again.

I acquiesced. I really didn't want to walk. If Tabby was in the middle of a perm, it would be an hour or more before she got here. Mark was already pissed. If Carl gives him a speeding ticket, and I'm betting that he will, Mark will be hotter than Maria Sanchez's pickled jalapeno peppers. When Maria's cooking, I give her a wide berth. It would be best if I avoid Mark for awhile too.

Luke took my arm and led me over to his Explorer. "Will you answer one question for me?"

I nodded warily.

"Why are you out here and on foot? Where's you car? Why aren't you at work?"

"My car's at Tabby's so I decided to walk home."

"Why?"

"Harry fired me." I crawled into the Explorer and buckled my seatbelt.

Luke slid into the seat and then turned to study me. "Did you know there were peanuts in that dessert?"

I glared at him mutinously. He was already over his quota of questions.

"Annie, answer the question."

"No."

"No?"

"No! I *didn't* know there were peanuts in the dessert."

"Fine." Luke started the Explorer, made a sharp u-turn, and headed back toward town.

"Did you ask Dr. Ramsey for sleeping pills?"

"No! Now don't ask me anymore questions."

"Did you …"

"Stop the truck and let me out!"

"Calm down Annie."

"No questions." I stared at my hands resting in my lap. I couldn't take anymore today.

"Okay."

We rode in silence for about a minute. Considering Luke's job, a minute was the best he could do. He had questions. If he didn't ask them, he would choke on them.

"Do you want to be dropped off at Tabby's or your apartment? Better yet, I'll take you over to your dad's. Dr. Ramsey didn't want you to be alone."

A minute is not very long, but it gave me a chance to pull myself together. Freaking out over Luke's questions would add credence to Mark's story. "Leave my dad out of this. And just for the record, Dr. Cantrell's my doctor, not Dr. Ramsey."

"What about the depression? Are you depressed?"

"Of course I'm depressed. I'm broke and unemployed. I'm sleeping in a sleeping bag instead of a feather bed. I've had to wear the same shoes for three solid weeks and I can't buy another pair. I gave up shopping for Lent. So if I'm a little depressed, I'm entitled."

Luke didn't look like he believed me. "I'll take you to Tabby's."

"I'm not depressed!"

"You just said you were."

Men! Are they all that thick headed?

"Fine, I'll take you home, but if you try to commit suicide, I'll kill you."

I glanced at him warily as I moved closer to the door.

"Annie, I was joking!"

"Death threats aren't funny."

"Okay, let's try this again. Mark's worried about you. Does he have reason to be?"

"Mark's lying!"

"Annie, calm down."

"Why? You already think I'm depressed and suicidal. I might as well add a little hysteria to the mix. Maybe I should throw a screaming temper tantrum. You might listen to me then!"

"Calm down!" Luke's radio crackled. He mumbled an explicative that warranted a whole bar of soap before picking up the mike and responding.

"Luke, you need to go talk to Clyde McDuffy. Someone spray painted Dick Head on the side of his barn again." I could hear the laughter in the day shift dispatcher's voice.

Luke sighed. "Ten-four."

"Drop me off at the Copper Kettle. Tabby will come and get me."

Luke sighed again. "I'll take you home, but this conversation is not over."

"What's to talk about?"

"Annie … fine. We'll discuss it later."

We rode in silence until Luke pulled to the curb in front of Grammy's. I was immensely grateful for the reprieve, but I knew it wouldn't last. Luke was a detective. Detectives, just like gossips, had to know all the dirt.

"Annie, we need to talk, and not just about what happened back there."

I glanced over at Luke. I didn't like being indebted to him. He saved my life. It might be years before I have a chance to return the favor. The least I can do is save him a little work. "Luke, my mother's not dead."

"Are you sure?"

"Yes. I got a card from her awhile back, and as far as I know, the post office doesn't deliver mail from beyond the grave."

CHAPTER ELEVEN

I slept. It surprised me that I did. It might have been simple exhaustion, but I figured it was more likely the comfort and security of home. Here, Grammy was always watching over me. Bracing a chair under the doorknob and Ralph's spare cane tucked in beside me may have factored in as well.

Tabby's call woke me up. "Hey, it's after six. Are you working overtime or did you scrounge another ride home?"

I rolled off the sleeping bag and sat up. "I don't need a ride. I've been at home most of the day."

"So you decided to take another day? Good. You needed it."

"Wrong." I groaned as I crawled to my feet. "I went into work this morning, but Harry fired me."

Tabby didn't respond to that. She'd warned me, but I thought Harry's business sense would prevail. I was wrong.

"What are you going to do?"

"I don't know." I made my way out to the kitchen as we talked. "Harry told me to buy some fancy underwear and a negligee, and then go home to my husband. If I was a better wife, Mark wouldn't be preying on innocent girls."

Tabby choked. "You're kidding."

"I think he's afraid I'll divorce Mark and then he'll marry Amy. He knows Mark's a leach and doesn't want him for a son-in-law."

"Mark's not a leach. He's an asshole."

"I told Amy she could have him."

"When did you talk to Amy?"

"Harry hired her. She's my replacement." I opened the refrigerator and pulled out the ice tea.

"He'll regret it."

"I think you're right. Well anyway, I was upset and decided I wanted to walk for awhile, try to make sense of this mess. I was going to call you when I got to The Copper Kettle, but I didn't get a chance."

"What happened?"

"Mark showed up and strong armed me toward the car. He scared me Tabby. I think he wants to kill me."

"That's crazy. He'd never get away with it."

"I'm not so sure about that. He told Luke that Dr. Ramsey thinks I'm suicidal, and Dr. Cantrell's covering for me because of her friendship with dad."

"You're not, are you?" Tabby asked hesitantly.

"Tabby!"

"Sorry, but I had to ask. In the last two weeks you've caught your husband screwing his secretary, you got into a fight, you're covered with bruises, you lost your job, you're living in an empty apartment, you're broke, and you just found out that the mother you thought was living the high life in the Bahamas may have been murdered ten years ago. Who could blame you?"

"That's my point."

"Annie, Mark's not trying to kill you. He wants you back."

"You don't believe me."

"Okay, just for argument's sake, what would be the point? Why kill you?"

"I don't know." My argument petered out. Mark wasn't the type to put forth an effort if there wasn't anything to gain from it. Kill me and he'll inherit an apartment building mortgaged to the hilt, a car that's about to be repossessed, and 48 pairs of shoes.

I glanced up when I heard the quiet knock on the patio door. I lifted the broom handle and slid the door back. Miguel stepped around me and headed for the ice tea sitting on the counter.

"Are you feeling better now?"

"I guess."

"Good. Where are you? Are you still at your dad's?"

"No, I'm home."

"Did Miguel bring the truck back?"

"Yes."

"Good. You want me to run your car over?"

"You don't mind?" I asked hopefully. I wanted my car, but I didn't want to go out tonight. I was *too depressed.*

"Should I pick up some Chinese while I'm at it?"

"Chinese?" I glanced over at Miguel and lifted my brow in a silent question.

Miguel nodded. "That sounds good. Get enough for three."

"Miguel?"

"Yes."

"I'll see you in a half-hour, 45 minutes tops."

I closed the phone and set it on the counter. I glanced up at Miguel and then dropped my gaze. I'm not sure how I feel about our changing status. For 12 years we barely said ten words to each other. It hurt. Miguel and Tabby were my best friends for as long as I can remember. Losing Miguel's friendship was like getting an arm cut off. I could learn to live without it, but it would never be the same.

"Did you know there were peanuts in that dessert?"

My head shot up. "How long were you listening at the window?"

Miguel waved my indignation away. "Did you?"

"No! My life's pretty screwed up right now, but I'm not suicidal."

"Okay. Why did Harry fire you and hire Amy?"

"She needed a job. Mark fired her Friday."

"Why?"

I shot Miguel an evil look before responding. I might as well answer his questions. He has the tenacity of a teenage boy trying to talk his girlfriend into the back seat of his car. He wouldn't stop until he got what he wanted. "He said he didn't want Amy coming between us again."

"He wants you back."

I shrugged and turned away. "Yes."

"Why?"

"I don't know!"

"There has to be a reason. Did you inherit a million dollars from some great aunt I don't know about?"

"Maybe he loves me."

"Loving husbands don't fuck their secretaries over their lunch break." Miguel's words were blunt leaving no room for argument.

I shoved my hair back from my face to better glare at him for stating the obvious. The sleeve of my pajama top slid up my arm.

Miguel swore. He latched onto my left hand, shoved the sleeve of my pajama top the rest of the way up, and studied my arm. He slid his hand over the bruise measuring it for size. "Amy didn't do this."

I tugged on my arm. "Miguel, don't."

"Did Rosetti put those marks on you?"

"Miguel, stay out of it. Mark's my problem, not yours."

"He hurt you."

"No he didn't."

He stepped forward backing me against the counter. His hands came up and framed my face. "You're a lousy liar."

I stared into his eyes mesmerized.

He gently brushed a strand of hair from my face. "Annie, I miss you. I miss your friendship." He let his hands slide over my hair. His hands dropped to his sides and he stepped back. "Do you think we can ever be friends again?"

"I don't know." I turned and stared out the kitchen window for a moment before turning and walking out of the room. "Let me know when Tabby gets here."

I studied my bruised and battered body in the mirror before stepping into the shower. The bruises on my left arm were new as were the bruises along my ribs. All things considered, I was lucky. Mark was vicious when he was angry.

Damn straight. He wanted to hurt you and if he managed to get you home, he would have slapped the shit out of you.

I didn't acknowledge the thought. What good would it do? It was true. I just didn't know what to do about it.

I stood under the shower until the water turned cold before climbing out of the tub. I dried quickly and dropped the towel before reaching for my clothes.

"Annie!" Miguel pounded on the door. "Get dressed! Hurry!"

I yanked my sweatshirt into place and pulled the door open. "Why? What's wrong?"

"Tabby's been in an accident. They're transporting her to the emergency room now."

I grabbed my shoes and shoved my feet in them, sans socks. "What happened?"

"She ran a stop sign. She came barreling out of the alley and into the oncoming traffic."

"That doesn't make sense. She knows how busy Lexington Avenue is at this time of day." I snatched my purse off the counter and followed Miguel out the door.

Miguel glanced over his shoulder. "She told Chris she didn't have any brakes."

* * *

"Hey! You can't go in there! Dr. Ramsey's with her."

I ignored the receptionist. "Tabby!" I grabbed the first curtain and yanked it back.

"Hey!"

"Oh, gross!" The two teenager girls sitting in the waiting room squealed in horror. I yanked the curtain back into place blocking the view. I understood the girl's sentiments. One look at Chester Olson's scrawny body and swollen testicles was enough to put any girl off men forever.

I tugged on the curtain surrounding the second cubicle with a little more caution. "Tabby?" The bed was empty, but the room hadn't been cleaned. Bloody bandages and gauze littered every surface. I sucked in a breath as I whipped the curtain closed again. That's not Tabby's blood!

"Tabby!"

"Annie?"

I turned toward the voice and whipped the third curtain aside. "Tabby?"

Tabby pulled her face out of Dr. Ramsey's grasp, turned toward me, and raised her hand.

"Oh, Tabby." I cried as I ran into the cubicle and wrapped my arms around her. "I was so scared. I knew you were hurt, but I didn't know how bad."

"Hey, you can't come in here! I'm trying to examine my patient."

I scowled up at Dr. Ramsey. "Well get on with it."

"You're not family."

I sat down on the edge of the bed. "Close enough."

Dr. Ramsey pointed toward the gap in the curtain. "Get out!"

I ignored him and turned to Tabby. "Tabby, do you want me to leave?"

Tabby grabbed my hand.

I glanced up at Dr. Ramsey with smug satisfaction. It would take more than an ill-tempered doctor to get me out of this exam room.

"Annie!"

My head shot up.

The curtain was yanked back again, and Mark came barreling into the exam room. He snatched me up, wrapped his arms around me, and squeezed. "Thank God you're all right. I thought you were dead!"

I bit my tongue to keep from crying out.

Mark eased his grip, but didn't let go. "I knew I should have taken you home this morning. You were in no condition to drive."

I pulled out of his arms with an ill tempered jerk and glared up at him. "I wasn't driving, Tabby was."

Mark's eyes widened and then the blood leached from his face. His gaze shifted from Dr. Ramsey to Tabby and back again. "Tabby was driving your car."

The curtain was tugged back again, and Miguel stepped through the opening. He pulled up short when he saw Mark. "What the hell are you doing here?"

"Back off, Manning." Mark snarled. "I have every right to be here, you don't."

"Since when?" Miguel crossed his arms over his chest and glared at Mark.

Dr Ramsey started to say something, but Mark cut him off. "Annie's my wife! I'll take care of her."

"Tabby was in an accident, not Annie. But you're right, Annie's hurt. Is that how you *take care* of your wife?"

Dr. Ramsey tried again. Both men ignored him. They were posturing like a couple of rutting bulls.

Mark stepped forward getting right in Miguel's face. "I don't owe you any explanations!"

"Gentlemen! You need to ..." The curtain fluttered again and Luke stepped through the opening.

Mark took a hasty step back. I almost laughed.

Dr. Ramsey yanked off his gloves in disgust.

Luke's eyes traveled from Mark to Miguel, then back to Mark before settling on Tabby. "Are you all right?"

A tear leaked out and ran down her face. "I didn't have any brakes. I didn't know what to do."

Everyone started talking at once. Arguing, questioning, discussing, reassuring ...

"Get out!" Dr. Ramsey's voice rose above the den. "Let me treat my patient so I can go eat my dinner!"

Silence descended.

"Tabby?" I asked quietly. She bit her lip.

"Fine. Annie can stay. The rest of you buffoons can wait in the lobby." Properly chastised, the men filed out.

I patted Tabby's hand to reassure her. I've been in and out of emergency rooms all my life, but it was a new experience for Tabby.

"Annie, get off the table and sit in the chair."

"But ..." Tabby needed my moral support.

He held up his hand. "Not one word."

✳ ✳ ✳

I slipped out of the exam room once Dr. Ramsey turned Tabby over to the nurse and walked toward Miguel and Luke. They were talking quietly as they watched Mark pace back and forth in front of the entrance. I didn't know why Mark was here. Maybe he was genuinely worried about me. It didn't seem likely, but it was possible.

He's worried about the car. The loan is in his name but the insurance is in yours.

I smiled at the thought. He had no business using my car for collateral without my permission. I'll take the insurance money and buy myself a truck.

I glanced at the men again and my smile turned into a frown. Why was Luke here? The accident happened inside the city limits. The police would be investigating, not the Sheriff's Department.

"Annie said you talked to her this morning." Miguel said quietly.

I stopped dead in my tracks.

"No, we didn't talk. I came across Rossetti trying to persuade her into going with him and intervened."

"Persuade?"

"He was dragging her toward his car. I didn't care for his methods, but I think he was genuinely concerned about her."

I stood there rooted to the spot. They were discussing my personal business as if they had every right. It was mortifying.

"Why?"

"Dr. Ramsey thinks Annie is depressed, even suicidal."

"Do you believe that?"

"I don't know. She was pretty distraught this morning."

Who wouldn't be? Mark threatened to beat me!

"Did Rossetti put those marks on her arm?"

"I can't swear to it. You need to ask Annie that question."

"What good would it do? Annie's an expert at ignoring problems. She figures if she ignores them long enough they'll go away."

Now he was making me sound like a ninny. I don't ignore my problems. I just need time to think them through. I can deal with Mark. If he thinks I'll commit suicide rather than endure another scandal, he's in for a surprise. I can sling mud with the best of them.

"I need to talk to her." Luke responded bluntly.

Why? There's nothing to talk about. I'll deal with Mark in my own good time. As far as the other goes, Lynette's not dead so there's no reason to talk. She's living in the Bahamas soaking up the rays by day and dancing the night away.

"Have you sent the evidence to the state lab?"

"What's it to you?"

"I don't want Annie hurt again."

"Annie doesn't believe her mother's dead."

"Annie doesn't want to believe her mother's dead." Miguel corrected. "One birthday card in ten years isn't much to go on."

No! Mama's not dead!

"Did she keep the card?"

"I doubt it. Annie loved her mother, but Lynette left without saying goodbye. It hurt Annie more than she likes to admit."

"I need to talk to her."

"Talk to Tabby. She might be able to talk Annie into cooperating."

"What about you?"

"The past doesn't interest me. I'm far more concerned about the present." Miguel continued to study Mark through the glass door.

"What are you going to do?"

"I'm going to do a little investigating on my own."

Luke nodded.

Why didn't I think of that? Miguel doesn't *go* to work. The work comes to him. He spends hours on the computer every day. No secret is safe from his prying eyes. I wouldn't be a bit surprised if Saint Peter turned to Miguel for background checks on inductees. If my deepest, darkest secrets ever come back to haunt me, I know who to blame.

"If you come across any interesting tidbits like Lynette's address, I would appreciate it if you'd pass it along to me."

Miguel responded to Luke's veiled request for information. "Lynette doesn't have an address. She doesn't have a current driver's license in any of the 50 states, she hasn't filed an income tax return in ten years, and she hasn't touched the money she has stashed in a savings account in Charleston."

"She's dead."

"That would be my guess."

A strangled cry alerted Miguel and Luke to my presence. They both spun around with identical expressions of surprise on their face. I would have laughed if I wasn't already crying.

"Annie." Miguel stepped forward reaching for me. I stepped back.

"Dr. Ramsey's releasing Tabby. She needs some clothes to wear home."

Miguel let his hand drop. Profound frustration etched his face. He glanced at Mark through the glass door again then turned to Luke. "Stay with them until I get back."

"That's not necessary!" I wiped the tears away with the back of my sleeve.

Luke nodded.

Mark came in through the door as Miguel was going out. The macho chest beating stuff must be a genetic thing linked to the Y chromosome. They both stopped, each giving the other a once over as if sizing up the competition. I didn't know if they thought of me as a prize turkey or the spoils of war.

Miguel held Mark's gaze for a moment, before pushing the rest of the way through the door, and heading for his truck.

Mark stood in the doorway and watched Miguel climb into his truck before turning to me. "Annie, are you ready to come home?"

I couldn't believe it. He still thought I would come back to him. Was the man brain dead or what? No, Mark's not brain dead, he's a toad. Not a regular toad, but one of those great big bullfrog-toads. He's a bully-toad, and a bully has to win even if he's not interested in the prize. Avoiding him hasn't worked, the only way I can accommodate him is to give in, and he laughed when I tried to assert myself. There was only one thing left to do. Play the game and hope I survived.

"I'm spending the next few days with Tabby. Dr. Ramsey doesn't want her left alone."

Mark nodded. "Okay, I'll see you this weekend." The triumph in his voice was unmistakable.

I lowered my gaze instead of nodding.

"You're going back to him?" Luke asked after Mark left. His voice was flat.

"No, I'm just buying some time."

CHAPTER TWELVE

"Thanks for the ride, Dad." I climbed into the pickup and shut the door.

Dad shoved the truck into gear. "How's Tabby doing?"

"She's better now that her mom is here." Tabby's mom was in Florida. The minute she got the call, she threw her suitcases in the car and headed back. Would Lynette ever come running if she knew I needed her? I knew better.

"Annie?"

I jerked back to attention. "Sorry, what did you say?"

"How bad was she hurt?"

"She's stiff and sore. The airbag caught her in the face so she's got the raccoon thing going." I stared at my hands clasped in my lap. "It could have been worse."

"It could have been you!" Dad spoke through clenched teeth. "It could have been you. I could have lost you."

"Daddy ..."

"I can't take this any more. I want you to come home with me. That way I'll know you're safe."

"I'm fine! Tabby was driving the car, not me."

"It was your car!"

"So?"

"Your brakes were gone!"

"I know!"

"Why?"

"I don't know, but you know my luck." Dad didn't know how to respond to that. Psychics have receptors that pick up excess energy. That's how they know when ghosts and goblins are around. I'm not psychic. If I saw a ghost, I would die of a heart attack or wet my pants which would be worse. No, psychics pick up excess energy. I pick up excess bad luck. If there was a rabid skunk within a hundred miles of town, I would be the one to stumble across it. I wouldn't get bitten. I'm lucky in that regard, but I would stink for a month.

"You want to brush this off as a bit of bad luck, a twist of fate?"

"Daddy, don't make it into something its not."

"What if someone tampered with the brakes?"

I swallowed hard. "Why? What would be the point?"

"I don't know, but until I do, you're staying with me."

"That's not necessary."

"I say it is."

"You're being unreasonable."

"Fine. Move back in with Mark. He'll keep you safe."

"What!"

"Tell him if he cheats on you, I'll castrate him. That should keep him in line."

"Dad, I'm not going back to Mark, and I'm not moving in with you."

"Your brakes were gone, not sluggish, gone. Things like that don't just happen."

"That's crazy. No one's trying to kill me."

"Are you sure?"

"Okay, fine. Tabby was driving my car. Maybe someone was trying to kill her."

"Why?"

"Maybe she screwed up someone's perm and ruined their life. That's a pretty good motive for murder."

"Annie, be reasonable. No one's trying to kill Tabby."

"Oh, but it's reasonable to assume someone's trying to kill me?"

"It was your car."

I crossed by arms and sat back. "So? Tabby was driving, not me."

"*That* was a twist of fate."

* * *

Dad dropped me off at my apartment assuming I would stay put, but I needed to think. Some women don their garden shoes and head for the weeds when they need to think, others pour a glass of wine and crawl in the bathtub, I shop. I can't afford to shop, but I can afford to look. Besides, with one arm bandaged and the other too bruised to move, what else can I do? I climbed into Tabby's truck and headed for the mall.

I wandered from store to store with my father's words dogging my steps. Why would anyone tamper with my brakes? What would be the point?

Someone wants to kill you.

Why?

How should I know, it's your life.

I rolled my eyes, shoved the depressing ruminations out of my mind, and started making plans.

I bought some time last night and today I bought a 34 oz Louisville slugger, cleaning supplies, a coffeepot, a cookie sheet and mixing bowl, plant food, cat litter, and a mattress and box spring.

I pulled up to the apartment and glanced around. A quiet breeze stirred the trees. The leaves rustled. A dog barked off in the distance. I was home, safe from prying eyes and wagging tongues, insolent husbands, and pesky detectives. I felt the tension ease.

I grabbed a couple of bags and headed in.

A creepy, uneasy feeling settled over me the moment I opened the outer door. I glanced around. I could hear the TV blaring from Sam's apartment and an indistinct odor wafted from Ralph and Martha's. Sam always had the TV blaring and Martha's cooking defies description.

I headed down the hallway, set my bags down, and dug around in my purse for my key. I unlocked the door and pushed it open. With a cry of dismay, I slammed the door shut again.

* * *

I sat on the stoop and waited for the police to arrive. I didn't want to call them. There was absolutely nothing in my apartment worth stealing. I didn't have any electronics. The only jewelry I could lay claim to was the pendant hanging around my neck.

I called them anyway.

I stood when Chris Addison's patrol car pulled to the curb, and then snarled when Luke pulled in behind him. I know I need to talk to him, but until I do, I can pretend Mama's shagging on the beach in Charleston.

Chris stopped directly in front of me and pulled out his notebook. "Dispatch said you had a break-in."

"Yes, and he has to be the dumbest B and E guy on the face of the earth. The only thing in my apartment worth stealing is Grammy's Schwan's Ice Cream tins. They're maybe worth ten dollars apiece."

"Let's take a look."

Chris took the lead. He eased the door open slowly. I hunched down making sure his body blocked me from view. The apartment was empty, but I didn't see any point in taking chances.

I heard a hiss. Chris froze. *Mascara and Palmer!* How could I forget my babies? "Mascara!" I shoved Chris forward intent on clearing the door and rescuing my cats. "Palmer!"

Mascara darted past Chris, and started clawing her way up my leg. I reached down and plucked her off my jeans and into my arms. "Poor baby." I crooned. "It's okay. Mama's here now."

Luke stepped around me, and followed Chris into the apartment. He glanced around before stepping into the kitchen.

"Shit!" Luke yelped.

I tightened my grip on Mascara. "What's wrong?"

"M-e-o-o-w!"

"Palmer!"

"Ugh! Ouch! Damn it!" Luke's expletives bounced off the walls. I knew what was happening. Palmer's claws are sharp.

I ran into the kitchen. Palmer was clinging to Luke's shoulder, hissing and spitting. He doesn't like strangers.

"Damn cat! Get off me!"

"Don't hurt him!"

"Ow!"

"*Meow!*"

A flash of black streaked past me. "Palmer! Come back here!" I turned and ran back toward the door. I dropped Mascara and slammed the door shut behind me. Tears welled up when I reached the outside door in time to see my baby disappear into the trees.

"Damn cat clawed me." Luke growled behind me.

I closed the door quietly and turned around. "He was scared." Eyes downcast, I walked back to my apartment.

"Annie, he'll come back."

I glanced around my apartment. It was better to focus on the here and now, rather than the all too familiar feeling of abandonment. Palmer, like my mother, will come back … eventually.

"Why would anyone break in to my apartment? I don't have anything worth stealing."

Luke took my arm and pulled me along. "The kitchen's tossed."

"Oh my God!" Every drawer hung open and the cupboards were gaping wide. My solitary plate lay shattered on the floor. Talk about kicking a dog while he's down. I had to eat out of the can now.

Chris glanced around before crossing the threshold. "The bedroom's tossed too. They even opened the tins stacked in the corner."

I closed my eyes and rubbed my temples. How could I have been so stupid? When Harry's crew dug up the purse and the shoe, the gossip started again.

"Annie, what was he looking for?"

"A pot of gold lined with $250,000."

Chris slapped his notebook shut with a snort. He knew what I was talking about. "Your mother's not a leprechaun. If she embezzled that money, there wouldn't be enough left to hide. A quick trip to the mall and she would have blown the whole wad."

Until my foray into Mama's safety deposit box I would have agreed with him.

I carried in my purchases as Chris and Luke wrestled the box spring and mattress into the apartment. The police were hired to serve and protect. They couldn't do anything about the break-in, so I didn't feel guilty asking them to help carry in my bed.

Chris gave me a jaunty salute before heading out the door.

Luke stayed.

I glanced at Luke before swinging my gaze back to the door. I glanced at Luke again. He shook his head.

"Fine." I cut through the living room and into the kitchen. I opened the refrigerator, pulled out the ice tea, and poured two glasses. I wasn't being hospitable, just stalling for time.

The longer you stall, the longer Luke will be here.

I drew in a deep breath, turned around, and faced the truth. "You think my mother is dead."

Luke sighed heavily before taking the glasses from me. He set them on the table and gestured for me to sit down before answering. I shook my head. I didn't want to sit down. I'll take the news standing up.

"Annie …"

I shook my head and clutched the counter behind me.

"You're right. We have reason to believe your mother is dead."

I closed my eyes and sent a prayer heavenward. "Murder?"

"That would be my guess."

"What about the birthday card?"

"You received the card seven years after your mother disappeared. At that point you could have had her declared dead."

"Why would I do that? She left a note and then took off. As far as I knew, she was living on Mai Tai's in Tahiti."

Luke bent down and picked up an empty drawer that was lying on the floor and slid it back into place. "What was he looking for?"

"What does that have to do with Lynette?"

"Good question."

"What are you getting at?"

"What did your mother leave behind?"

A big fat envelope of money.

I turned my back on Luke and stared out the window. My mother took first place in the liars marathon sponsored by State Liars Association three years in a row. She was an awesome storyteller. I'm not. I didn't want to be caught in a lie. "I don't know. You'll have to ask John LeBlanc that question. She was married to him when she disappeared."

"Annie, don't lie to me."

I swung back around, vexed. "I'm not! She *was* married to John at the time."

"That's not what I meant and you know it."

The money in the safety deposit box has nothing to do with the $250,000 embezzled from the bank. There was only $100,000 in the safety deposit box. In spite of what Chris said, no one, not even Lynette O'Reilly could spend $150,000 that fast.

What about her journals?

That had to be it.

"Annie, the bastard will keep harassing you until we figure out what he's looking for. Cooperate with me."

"Do you think the break-in has something to do with my mother's death?"

"Yes."

"Are you in charge of the investigation?"

Luke huffed out a breath. "All I have is a hunch. Until I have proof that your mother is dead, I can't …"

"You're not going to investigate!"

"Not officially."

"Then why are you here?"

"If Lynette left something behind that can point me in the right direction, I might have a chance of figuring it out."

"Hah! You're not fooling me. The sheriff already nixed the investigation. As you're not investigating, I'm not giving you squat."

Luke's lips compressed and his eyes narrowed to little slits.

I turned away. His anger would not sway me. I'm not giving him the journals. How can I? They would end up in the sheriff's hands. The sheriff would either torch them, or use them to supplement his late night reading. Either way, there would be no investigation.

You can hire a private investigator.

"I'm broke."

Let it go.

"I can't."

What are you going to do? Investigate on your own?

"How hard can it be? Ask a few questions …"

"Are you nuts!"

I turned around and scowled at Luke. "Eavesdropping is rude. You had no business listening in on a private conversation."

"Who were you talking to?"

"Myself."

Instead of apologizing like he should, Luke blasted me. "Stay out of police business!"

"If you're not investigating, it's not police business."

"I can't let you do it."

"What I do or don't do is none of your business!"

"You step on the sheriff's toes and it's *my* ass he'll kick. I'm not going to stand by and let you stir up a bunch of trouble."

My phone rang. I grabbed my purse and dug for it. I didn't care if it was a telemarketer offering a cure for baldness or someone doing a survey on the frequency and duration of sexual fantasies. I didn't care as long as it put an end to the argument.

R-i-i-i-ng.

I left Luke standing in the kitchen and stepped into the living room.

"Annie? What took you so long to answer the phone? I was ready to hang up."

"Sorry Doug. I didn't realize you had my number."

"I asked Harry for it yesterday. I stopped by the office to talk to you, but he said you were off."

"Off? Harry fired me yesterday."

Doug sighed heavily. "He was really pissed when the Sheriff's Department put a stop to the work."

"It's not my fault!"

"Harry was angry and you were a convenient target. He didn't mean it."

"Yes he did! He hired Amy to replace me."

"Annie, you're wrong. Amy works for Mark. You know that."

"No she doesn't. Mark fired her on Friday."

"I stopped by Mark's office and dropped off a bid for Harry on my way home yesterday. Amy was at her desk, as usual."

"I'm not making this up!" I paced back and forth. I'm not losing my mind! I know what happened. Why doesn't he believe me?

"Mark's worried about you."

"Doug! I'm not crazy!"

"Annie! Calm down."

"Do you believe me?"

Doug hesitated. "Annie, you've been under a lot of stress lately. You might want to take a few days off."

I grabbed a handful of hair and yanked it, hard. Maybe a little pain would bring my world back into focus. "Doug, I have a good imagination, but I didn't imagine this. Mark told me he fired Amy. That's what led to the fight in Bi-Lo. When I went into work yesterday, Harry fired me. Amy was there when I left."

"Mark could have sent her over with some papers for Harry. You know they're working on merging the two companies."

"Doug …" I let the subject drop. Doug wasn't listening to me. I know what happened. I was there and he wasn't. I closed my eyes and drew in a deep breath. I'm not distraught, depressed, suicidal, anal retentive, or sexually dysfunctional. "Can you come over and replace the lock for me?"

I heard Doug sigh in relief. "I told you I would."

"Can you do it now?"

"Why? What happened?"

"Nothing."

"Yeah. Sure. I believe that. I'll be over in about an hour."

I closed the phone slowly. Luke was waiting in the kitchen with every intention of resuming our argument. I wasn't up to it. I didn't need another problem added to my repertoire of problems. I already feel like a juggler trying to keep a dozen balls in the air. When I try to focus on one thing, I get bonked on the head by another. If this keeps up, I'll lose all my marbles.

I started rooting through the bags sitting on the loveseat. Lynette was dead. It took me over a week to come to terms with that. It wasn't easy, but now that I have accepted it, I want something done about it. I want her murder investigated and the bastard behind bars.

Luke's not going to investigate. He would if he could. At least I'd like to believe that. No, it was the sheriff that nixed the investigation. So, they don't have a body, big deal. A good investigator wouldn't let that stop him.

"Annie." Luke came into the living room. His patience was running thin. I could hear it in his voice. "What did your mother leave behind?"

I sighed heavily. "Luke, my apartment was broken into six times the first two years I lived on my own. Nothing was ever taken."

"What were they looking for?"

"Money. My mother *supposedly* embezzled $250,000 from the bank. Someone thinks I'm holding it for her."

"Why now?"

"When Harry's crew dug up Lynette's purse, the talk started again. Had I been thinking, I wouldn't have called in the break-in. Filing a report was a waste of time."

It was the truth, at least most of it. Once I got the locks changed, rescued my shoes, figured out how to support myself, came up with the money to hire a lawyer, bought a car, and figured out why Mark's trying to convince everyone that I'm suicidal, I'll worry about nailing my mother's murderer. As Luke's not investigating, the pesky detective had to go.

"Why don't you stay with your dad for a while? You'll be safer."

No! I'm not moving in with dad. He'll screen my calls, make me account for my whereabouts, and would implement a curfew that would make a ten-year-old cringe. "Doug's on his way over. He promised to change the locks for me. I'll be fine."

"Fine, but I'm staying until he gets here."

"Fine!" I mimicked in response. "Do what you want."

I pulled the cookie sheet and mixing bowl out of the bags on the loveseat, and disappeared into the kitchen. I dumped the stuff on the counter, shoved all the drawers back into place, and swept up my broken plate. Luke came to a stop in the doorway between the kitchen and the living room.

"Tell me about your mother."

"Why?"

"I'm curious."

I started mixing the dough for chocolate chip cookies. "What do you want to know?"

"Anything. What was she really like?"

I set the cookie sheet on the counter and started dropping little balls of dough on it. "My mother believed in fairytales."

"Fairytales?"

"She was looking for the happy ever after."

Prince Charming is out there waiting in a room full of toads. Kiss enough toads and you'll find your Prince Charming.

"Did she find it?"

"I don't know. She was married to John LeBlanc for four years. It was a record for her. Maybe she was happy, but I don't know. Things sort of fell apart when Grammy died. Lynette couldn't sell the house until I turned twenty-one, and I refused to move in with her. As long as I was living with Grammy, dad had to pay child support. Once I moved in with him, the money stopped. It caused a rift between us. My mother put a lot of store in money."

I slid the pan of cookies into the oven. "It's your turn. Tell what you found up at the construction site."

"You already know."

"Tell me anyway."

"We found a shoe and your mother's purse. Her wallet and all her junk was still in there."

Goosebumps danced up my arm. "If you have her wallet, you know it's her."

"Annie, there's no body. There was evidence of digging, so we're guessing the perp went up there, dug up the body, and moved it when Harry got the go ahead to build. He didn't leave a single bone behind. If he had, we could have done a DNA match …"

"Bones!" I grabbed onto the back of a chair as my vision grayed and my ears rang. My mother was nothing but a bag of bones.

"Shit!"

I heard a chair scrape back, but I didn't pay attention to it. I kept hearing Jack Skeleton chanting. *This is Halloween … This is Halloween … This is Halloween …*

Luke pushed me into a chair and shoved my head between my knees. "Push back against my hand."

"No! Let me up!" I've never passed out a day in my life, well except when Jessie Addison shoved a toad in my face. She wanted me to kiss it and turn it into a prince.

"Push! Don't you dare pass out on me and make me feel like an ass."

"You are an ass!"

"Shut up and breathe, slow and deep."

The timer on the oven dinged. I pushed harder. "Let me up!"

"Stay put. I'll take the cookies out."

"Don't touch my cookies!"

"Annie! Don't move or so help me God …"

With a strangled cry, I threw my arms up over my head.

Ding … ding … ding …

"Calm down! Jesus Annie." He sounded both appalled and frustrated.

Ding … ding … ding …

Luke swung around. He turned off the timer, pulled the cookies out of the oven, and dumped the pan on top of the stove.

I sat up slowly.

Luke stood at the stove with his back to me. "Jesus Annie."

It was the tone, not the threat that had me ducking and covering. I didn't mean to hurt his feelings. I stood, nudged Luke aside, and picked up the spatula. I transferred the cookies to the wax paper on the counter before addressing him. "I'm sorry. It was stupid of me, but I always pictured my mother with her hair perfectly coiffured, her face made up, and wearing her favorite dress."

"I don't want to talk about your mother. I want to know why you reacted ..."

"Damn it Annie!" Doug's bellow bounced through the apartment. "What good are locks if you don't lock the door?"

I scrambled out of the kitchen. I was so thankful for the interruption that I considered kissing Doug's feet. "Thanks for coming over."

"Who's here and why are you driving Tabby's truck?"

"Luke's here."

Doug paused in the process of pulling off his boots. He straightened and touched my cheek. "Are you all right?"

I took his hand and gave it a quick squeeze. "I will be."

"Okay, why are you driving Tabby's truck? Where's the Mazda?"

"Um, well ..."

CHAPTER THIRTEEN

My mother kept a journal. It was one of the few habits I picked up from her. Like Lynette, I write down everything, every thought, every fear, every daydream. I never really thought about it. I just did it.

I have my mother's journals. I wish I didn't have to read them. I wouldn't want my personal thoughts scrutinized after I'm dead and gone. It's an invasion of privacy, but they're the only lead I've got. I have to read them, but as of today, I'm using my journal like I originally intended to help organize my life. I sat down and started making a list.

The other day I compared my life to a juggling act in a three-ring circus. It is a pretty good analogy. I can juggle a lot of stuff, but even I have my limits. As I'm not willing to give up any of my marbles, I had to prioritize and resolve some of the issues.

Mark threatened my shoes.

I returned Tabby's truck and appropriated dad's this afternoon. I waited until he opened the Mountain and then left him a note. I didn't ask him, I just took it. He'll plotz when he finds out, but he would ask questions. I can't tell him what I'm up to. It's a covert operation and I'm going in alone.

I'm rescuing my shoes. Mark threatened to rip out their soles. I don't think he meant it, but I'm not willing to risk it.

The house is Mark's and he can have it, but why should he keep all the Tommy Hilfiger Signature towels when I'm stuck with a faded Garfield beach towel? And what about my antique turtle shaped watering pot? Mark doesn't need it. He doesn't even know the difference between a rubber plant and a philodendron.

I'm not going to argue about the plasma TV and I don't mind leaving the Tiffany lamps behind, but I want my shoes and a decent bath towel. I might as well take the food mill while I'm at it. Mark wouldn't have a clue what to do with it anyway.

It's Saturday night and there's a chance Mark will be home, sitting in front of the TV in his underwear, drinking beer, and eating pizza, but the odds are against it. It's his last night of freedom before his renegade wife returns to the fold. He'll make use of it.

I don't think it even occurred to Mark that I would take matters into my own hands. He treated me like I was as dumb as a box of rocks. Okay, so I didn't go to college, I could have. I graduated sixth in my class and was accepted at the University of North Carolina. I opted not to go. Dad said that was a mistake. Maybe it was, but the only *dumb* thing I ever did was marry Mark. Mistakes don't count.

I fished my keys out of my purse and headed out the door. Mark knows how many pairs of shoes I have. When I brought home a pair of black velvet pumps, it was an after Christmas sale and they were a steal, he hit the roof. He pulled all my shoes out of the closet and started pitching them back in one-by-one. By the time he reached 20, his face was red and he was bellowing out the numbers. Topping 30 I thought he was going to have a heart attack, but when he reached 40, his voice dropped to a whispered hiss. Thank God he ran out of shoes before he reached 50. At that point I think he was contemplating murder.

I have 48 pairs of shoes. Forty-nine if Mark thought to count the pair I was wearing. I still have 49. I haven't dared buy any shoes since then.

At least I'm not obsessed with shoes like my mother was. I packed up 62 pairs of shoes and put them in the attic after she disappeared.

Mark may know how many shoes I have but wouldn't know a Via Spiga from a Franco Sarto or an Adidas from a Nike. I'm counting on that.

I climbed the stairs and walked to the end of the hallway between the two upstairs apartments. I didn't give myself time to think. Reaching up, I grabbed the cord, pulled the door down, and unfolded the steps.

The steps creaked and groaned as I climbed. Reaching the top, I swung my arm through the darkness until I found the cord for the light and gave it a yank. I glanced around. A thin layer of dust lay over everything, and the space smelled musty.

I crawled up into the space and shifted around until I was sitting in front of the boxes I put up there ten years ago. I tore open the first box, started scooping up the shoes, and began dumping them into a trash bag.

Only 22 pairs of shoes fit in the bag. I wanted to rescue all 48 pairs but 22 was a good start. Gathering up the bag of shoes, I started back down the steps.

"Let me get that for you."

Startled, I jerked upright with a cry of alarm. My foot slipped on the step. I grabbed the ladder to keep from going down, but I lost my grip on the bag of shoes.

"Ow!"

I glared down at the man rubbing the side of his head with shoes scattered around his feet. "Serves you right for scaring me like that."

It took a conscious effort to ease my grip on the ladder and climb the rest of the way down. I wasn't scared of heights or anything. I just needed time to marshal my thoughts before I confronted Jay. He was the last person I expected to see. I wasn't sure why he was here, and I wasn't sure I wanted to know.

I folded the steps back into the hatch and eased the trapdoor back into place. I dropped down to my knees and started gathering up the shoes.

"What's with the shoes?"

"They're my mother's. Detective Sheridan wants them. Don't ask me why, I don't know."

Jay bent down and scooped up the last pair of shoes, dumped them in the trash bag, snatched up the bag, and started walking down the hallway. "Yeah. I believe that."

"Hey!" I ran after him. "What do you think you're doing?"

"I want to talk to you."

"Well I don't want to talk to you."

"I figured that. That's why I'm keeping the shoes until you do."

"Jay!"

He stopped in front of my apartment. "Unlock the door Annie. I'm asking for five minutes, that's all."

I studied his face for a moment before I relented and unlocked the door. The sneer was gone. I took that as a positive sign. "Come on in."

Jay glanced around the apartment. It wasn't empty. I had a chair and a loveseat and about a 100 house plants. Well, not a 100. It was closer to 20. At least they gave the apartment a lived in feel. "You've been screwed."

"No, that honor goes to Amy."

"Touché."

I gestured to the chair. "What do you want Jay? Why are you here?"

"Mark said you were spending a few days with Tabby, but you were coming home tomorrow night. I want to know why."

"Why do you care?"

"I don't. Not really. I don't like you any more than you like me, but we were both played for fools. That puts us both in the same corner. Amy asked me out, but if you listen to the gossip, I was panting after her."

"I'll bet that didn't stop you."

Jay shrugged. "What can I say? Amy is hot."

It's the boobs. It's not too late. Thirty-six double-D's and you'll be hotter than Amy.

I don't want a boob job. I don't want a bunch of macho, chest beating, Neanderthals panting after me. Hot, sweaty sex isn't all it's cracked up to be.

Liar.

All right! Celibacy sucks, but men are more hassle than they're worth. I don't need a man. I have a pulsing massage showerhead. It's a great way to relieve stress. My *toys* are back at the house, but I'm picking them up tonight. As long as I have them and the shower, I can buy stock in Duracell and live happily ever after.

"What do you want, Jay?"

He jiggled the keys in his pocket. "Do you remember the day you walked in on Mark and Amy?"

I rolled my eyes. How could I forget? My life's been a roller coaster ride ever since. I've always avoided rides like that. They make me sick to my stomach.

"Amy called you?"

"Yes." I responded impatiently. I didn't see any point in belaboring the point. I wanted him to get to the point of this discussion and then leave.

"An hour later you walked in on them."

"What do you want, proof? I didn't happen to have a camera handy, but Amy has a butterfly tattoo on her right cheek and she shaves her pubic hair to hide the fact that she's not a natural blond."

"Okay! Okay! I believe you."

"Why would I lie about that? Mark and I were only married for two years. It doesn't say much for my skills as a wife or a lover."

Jay was quiet. He didn't know how to respond to that. I glanced at my watch. He took the hint and started talking again.

"I was in the office the day you walked in on them. I heard Amy make the call." Jay's eyes shifted to mine. "Mark heard it to."

The bile started backing up in my throat. That's been happening a lot lately. It's not a pleasant feeling. It was bad enough knowing Mark cheated on me. I didn't need to know that he deliberately rubbed my face in it. Jay was either oblivious to my discomfiture or didn't care. He kept right on talking.

"You walked out on him, but you kept your mouth shut. No one knew why you left him."

"My mother enjoyed the notoriety, I don't."

"I know. I knew you were working at the Mountain the night we argued. Mark told me."

"He knew you would needle me and he knew I would get pissed and spill the beans. At least we're predictable." I responded morosely. "If he went to such lengths to make sure I knew he was cheating on me, and wanted the whole town talking about it, then why is he making such a big deal out of wanting me back?"

Jay stood. "Have you ever played chess?"

I wrinkled my nose. "That's Mark's game. He tried to teach me once, but he finally gave up. He said I was hopeless. Why? What does that have to do with it?"

"Why did he say you were hopeless?"

"I refused to sacrifice the pawns. The rooks and bishops can defend themselves, but the pawns are so small and insignificant. Someone needs to look out for them."

"The pawns are meant to be sacrificed."

"That's barbaric."

"That's life."

* * *

I tried not to think about my conversation with Jay as I drove across town. If I'm a pawn in one of Mark's elaborate games of chess, I'm in trouble. I can't out maneuver him, not without understanding his strategy. Besides, pawns can only do one thing, move forward, one step at a time.

That's my strategy, one step at a time. Tonight I'm rescuing my shoes. Once I've accomplished that, I'll move onto the next problem on the list.

I watched a patrol car drive by and hastily crossed myself. Breaking into the house the other day was easier. I didn't have time to think about it, didn't have time to think about the potential consequences of getting caught.

I wiped my hands on my jeans. I planned it well. I have nothing to worry about. Mark's out. I called the house and didn't get an answer. If he was there, he would have picked up the phone.

Not if he was in the shower.

Okay, I'm nervous and I have reason to be. There are a million things that could go wrong. I'm counting on God and a little bit of luck to see me through.

Thou shall not steal. I don't think you can count on God bailing you out of this one.

I'm not stealing! The shoes are mine. Mark wears a 12, not six-and-a-half. I bought the towels and all the kitchen equipment too.

With his money.

So I used his money. I cooked meals for both of us and Mark used the towels too. If I let my conscience be my guide, I would still be living with dad and waiting for the Easter Bunny. I know what I'm doing.

I wiped my hands on my jeans again.

R-i-i-i-ng!

I fished out my cell phone while I waited for the light to change. I glanced at the monitor before putting it to my ear. I don't like talking on the phone while driving, but I'm on a tight schedule. I want to be in and out of the house before last call. "Hey Tabby, how are you feeling?"

"Annie, you've got to help me."

"What's wrong?"

"Mom's driving me nuts."

"Tabby, it's only been three days."

"Humph! Did you know the accident never would have happened if I was married and raising babies?"

I grinned at that. Louise is greedy. She already has three grandchildren, but she wants more. Tabby's 27. If Louise had her way, Tabby would be working on her fifth kid by now. "Maybe you should skip the marriage part and just get pregnant."

"Hah, hah, hah."

"At least your mom wants grandchildren. Dad practically had a heart attack when I told him I was marrying Mark."

"It wasn't the marriage, it was the man. Tony didn't trust Mark."

"If I brought Prince Charming home, Dad still would have objected."

"Tony was right about Mark."

I sighed heavily. "I know."

"So, can you come over?"

"Okay, but I have something to do first."

"What?"

"A little breaking and entering."

Tabby sucked in a breath. "Annie, what if he comes home? If he catches you he'll kill you."

I winced at that. I have a good imagination and Jay's cryptic remarks sent it into overdrive. I could almost see Mark killing me and
then playing the grieving widower. Mark looks good in black. He would
have no trouble wearing it for a year.

My world tilted.

I grabbed the wheel and swung over to the curb. Mark wants me
dead, but he doesn't want to do it himself. If I commit suicide or die in
an accident, he's home free. It's so typical of him. He wouldn't help
clean the house either. He wasn't about to get *his* hands dirty.

"I hope you know what you're doing." Tabby jerked me out of my
ruminations and back to the conversation.

I took my foot off the brake and eased out onto the road. "Mark's
not home."

"Come and get me. I'll stand lookout."

"What are you going to do? Crawl out the window? Your mother
won't let you go." Bad luck is contagious, just like the chicken pox I
gave Tabby when we were in second grade.

Tabby knew I was right. "Call Miguel. He'll back you up."

"Are you nuts? Miguel would shoot a hundred holes in my plan and
then call it off. Mark threatened my shoes. I have to do something."

"He threatened your shoes?" Tabby's voice dropped to a whisper.

"He said he'd rip out their soles if I didn't come back to him."

Tabby sucked in a breath. "He wouldn't dare!"

I smiled grimly. "I'll call you when I'm out."

"Let's synchronize watches."

"I don't think that's necessary."

"Yes it is, and if I don't hear from you by eleven, I'm calling the
police."

"Don't. The house is Mark's, not mine. The police will arrest me
and then *I'll* be wearing an orange jumpsuit. You know I would hate
that. Orange clashes with my hair."

"How can you joke about it?"

"I'm not joking. I'll call you." I dropped my phone in my purse as
I pulled into the driveway and eased up to the garage door. Luck was

with me. The house was dark and deserted. I hit the button on the garage door remote. The door slid up and the light came on. I eased the truck forward and let the door drop behind me.

I'm nervous, but not like the last time. Maybe I'm deluding myself and Mark is lying in wait for me. At least I had back up. If Tabby doesn't hear from me by eleven, she would sound the alarm.

I grabbed the bag of shoes and levered my way out of the truck.

I turned the light on over the stove. It was a risk, but a flashlight beam bouncing around the house would be worse. When Mark's neighbor's house was broken into, it was the flashlight beam that caught our attention. The police were waiting for the guy when he came out.

I steeled myself for the mess in the living room. If the mess wasn't cleaned up soon, the cockroaches would be moving in. I wouldn't wish that on my worst enemy, not even Mark. Cockroaches are nasty.

I stopped and stared at the living room, dumbfounded. The room was dark, but I could see enough. The place was immaculate.

Amy?

No, Amy wouldn't pick up after Mark. He must have hired a maid service. What surprised me the most was the realization that I didn't care. I didn't care if Mark hired a maid, and I didn't care if he was screwing Amy six times a day. I didn't love him anymore. To be honest, I'm not really sure I ever did.

I adjusted my grip on the trash bag and headed upstairs. I wasn't making the same mistake twice. Shoes first.

I pushed the bedroom door open and let the light from the hallway illuminate the room. The bed was made, but the comforter was folded down. I was right. Mark had plans for the night.

Rushing now, because I didn't know when Mark and Amy would show up, I quickly dumped the bag of shoes out in front of the closet. It wouldn't be a random grab. I have to give the selections some thought. I was rescuing 22 pairs tonight, but I may not ever get a chance to rescue the rest.

I picked up a pair of my running shoes, sat down on the floor, and slipped them on my feet. I've been wearing my flats for three solid weeks.

It wasn't as though I don't like them, I do, but if I have to choose between my flats and my Via Spiga ankle boots, the flats had to go.

I bagged up my selections then started fitting Lynette's shoes into
the empty slots. Finishing, I stood back and admired my handy work.
The switch out was perfect. Mark would never know.

Humming, I carried the bag out and set it in the back of the pickup.
I pulled another trash bag off the roll and headed back in. Linens and
towels were next on the list.

I worked diligently for close to an hour. I've given this a lot of
thought. If I took all the towels, Mark would notice. I took four of the
two dozen stacked in the linen closet. Just to make sure he wouldn't
notice, I took the matching hand towels and washcloths too. The spare
blankets and pillows were stored in the closet in the spare bedroom.
Mark wouldn't notice their absence for months, if ever.

I needed clothes. Again, I just took a few. My drawer of panties and
bras is half full now instead of three-quarters full. I left four pairs of
jeans hanging in the closet instead of eight. All total, I filled up five
more trash bags.

The kitchen was harder. Mark doesn't cook so taking the food mill
and the espresso maker wouldn't be a problem, but I need pots and
pans. I took some, but not nearly as many as I wanted to.

I glanced at my watch after carrying another load out to the truck.
I was pushing the time limit, but I had to make one more trip in. My
charge cards were in the desk. I didn't trust Mark. It would be just like
him to run up a bunch of charges and stick me with the bill.

I scooted back in and carefully rifled through the desk. I'm getting
pretty good at this. Maybe I should consider a career as a cat burglar. It
pays better than secretarial work.

Grammy wouldn't approve.

True. I tucked the charge cards in my back pocket and headed back
upstairs. There was one thing left to retrieve. I wanted my favorite toy.
Mark doesn't need a vibrator. He already has a penis.

I slipped back down the stairs. It was almost eleven. I needed to get
out of here. Tabby would make good on her threat. I looked at the

vibrator clutched in my hand and grimaced. Miguel would never understand.

I was sliding into the truck when I heard the familiar rumble of Mark's Porsche. *Oh God!* I slammed the door and dove for the floor. I listened to the garage door grind its way up with trepidation. I was doomed.

I listened while Mark pulled the Porsche in and killed the engine. The garage door started grinding again. The noise grated on taut nerves. A car door slammed. I winced.

"This is not my idea of a perfect evening! To think I bought a new outfit for this!" I could barely hear Amy's grumblings over the pounding of my heart. She was bound to notice the truck.

"Mark! Damn it, wake up. I'm not carrying you in!"

"I'm gonna be sick." Mark moaned.

I grinned. I know it wasn't prudent considering my current predicament, but when I heard the sounds of Mark's retching and Amy's cries of disgust, I couldn't help it. Mark wasn't a drinker. He was a toad. He could handle beer, but if he hit the hard stuff, he ended up sick as a dog.

"Help me baby." Mark whined. "I'm dying here."

"I just bought these shoes and you ruined them!" *Thump! Thump!* Something hit the wall. I was betting on the shoes.

"I'm going to bed." A door slammed. Apparently it wasn't just the Irish that have flaming tempers. Blond-headed bimbos can throw a pretty good temper tantrum too.

"Amy, please …" I heard a crash and a curse. I closed my eyes and visualized Mark crawling up the steps to the kitchen door. It was easy enough to picture. I've seen it a hundred times before.

CHAPTER FOURTEEN

I took another bite of pizza. "Yum. I didn't realize how hungry I was." I had called Tabby and then stopped and picked up a pizza on the way to her apartment. Louise was down for the count. As long as I took the pizza box with me when I left, she would never know I was there.

"I don't know why you think you're unlucky. What were the odds of Mark coming home shit-faced and not noticing your dad's truck in his garage?"

"Amy wasn't drunk."

Tabby shrugged. "For all she knew it was a company truck."

I shrugged at that. A little bit of good luck doesn't make up for all the bad luck. I was just thankful I was with Tabby instead of being strip searched by the night matron over at the county jail. I've heard stories.

Someone knocked on the door. Tabby jumped up and bolted for the door. She didn't want her mother waking up and crashing our party. "Don't open …"

Too late. Tabby jerked the door open. "Luke!"

My stomach rolled. What was I thinking? I should have skipped the pizza and stashed the loot. My shoes will end up in an evidence locker and … oh God! The whole town will know I broke into Mark's house to get my vibrator back. I'll never live it down. Every toad within a 50 mile radius will be offering to recharge my batteries.

"Is Annie here with you?"

"Why?"

I rose. I didn't want Tabby charged as an accessory after the fact. "What do you want, Luke?" When Doug showed up to change the locks, he booted Luke out of the apartment. He was upsetting me and that's all that mattered. I've been dodging his calls ever since.

Luke nudged Tabby back and stepped into the apartment. "Call your dad. He has half the police force out looking for you."

I winced. Dad left several messages on my cell phone. I was driving his truck and he wanted it back. I thought tomorrow would be soon enough.

I pulled out my cell phone and hit the speed dial. "Daddy?"

I jerked the phone away from my ear. Loud music may be the leading cause of hearing loss, but irate fathers come in a close second. "Daddy, calm down!"

"Where the hell have you been?"

The truth was out and if the police were looking for me, all my usual excuses wouldn't wash. My apartment would be the first place they would check. They knew I wasn't home. The library is closed and no one goes to the Laundromat on Saturday nights except drug dealers and prostitutes. "I went for a drive."

"What?"

"I went for a drive. I needed time to think, so I drove to Raleigh and back. When I got back, I stopped and picked up a pizza." I talked in a rush making up a feasible story as I went along.

"You took my truck then went for a drive!" His voice started out reasonable, but ended on a bellow. I jerked the phone away from my ear again.

"I'm sorry. I didn't mean to worry you."

"Get your ass home, now!"

"All right. I'm going." I grumbled.

"Not going, coming. Be *here* before I close the bar."

"Daddy …"

"Don't argue with me. You're not going to win this one." I winced when he slammed down the phone.

I closed my phone slowly, acutely aware of the fact that Luke witnessed my dressing down. It was mortifying.

"You drove to Raleigh."

I stiffened. Luke made the statement sound like a question. "So?"

"You stopped and picked up a pizza on your way back into town."

"Yes." I strove for confident rather than defensive.

"Why didn't you stop at Giovanni's instead of driving across town to Pizza Hut?"

"After last Saturday's fiasco, I didn't think they would let me in the door." How's that for fast thinking?

"Where were you this evening?"

"I already told you …"

"Don't lie to me!"

"What's it to you anyway? It's none of your business."

"I'm making it my business."

"What's going on? Tabby, why are all these people here?"

"Mama, go back to bed." Tabby stepped between me and her mother.

"Annie! What are you doing here?"

I gathered up my purse. "Don't worry. I'm leaving."

"Come on, I'll follow you to the Mountain." Luke opened the door and waited for me.

"That's not necessary." I turned to Louise. "Good night Mrs. Greenburg. I'm sorry we disturbed your sleep."

"Annie, are you going to your dad's?" Tabby didn't even try to keep the worry out of her voice. She knew what was in the back of the truck. Dad wouldn't understand anymore than Luke would.

"I don't have a choice. I'll talk to you tomorrow." I swept out the door and down the steps. I didn't give Luke the time of day.

* * *

Dad was watching for me. I could feel the anger radiating off of him the moment I stepped into the bar. He glared at me but didn't leave his post.

It's Mark's fault. If he hadn't told me to leave my purse in the car, I would have had my EpiPen when I needed it. My going into anaphylactic shock tends to wig dad out for a month or two. The bandages and bruises aren't helping.

"He's pissed."

My head swung around. I knew Luke was following me, but I didn't expect him to actually come in. The bar was closing in 20 minutes. "Go away, Luke."

"Tell me where you were tonight and I might help you defuse the situation."

"I don't need your help."

"You're probably right. Tony's an understanding guy. He understood when he caught you sneaking out of the bar with a six-pack of beer when you were 13. So I'm sure he'll understand why you went gallivanting across the country when there's a death threat hanging over your head."

No, dad didn't understand then, and he wouldn't understand now. I was 13 and smuggling beer to my friends. He was so pissed I thought he would have a coronary right there on the spot, and that really scared me. I didn't know CPR.

I can deal with dad's anger. It's when I scare him that he really lowers the boom. I didn't see the light of day for months and it took years to regain his trust. He was scared then and he's scared now.

I felt the blood leach from my face as the implications of Luke's words finally sunk in. "What death threat?"

"We need to talk."

"Luke … fine. Let me get you a beer."

I filled two mugs with draft and took them over to the table in the corner. I set one in front of Luke then slid in the seat across from him. "What death threat?"

"Your brakes."

"What about them? The inspection won't be done until Monday."

"True, but you know what they'll find."

I pushed away from the table. "Why are you doing this to me?"

Luke grabbed my arm. "You know I'm right."

"No I don't."

Tony will believe me even if you don't."

"That's blackmail." If dad thought I was in danger, he would lock me in the backroom and post a guard 24/7. I wouldn't see the light of day until travel agents started advertising weekend get-a-ways to the moon. I eased back down into the chair.

"Where were you tonight?"

"I don't trust you. You're already holding my father's over-protective streak over my head. What's to stop you using what I tell you against me too?"

"Nothing."

"That's comforting."

"Were you doing something illegal?"

"That depends on your point of view." I took a swallow of beer. My throat was dry, parched actually. Fear can do that, but Tabby and I shared a pepperoni and sausage pizza. It could have just as easily been that.

Luke sat back in his chair, his hand resting lightly on the handle of the mug. He was figuring the angles, trying to work it to his advantage. "Okay, from your point of view, you were doing something that was perfectly acceptable and on the right side of the law."

"Yes."

"If I was to hazard a guess, I would say Mark is the one who wouldn't see it that way."

My eyes widened.

He knows.

"What did you do, Annie?"

Confess. You'll feel better for it.

He's a cop, not a priest!

"Annie."

"I had to do it!" I responded, firing up at the injustice of it all. "Mark changed the locks and wouldn't let me in the house to get my stuff. He was holding my shoes hostage!"

Luke cringed. "You broke in."

"No, I used the garage door opener."

"You know, when he calls in the burglary, you'll be on top of the suspect list, and the whole police department knows you were AWOL tonight."

"Mark won't even know I was there. I replaced my shoes with some of Lynette's, and I only took enough clothes to get by."

"That's all you took, shoes and clothes?"

"No ..." I drew out the word. I could argue that the shoes and clothes were mine, but not the rest of the stuff.

"Out with it."

I winced. Luke's voice was harsh. "I took a few linens and some kitchen utensils too. Oh, and I took my charge cards out of the desk."

"That's it. You didn't take anything else?"

My face heated when I thought about the last item I took, but on threat of death I wasn't going to tell him about *that*. A girl has a right to a few secrets.

Luke sat back and studied me again. I hate when he does that. I feel like I'm under a microscope and am about to be dissected. "Where's the garage door opener?"

"It's in my purse."

"Give it to me."

I glared at him. "Why? Mark doesn't know I have it. As far as he knows, it's still in the glove compartment of the Mazda."

Luke didn't respond. He just held out his hand and wiggled his fingers. I pulled it out of my purse and slapped it in his hand. "There! Are you satisfied?"

"Not by a long shot."

"Are you going to arrest me?"

"I should, but I'll make a deal with you instead."

"What?"

"Back off. Stop pushing the sheriff for an investigation."

"No." I called the sheriff yesterday and left a message. When he didn't return my call, I called again. The fifth time I called, his secretary hung up on me.

"Annie, stirring things up won't make a difference. I don't have a body."

"I can't. My mother was murdered. She has as much a right to justice as the next guy."

"Keep it up and you'll be joining her."

"What?"

"Annie, someone's trying to kill you."

"Why?"

"We already talked about that."

"Okay, but Lynette disappeared ten years ago. If her murderer thought I was a threat, why did he wait until now?"

"Are you sure he did?"

"What do you mean?"

"How many near death experiences have you had in the last ten years?"

I swallowed hard.

"Good. You're thinking."

"What brought this on?"

"The break-in. You walk under a perpetual black cloud. Nobody's luck is that bad, not even yours. There's a pattern to your disasters."

"You're wrong."

"Do you remember the benefit dinner the Women's League sponsored last fall?"

"I told you I was jinxed. Who but me would trip and fall down the stairs in front of a hundred people? I was so embarrassed I felt like dying."

"You were lucky. You could have broken your neck. Did you trip or were you pushed? Who was standing at the top of the stairs with you?"

"I tripped and I thank you not to discuss it any more. It wasn't exactly the highlight of my life." Mark tried to catch my arm, but he wasn't fast enough. I tumbled ass over apex all the way down the stairs. It was humiliating.

"Fine. How many times have you been rushed to the hospital with an allergic reaction to a food you didn't know you were allergic to?"

"Counting Saturday, three times, but it was my fault. Luke, I'm allergic to peanuts. Peanut oil is common and sometimes I forget to ask. That's why I carry an EpiPen."

"You've eaten at the Copper Kettle a hundred times. Valerie knows about your allergies. She swears the salad dressing was made with canola oil. Even if it was an accident, what happened to your EpiPen? Every time you've needed it, it's gone missing. I don't think you're that careless. Not with something that could save your life."

I thought back to the incident at the Copper Kettle. When my EpiPen wasn't where I thought it was, I panicked. My throat was closing up and I couldn't breathe. If there hadn't been two EMT techs in the Copper Kettle eating lunch, I would have been deader than a doornail.

I almost died, but it wasn't attempted murder. I bought this really cute little purse at a clearance sale two days before. When I transferred my stuff, I thought I transferred my EpiPens too. I guess I didn't. I let Dr. Cantrell write a new prescription rather than admit to my carelessness.

Okay, you're clumsy and you're careless. What about the brakes? They were working just fine the last time you drove the Mazda.

"You've made your point." The incident at the Copper Kettle was my fault, but if Luke *thought* I was a target, maybe he would start investigating.

You're ignoring the truth again.

The Mazda hasn't been inspected yet.

Luke pulled my attention back to the conversation. "Are you going to tell me what your mother left behind and then lie low for awhile?"

"I'll think about it." Luke's jaw clenched and his eyes darkened. I don't think he liked my response.

"God you're stubborn!"

I sat back and crossed my arms over my chest.

"Fine." Luke pushed away from the table. "Tony will take the death threat seriously even if you don't."

"Don't you dare!"

"I have to. Someone's trying to kill you. The department can't afford protection. Tony will keep you safe and he'll do it for free."

"You rile up my father and you'll never know what my mother left behind."

"That's blackmail."

I sat back again. "Touché."

CHAPTER FIFTEEN

I paused to genuflect before sliding into the pew three rows from the back. Church attendance was down. That wasn't uncommon this time of year. Springtime in North Carolina is beautiful. Only the truly faithful would *waste* an hour of it sitting through Mass.

I'm not always as faithful as I should be. I skip church as often as I go, but I've never been targeted for murder before. In light of that, I really didn't want to piss off God by spending the morning on my knees scrubbing the toilet instead of praying for help and guidance.

I went back to my apartment last night. Dad's still mad at me, but he let me take the truck. Daddy's gruff and he does a lot of posturing, but he's a softy at heart. At least he's easier to get around than Luke.

Luke kept his mouth shut. He wasn't happy about it, but he wants my mother's journals. At least he would if he knew about them. I'll make a copy for him. A deal's a deal. Besides, I want Lynette's murderer caught. Not only for what he did to Lynette, but for messing with me. I loved my Mazda.

I pulled the kneeler down, crawled down on my knees, and made the sign of the cross. *Hail Mary, Mother of God, hear my plea …* It's springtime, a time of hope and new beginnings. God answers prayers. It's not always the answer I want, but I don't always see the big picture. In the grand scheme of things, my problems are pretty insignificant. I can see why peace on earth, feeding the hungry, and sheltering the poor would take precedence.

I ran through my list of petitions for the greater good of mankind and then started in on the ones closer to home. I prayed for Lynette. I

don't know why. I never bought into the idea that you could pray someone into heaven, nor could we buy our way in with money or good
deeds. We gained entrance by the grace of God. I prayed for her anyway. Who knows, maybe I'm wrong.

Maybe he'll let her in. Maybe he won't. That's between God and
Mama now. She'd liven up the place anyway.

I closed my eyes shoving that irreverent thought aside and focused
on the here and now. Someone was trying to kill me. Maybe. Luke's
story scared me last night, but in retrospect, I know my luck. Besides, if
Lynette's murderer was trying to silence me, he had ten years to do it
and hasn't succeeded yet. Nobody's luck is that bad, not even mine.

Mark used to fall in the middle of my petitions, but there's no point
in wasting my prayers on him. The prayer has to be sincere when praying about the prayee. Mark was unfaithful, he's spreading lies about me,
he cost me my job, and he held my shoes hostage. I'm sincerely pissed at
him. I can't kill him, but if he fell victim to the Black Plague or a rare
strain of Australian influenza, it wouldn't be my fault. A few "Hail Mary's"
and I could move on with my life.

It was hard to keep my mind on the Mass. Every time Father Nolan
paused to take a breath, I thought of another hundred things I needed
to do. If I kept this up, I would have to make time to go to confession. That would put me even further behind. It would be that much
harder to pay attention next week and then I would have to go to confession *again*.

The offertory plate made its way around the church. I dug in my
purse and pulled out a fifty-dollar bill. I had so much to be thankful for.
I have my shoes back. I glanced down and smiled at the strappy little
sandals I had on. I had a ham and cheese omelet for breakfast. I used my
very own omelet pan and ate it using a real knife and fork. Okay, so I
had to use a paper plate. Work with me here.

I dropped the bill into the offertory plate and passed it on. My car
was insured and the insurance was in my name. I no longer needed
Lynette's money to get my car out of hock.

With the last notes of the recessional, I shifted my purse onto my shoulder, and turned to slide out of the pew. Sonja MacDuffy, blocked my exit. Great, just great. Sonja is one of Edna's gossip mates. I didn't want a scene, not here in church. *Please Lord, get me out of here!*

"Good morning Annie." Sonja's smile and the corresponding gleam in her eye sent shivers down my spine.

"Good morning, Sonja. How are you?"

"I'm fine." She leaned closer and whispered. "Did you win the lottery?"

"What?"

"I won't tell anyone if that's what you want."

"No, I don't even play. What makes you think I won the lottery?" I eased forward hoping she would take the hint.

Sonja shrugged, but didn't budge. "Oh! I love those sandals. Are they new?"

"No." I bought the sandals at an end of summer clearance sale last August. I only wore them once before, but I had them for eight months so they didn't qualify as new.

"Well they look new. Are you sure you didn't get them the other day? Edna said you were out shopping."

I *got* them yesterday, but I bought them months ago. I glanced over her shoulder. "Oh look!"

Sonja swung around. "What?" Her laser sharp eyes scanned the thinning crowd. I used her momentary lapse in attention to squeeze past her.

"Sorry. I thought I saw Elvis. I guess I was wrong." I gave her a quick smile and headed for the door.

"Annie." A hand caught my arm halting my retreat. What's the world coming to? A body can't even go to church without be accosted by a bunch of busybodie's.

"Good morning Mildred." Mildred wasn't as bad as Edna, but she knew more than most. She's the day shift dispatcher for the Police and Sheriff's Departments. She sees and hears everything and has no compunction about passing it along.

"I heard about the accident."

"I'm sure you did." I tried to discreetly extract my arm from her grasp, but she tightened her grip. Her prey wasn't getting away until she had her say.

"What kind of friend are you? How could you let Tabby drive your car when you knew the brakes were bad?"

"I didn't know ..."

"Tabby was hurt. She could have been killed!"

"Mildred, it was an accident. There was no way of knowing the brakes would go out like that. Stop blaming the girl." Glen Eason came to my defense. I've known Glen all my life. One of the blessing and one of the curses of small town living. You know everyone and everyone knows your business.

Mildred's hands landed on her ample hips as she turned her ire on Glen. "Humph! None of this would have happened if she hadn't walked out on Mark."

I started backing away.

"Annie," another hand touched my arm. "Don't listen to her. The accident wasn't your fault."

I stopped, resigning myself to the small talk. At least it wouldn't be gossip. "Thanks Gloria, but Tabby was driving my car. I feel responsible."

"Don't." She let her hand slide down my arm and took my hand and squeezed it. "I'm sorry about your mother. No one deserves to die that way." Her lips compressed. "And to be left up in the woods without a proper burial, it's a sin."

"Detective Sheridan is working on the case. He'll find the guilty party."

"Yes, but it won't bring her back. How are you holding up? I know it's hard, but you need to hang tough. Stand up in the face of adversity."

"I'm trying to."

"Are you going to arrange a memorial service? I guess a funeral isn't necessary seeing as they haven't found the body, but a memorial service would be nice. It would bring closure for you and your mother's friends."

Friends? Lynette didn't have any friends, just lovers and husbands. Gloria meant well. She's Father Nolan's secretary and looks at the world through the proverbial rose-colored glasses. She would find something good to say about the Boston Strangler, and in her eyes, Jack the Ripper was just looking for companionship.

"Talk to Father Nolan before you leave today. I'm sure he will help with the arrangements. The church is available and if you have it on Wednesday, the Ladies Auxiliary can serve lunch."

"You want to have Lynette O'Reilly's memorial service *here?*" When Mildred waylaid me, several people crowded in to watch the scene. Watching a gossip filet her prey is almost as good as watching a horror flick. There's no real point to it, but there's always plenty of blood and mindless brutality.

When the conversation switched to Gloria and me, they continued to mill about. The feature was a bust, but there's always hope for a dollar theater flick. It's not as bloody, but just as entertaining.

"Better to have it at the bar during happy hour. We could lift a beer in her honor." The group broke into laughter.

I jerked my hand free of Gloria's grip, swung around, and glared at the group. "How dare you!" The snickers subsided. The men shuffled their feet and the women scurried back.

"Now Annie, don't get in a thither." Paul Gelspy spoke up. "We were just joshing with you. We didn't mean anything by it."

"My mother was murdered!" I pointed my finger at the group. "The bastard responsible lives in this town. It could be any one of you. It could be your neighbor, your drinking buddy, or a boss or co-worker." I turned and glared at the women. "Do you feel safe knowing there's a murderer amongst us? Do you think it's funny?"

"Annie, you're wrong. Someone passing through town killed your mother. She was in the wrong place at the right time, 'tis all."

"Oh, and this transient came back ten years later, dug up the bones, and moved them. That makes perfect sense."

"Annie, enough." The group parted like the Red Sea. Father Nolan glanced around at the crowd. "It's nice to see so many of you waiting for your turn in the confessional. I'll be in there shortly." The crowd dispersed with frightening speed.

Father Nolen turned back to me. He didn't say anything, just stared at me with those quiet, serious eyes of his.

"I'm sorry Father."

"Why are you sorry?"

"I didn't mean to cause trouble."

"You've been stirring up trouble since the day you were born."

I cringed at that. "That was my mother's forte." It was disheartening to know that even Father Nolan considered me my mother's daughter. In a word, *trouble*.

"Not all trouble is bad."

"I couldn't just stand there and listen to them berate Lynette. Whatever her faults, she was still my mother."

"Do you want a memorial service?"

"I don't know." I responded miserably. It didn't even dawn on me until Gloria mentioned it.

Father Nolan patted me on the shoulder. "Think about it. A memorial is as much for the living as it is for the dead. Your feelings matter too."

"I'll think about it."

* * *

I had too much to think about and too many things on my mind. To block it all out, I threw myself into a cleaning frenzy. It worked. At least it did until Luke's phone call forced the issue.

"Will you please stop stirring up shit?" Luke growled at me over the phone.

"What?" I threw the scrub brush in the bucket and sat back on the bathroom floor. It was clean enough to eat off of.

Yuck!

"It's just a phrase!"

"What?"

"Never mind!"

"Annie! Did you or did you not cause a scene in church this morning?"

"I didn't ..."

"Dispatch is going nuts. The patrol units have responded to 32 different calls. Any sound out of the norm and the dang fools think they have a murderer lurking around their house. It has to stop."

"It's not my fault."

"Annie, did you announce after Mass that there was a murderer lurking around town?"

"I didn't mean to, but Paul Gelspy said Lynette was killed by a transient. I had to set him straight."

"I'm having a hard enough time separating fact from fiction without you stirring everyone up."

"Mildred started it!"

"Mildred?"

"Mildred was telling everyone that Tabby was hurt because of me. The accident never would have happened if I hadn't left Mark."

"Mildred wouldn't say that."

"Are you calling me a liar?"

"No, but …"

"Fine. Believe what you want. I don't care anymore. You said you would investigate but you're not. You *lied* to me."

"Are you always this difficult?"

"I'm not difficult!"

"Rosetti deserves a medal. If you were married to me, I would have murdered you inside a month."

I sucked in a breath.

"Annie, I didn't mean that. I'm sorry."

I closed the phone and threw it aside. I might as well buy a jar of peanut butter and satisfy my curiosity. Mark's telling everyone I'm depressed and suicidal. I wouldn't want to make a liar out of him. Why wait until some unknown assassin pushes me down the stairs, or Luke loses his temper and puts a bullet between my eyes.

Anaphylactic shock is fast, but it is sort of scary. Maybe sleeping pills would be a better choice …

I sat down hard.

Was this Mark's plan all along? Were the confusing dialogues and overt concern just a part of his master plan? Am I a pawn?

What master plan? You still don't know what game he's playing. He wants you dead, but you still don't know why.

True.

I pondered the problem for a moment, and then shoved it aside. Mark's master plan had to wait. Luke was gunning for me. I didn't know where he was calling from, but it only takes 20 minutes to drive from one side of town to the other. He could be pounding on my door any minute.

I grabbed my purse, my copy of my mother's journals, and headed for the door. The sooner I made a copy for Luke, the sooner I saw the back of him.

With Luke off my back, I just had to deal with Mark and the assassin. As I really didn't think the assassin, that's what I've dubbed Lynette's killer for lack of a better name, was after me. That left Mark. Mark didn't scare me. I may be short, but I can defend myself. My mother's third husband, Doug's dad, gave me a gift certificate for karate lessons when I was eight. I made it all the way up to yellow belt before Lynette packed us up and we moved back to Grammy's.

I turned onto Brandywine Boulevard and headed across town. Office Max has a Xerox machine. Once Luke catches up with me, he'll demand the journals.

He doesn't know you have them.

That's not going to stop him.

R-i-i-i-ng!

I reached into my purse and pulled out the phone. I glanced at the monitor. Luke. Forget that.

The phone started ringing again as I pulled into the parking lot in front of Office Max. I picked it up, glanced at the monitor, and grimaced. Dad's call following on the heels of Luke's didn't bode well. If he riled up my father I was going to kill him.

R-i-i-i-ng!

I crossed my fingers and answered the phone. Murder is a mortal sin. Kill Luke and I would be on my knees forever. "Hello."

"Where are you?"

I winced at the tone. Luke's a dead man. A little strychnine in the coffee or arsenic in his tea … Can hemlock be bought over the internet?

"Hi Daddy."

"Answer me!"

"Whatever Luke told you, it's not true."

"Your brakes were tampered with."

"Luke's guessing." Panic crept into my voice. Dad's a formidable jailor. "The Mazda hasn't even been checked out yet."

"Go home Annie. Better yet, come here. I'll make pasta primavera for dinner."

Dad knows what he's doing. Pasta primavera is really good bait. If mouse traps were baited with pasta primavera rather than cheese, mice would be wiped off the face of the earth.

I'm not a mouse.

"Daddy, you're over reacting. I have some shopping to do and I'm going to do it."

"Where?"

"Bi-Lo."

"Tell me what you need and I'll pick it up for you."

"I'm not going to spend my life hiding because of some perceived threat. No one's after me. The accident was just an accident."

"What do you need?"

It was like talking to the wind. Fine. "Are you sure Daddy? I know how you hate to shop."

"What do you need?"

"I need some tampons."

The silence was broken with a sigh. "Go pick up what you need, but call me the minute you get home."

"Don't worry, Daddy. Nothing's going to happen to me."

"I wish I could believe that."

* * *

Over an hour had passed before I pulled up to the curb in front of my apartment. The stupid Xerox machine kept jamming. I managed to copy three of the journals, but gave up on the rest of them. I was out of time.

I glanced over at the apartment and groaned. Some days it just doesn't pay to get out of bed. First the incident at church, then the argument with Luke, jammed copy machines, and now Miguel was sitting on my stoop. He spotted me, pulled out his cell phone, and punched in some numbers. I didn't know if he was checking in with Luke or with dad. I didn't care. I've had it with the lot of them.

"She's here."

I came to a stop and scowled at him.

"I'll tell her."

He closed his phone and his gaze shifted to the bag in my hand. "That's not a Bi-Lo bag."

"Pretend."

"Where were you?"

"Why? Are you reporting to dad or are you reporting to Luke?"

"You might want to cut them a little slack. They're worried about your safety."

I pushed past him and headed in. "Why should I? Dad's treating me like a ten-year-old, and Luke says Mark deserves a medal for not killing me."

I dropped my purse on the counter, dug for my phone, and called dad. I paced back and forth while I listened to him lecture me. By the time I hung up, *I* was ready to kill someone. *I'm not an irresponsible little fool.*

Miguel was standing between the kitchen and the living room. His arms were crossed over his chest and his feet spread. He reminded me of a mountain, just as big and totally unmovable. It could be done, but it would take ten lifetimes to make any headway. "What?"

"Where were you?"

"I can't tell you. You'll tell dad and then dad will tell Luke, and I'll be right back where I started."

"Where were you?"

"What are you? Part bloodhound?"

"Someone tried to kill you. They'll try again. I'm not going to stand by and let them succeed. If you don't tell me where you were, I'll tell your father you can't be trusted."

I sighed heavily. Miguel didn't bluff. He would talk to my father and what little freedom I had would be curtailed. "Luke wants my mother's journals. I made copies on Friday and put the originals in a safety deposit box, but I don't want to give Luke my copy."

"Why? Don't you trust him?"

"Yes. No. The sheriff refuses to call it a homicide. They're not even investigating. So I thought …" I bit my tongue in an effort to stem the flow of words.

"Annie!"

"What?" I asked innocently.

"So I thought … " Miguel mimicked.

"I don't know what you're talking about."

Miguel studied me for a moment, eyes narrowed. I stared right back at him.

Miguel dropped his gaze first. That was a first. He knows I'm right. *You didn't tell him anything.*

So?

"What are you going to do, Annie?"

"I'm going to find Lynette's murderer and I'm going to expose him."

Miguel raked his fingers through his hair in a gesture that reminded me of dad. I guess he didn't like my plan. "Annie, you don't know the first thing about investigating a murder."

"I'll learn."

"You'll stir up a bunch of trouble and get yourself killed."

"According to Luke, this guy is already gunning for me. At least this way I have a fighting chance."

Miguel didn't respond. The water dripping in the sink was the only thing that broke the silence. If he blew the whistle, I would lose what little advantage I had. It wouldn't stop me, but it would make it that much harder. Gloria was right. I needed closure. A memorial service wouldn't give it to me. Justice would.

"Give me the copies. I'll scan them into the computer."

Thank you Jesus! "I started to make copies, but I ran out of time."

"Where are they?"

"They're behind the seat in dad's truck." I dug the keys out of my purse and handed them to him. "I really appreciate you doing this for me."

"I'm not doing it for you. I'm doing it for me. If the death threat and your mother's murder are connected, we need to know. I hate funerals. I would rather not go to yours."

CHAPTER SIXTEEN

I need to buy a TV. I'm not particularly interested in watching TV, but it would make great background noise. It might even dispel the feeling of isolation.

I'm used to living alone. My short stint as a wife didn't change that. It's the perpetual fear and tension that has my nerves stretched taut. The windows are closed and the door is locked. I don't like living like this. I feel caged in.

The scratching at the patio door had me whipping around. Someone was out there. It takes a lot of nerve to break in, in broad daylight. I didn't like to think I underestimated the opposition. Underestimating the opposition has cost more than one politician their livelihood. Would it cost me my life?

The scratching started again. I almost jumped out of my skin. I glanced around franticly for something to use as a weapon. Where's my bat?

Scratch. Meow!

"Palmer!" I ran to the patio door, shoved the blinds aside, and started flipping the locks. He has been out in the cold, cruel world for over 48 hours. He was probably scared for life.

"Come here baby." I slid the door back and scooped him up. He wiggled in my arms and licked my face as I carried him into the kitchen. "Why did you run away from me? I wouldn't let that big ol' mean detective hurt you." I shifted Palmer in my arms and opened a can of cat food. I set him on the counter in front of me and stroked his back while he ate.

Mark said Palmer and Mascara were spoiled and he's right. They are my babies. I can always count on them when the world turns its back on me. Mascara wove around my feet. She purred loudly. I wasn't the only one happy to see Palmer back home. I scooped her up and rubbed my face against her fur.

When I married Mark, I gave him my heart and the key to my soul. Instead of cherishing them, he stabbed me in the heart and smeared peanut butter on my soul. The little bit of loving that Palmer and Mascara offered was all that kept me from curling up and dying.

I lowered Palmer and Mascara to the floor and watched them scamper off. My thoughts were maudlin, but I figured I was entitled to an occasional pity party. I've had a rough week.

Miguel stopped by. He gave me the copies of my mother's journals to pass on to Luke, but damn him, he kept the other copies. He told me to give Luke a chance before I started meddling in police business.

I know what I'm doing. Well, no I don't, but nowadays most jobs are learned by OJT, on the job training. Detecting can't be that hard. If the books I've read are to be believed, it's mostly stakeouts and research anyway. Besides, the good guys always win.

I heard a car screech to a stop in front of the apartment building. My heart jumped up into my throat. It sounded like Mark's Porsche.

I crept to the window and eased up one of the blinds. Yep. The Porsche was parked behind dad's truck and Mark was coming across the yard. He wasn't running, but he wasn't walking either. It was more of a ground-eating stride that emanated anger. The stride matched the set of his jaw and the fire in his eyes.

A confrontation was inevitable, but I wasn't expecting it so soon. Mark expected me home this evening, not this afternoon.

"Annie!" Mark pounded on the door. "Open up!"

What? Does he think I'm stupid? I'm glad I bought the 50-dollar lock instead of the 20-dollar one. "Go away Mark. I'm not letting you in."

"Open the door!" He kicked the door and cursed.

"Stop kicking my door, you big jerk! If you put a dent in it I'm making you pay for a new one." It's easy to be brave when there's a steel door between me and the threat. The door was strong and the locks new.

I felt a breeze ruffle my hair. I swung around and gaped at the open patio door.

I dashed across the room, slid the glass door shut, and fumbled with the locks. Mark wasn't going to outflank me today.

"Annie! Open the God damned door! I just want to talk to you."

Yeah, and the serpent just offered Eve a taste. "If you don't leave, I'm calling the police." Why didn't I think of that before? I ran back into the kitchen and snatched up my phone before creeping back into the living room.

I was met with silence.

I lifted one of the slats on the blinds. Mark had the trunk on the Porsche open and was shifting through the contents. He straightened with a crowbar in his hand, slammed the trunk shut, and started back toward the apartment. I opened the phone and started punching numbers as fast as I could.

Tabby answered the phone. It goes to show just how scared I was. I automatically dialed her number instead of the police. "I'll call you back."

I scrolled down the address book in my cell phone. It didn't take long. There were only two numbers. That was Mark's fault. My old phone had the police department's number already programmed in. I glanced around. Where's the phone book?

Call 911!

Right. I heard the wood splintering. I started punching in the numbers. It took three tries. My fingers were shaking and I kept hitting the two instead of the one. I succeeded, finally.

"Sheriff's Department, may I help you?"

"There's a madman beating down my door!" *Screech! Pop! Snap! Rrripp!* I scurried into the bathroom and threw the lock.

"Give me your address and I'll send a unit."

I rattled off my address in a panicked hush as I huddled on the floor next to the toilet.

"Annie? Is that you?" The dispatcher asked.

"Melinda?"

"What's going on?"

"Mark is tearing down my door! He wants to kill me! Send someone. Hurry!"

"Keep calm. There will be a patrol unit on the scene in just a few minutes."

"I'll be dead by then."

"Annie …"

"Will you adopt Palmer and Mascara? I don't want them going to the SPCA."

"Annie …"

"I don't have a will, but I want daddy to get the apartment building. He'll take good care of it."

"Annie, you're overreacting."

"I would like for Tabby to get my shoes." I heard the frame splinter and the door slam against the wall.

Hail Mary, Mother of God, hear my plea …

The bathroom door was wrenched open. A small, strangled sound escaped from the back of my throat.

Mark reached down and grabbed me by the front of my shirt. He yanked me up off of the floor and shook me. The phone flew from my hand. The whimpers turned into a cry and then blossomed into a full-fledged scream.

"Shut up!" He gave me another teeth rattling shake. "Where did you get the money?"

My head snapped back and forth. At least Mark got his wish. I wasn't screaming any more. Fear froze my vocal cords. I stared at him, mute. Money? What money? I heard the sirens off in the distance. They were too late.

He shook me again. "Answer me!"

I forced some air past my vocal cords. "What money?"

"If you could afford to drop a 50-dollar bill into the collection plate, you've got money to burn."

Sonja. If I live to see another day, I'm going to kill her. It was an empty threat. I was dangling a foot off the floor and in the clutches of a madman. He would kill me now. *Until death do thee part …* I guess Mark really meant it.

I felt Mark stiffen. I like to think he was having second thoughts. Murder is a mortal sin and he would have to go to confession. I know he'd hate that, but I don't think that's it. It was the sound of a patrol car screeching to a halt right in front of the building that changed his mind. Getting caught wasn't part of the master plan.

"Shit!" He swung me around like a rag doll and dropped me on my knees in front of the toilet. His hand clamped down on my neck holding me in place.

"Mark, please!"

He's going to drown you in the toilet!

Oh God, no! Please! Kill me if you must, but not like this! I'll never live it down. "Mark, no!"

"Shut up!" I heard a pop. The lid of a prescription bottle bounced on the floor and then skidded to a stop next to the sink.

Plop, plop, plop. Little white pills spilled into the toilet bowl splashing water up in my face.

I braced my hands on the seat and tried to push away, but Mark's strong. My pitiful efforts didn't even faze him. He stuck his hand in the toilet and swirled the water around and then brought it up to my face.

I didn't realize his intent until it was too late. I opened my mouth to scream. It was a stupid move on my part. I gave him an opening. He shoved his long fingers down my throat triggering my gag reflex.

Lunch was hours ago, but my stomach wasn't empty. It was nasty tasting stuff. If I wasn't already gagging, I would have gagged on it.

Mark pulled his fingers out of my mouth, wiped them on *my* shirt, and then shoved them down my throat again. I gagged again. He leaned close to my ear and whispered. "You'll never talk your way out of this one."

Outraged, I clamped down on his fingers.

"Ow!"

"What's going on here?" I glanced up and spotted Jed Stevenson coming through the door with his hand poised over his holster and his eyes wary. Jed spotted Mark and relaxed his stance.

My luck was holding. During their glory days of high school football, Mark and Jed were teammates. As a quarterback, Mark carried the ball to victory. It was easy enough to do once Jed plowed a path for him. They put aside the football uniforms twelve years ago, but Jed was still clearing the path for Mark.

There was another police officer two steps behind Jed. Would he be my salvation?

Not.

The kid's uniform was pristine. It probably came out of the package two days ago. If Jed and a rookie were my only hope, I was doomed.

Mark's demeanor did an abrupt about face. His hand came up and brushed the hair from my brow. "You'll be all right, baby. I'll take care of you." The grip on the back of my neck eased as he pulled me back from the toilet bowl.

"What's going on, Mark?"

"Annie swallowed a bunch of sleeping pills." He wrapped his arm around me and pulled me close.

"No! That's not true!" I tried to push away from him, but his arm was like a vice grip.

Jed stepped forward, glanced in the toilet, and grimaced. "Is she finished?"

"I think so." Mark stood dragging me up with him and stepped out of the bathroom.

I twisted and squirmed in his grip. "No!"

"Maybe she needs to puke again."

"No. She's distraught." He turned his attention back to me. "Calm down Annie. I'll take you to see Dr. Ramsey. He'll know what to do."

"No! Don't let him take me! He's trying to kill me!"

Mark's grip tightened, painfully. I fought as if my life depended on it. It did. I started screaming.

"Annie, calm down!" Mark's solicitous demeanor started slipping.

"Don't let him kill me!" I wiggled and kicked and pounded. Jed stared at me slacked jawed and the rookie backed up a step. I think they were waiting for my head to rotate. I wasn't possessed like poor Regan in the *Exorcist*, but I was caught in the demon's clutches. The devil made her puke too.

"Annie!" Mark couldn't subdue me without resorting to brute force.

"I think you better put her down." The rookie glanced over at Jed as if expecting to be slapped down for making a suggestion.

"She can't be left alone. Surely you can see that." Mark grabbed my flailing arms and pinned them to my sides.

"Put her down, Mark." There must be a limit to how much Jed was willing to let slide.

Mark's jaw clenched, but he did what he was told. My feet touched the floor and I shoved away from him. I was wobbly and weak from my communion with the toilet and Mark's rough treatment, but that didn't stop me. I scurried away from him, putting as much distance between Mark and me as I could. It wasn't much. Three steps and my back was against the wall.

Jed took a step forward putting his body between Mark and me. He glanced at Mark and then at me, finally shifting his focus back to Mark. "What's going on?"

"I already told you. Annie tried to kill herself."

"I didn't try to commit suicide! Mark's trying to kill me."

"Okay …" Jed drew out the word. He wasn't happy. He didn't want to question Mark, but he didn't dare ignore my claims. "Why does he want to kill you?"

Good question.

"Enough of this! I'm taking her to the emergency room." Mark stepped forward reaching for me again.

I threw up my hands and slid down to the floor. "Don't let him hurt me!"

Mark grabbed my arm and jerked me back to my feet. "Annie! Cut it out!" My bruises were finally starting to fade and now he was giving me a whole new set. If this keeps up, I'll have to move to Alaska so I can wear long sleeves year round and not look out of place.

With a cry, I grabbed his hand and tried to pry my arm free.

"Let go of her!" Jed's voice was sharp.

Mark dropped his hand and stepped back. "She's distraught."

I leaned against the wall for support as I tried to reel in my terror. Jed stepped between Mark and me again, nudging him back another step. "No, she's scared."

Mark raked his fingers through his hair. "Do you really think I tried to kill her?"

"No, but ... shit Mark! What the hell do you expect me to do? Annie made the call. I can't just ignore it." Frustrated, he gestured for Mark to take another couple of steps back and then pulled out his cell phone before addressing the rookie. "Keep them separated while I call the watch commander. He can make the call on this one."

I watched Jed disappear into the kitchen before glancing around the apartment. My door was ruined and my serenity shattered. It was so *depressing.* I wanted to break down and cry. Scratch that. I was already crying. Mark wasn't going to get away with this.

Yes he is. Jed thinks you're crackers and the watch commander will agree. They're going to haul you down to the emergency room. Dr. Ramsey will fill out the commitment papers and Judge Swenson will sign them. You'll spend the rest of your natural life in a rubber room.

No! I turned to the rookie, he was my only hope, and pleaded my case. "You've got to believe me!"

The rookie hesitated. I don't think there was anything in the training films that prepared him for this. His eyes widened and a grin split his face. "Hey, I know you. It took a minute for the name to click. You're Lynette O'Reilly's daughter and ..." He turned and smirked at Mark. "This is your adulterous husband."

Mark's lips compressed. "I told you she was suicidal, and I know my actions added to her distress. You don't have to rub my face in it."

The rookie glanced over at me and sobered. "Killing yourself is not the answer."

Pawns are meant to be sacrificed.

The fear eased just enough to let the anger in. Mark's not getting away with this! He wants to kill me. There was only one thing left to do, prove it. "I didn't try to kill myself. Mark tried to kill me!"

"Why?"

"Because of my ring," I sniffed.

Mark's head shot up.

"I didn't have any money and I needed to eat." I took a discreet step to the left. Mark's fuse is short and his temper volatile. Maybe I am crazy and need to be committed. Goading him into exploding could backfire. Jed would arrest him, but what good would that do me? I'd be dead.

Mark's eyes widened and then they narrowed. "What did you do with your ring?"

I kept my eyes on the rookie when I responded to Mark's question. The rookie was all that stood between me and certain death. "I pawned the ring." I wiped a tear away with the back of my hand. "The man said I had ninety days to get it back, but then I bled all over the receipt. I didn't mean to throw it away."

Mark lunged at me with a roar. "That ring was a family heirloom!"

I darted around the chair, but I wasn't fast enough. Screaming, I hit the floor hard with Mark sprawled on top of me. His hands wrapped around my throat and squeezed off my air.

I barely had time to register the fact that my plan backfired when Mark was knocked off his perch with perfectly executed tackle. Well, maybe not perfect. It knocked Mark off me, but it didn't break his hold on my neck. Mark rolled over onto his back with me sprawled on top of him. The rookie landed on top of me with a thump.

"What the hell …" Jed cursed, loudly.

I clawed at Mark's hands.

The pressure on top of me shifted and moved. I didn't pay much attention to it. The blood pounded in my ears. My lungs burned and my vision was fading in and out. Desperate, I pushed up from the floor with my feet, pulled my knee forward, and then dropped back down again.

I caught him square in the nuts.

Mark's hands fell away and I sucked in a greedy breath. I was jostled aside when Mark rolled into a fetal position. He was wheezing louder than I was.

The rookie grabbed Mark's right arm and slapped the cuff on it. He rolled him onto his stomach and reached for his left.

Mark whimpered.

The rookie glanced over at me and grinned. "His secretary's gonna be pissed. I think you broke his woody."

CHAPTER SEVENTEEN

Sometimes you can't win for losing. My door was smashed in. I was the one harassed and terrorized. It was my life that was threatened, so why was everyone mad at me?

Doug and Miguel nailed a piece of plywood over the hole in the wall that used to be my door. Both men were furious. Doug's anger was predominantly aimed at Mark, but Miguel saved some for me. I'm used to depending on myself. Miguel lives right next door, but it didn't dawn on me to call him when Mark showed up.

I underestimated Mark. The people I trust no longer trust me. Mark was lying through his teeth. Even if I convinced everyone I was telling the truth, there would always be a shadow of a doubt.

Dad believes me, but I almost wish he didn't. He hasn't said ten words since he got the rundown on the incident. He's been sitting at the table since Miguel dropped me off, sharpening one knife after another. I think he's planning something that'll land him in the chair.

Luke is on his way over. He sounded mad too. At least he got his way. Until the hole in my wall is fixed, I'm back to living with my dad.

When I was growing up, dad's apartment, like Grammy's apartment, was home to me. My mother had primary custody, but I spent most of my time at Grammy's or with dad.

Dad lives over the Mountain. The apartment takes up the entire second floor of the building. There's one set of stairs leading down to the bar and another that climbs the outside of the building. The outside stairs were added when I was thirteen. Dad didn't want me stepping foot in the bar.

I heard someone climbing the steps that ran up the back of the building and rose. Dad turned around and glared at the closed door. He had a twelve-inch hunting knife clutched in his hand. "Relax Dad. It's Luke. He called a few minutes ago." Dad nodded and went back to sharpening his knives.

I pulled the door open and stepped out on the landing.

Luke came to a stop two steps from the top. "Come on. Let's go for a drive."

I shuffled my feet but didn't move. His quiet tone wasn't friendly. He was an avalanche waiting to happen. Step wrong and it would come down on my head. Going with him didn't seem prudent. "I'd rather not."

Luke stepped past me and opened the door. "Tony, Annie and I are going out. We'll be back in an hour or so."

"I don't want to go with you!"

"Tough." He grabbed my hand and started pulling me down the steps.

"Luke!"

"Get in the truck and shut up. You've got some explaining to do."

Now that makes perfect sense. How can I explain when he told me to shut up? I buckled my seatbelt, crossed my arms over my chest, and stared straight ahead.

Luke slid into the seat and closed the door. He just sat there for a minute before starting the truck and pulling out of the parking lot. We rode in silence. Reaching the outskirts of town, Luke turned onto Highway 10 and headed toward the lake.

"Why did you hide it Annie? Why didn't you leave him or ask for help?"

I wrapped my hands around my arms. The dynamics of my marriage are no longer relevant. I didn't want to discuss it with Luke. "It doesn't matter anymore. Mark's in jail."

Luke pulled into the county park and wound his way around to the lake. He pulled the Explorer to a stop, killed the engine, and then turned in his seat to face me. "You're scared of him."

"Yes."

"He was abusive."

"No."

"You said you were scared of him."

"I am."

"So he was abusive."

"No."

"That makes absolutely no sense. Was he abusive or not?"

"No, Mark wasn't abusive, and yes I am scared of him."

"Why?"

"He wants to kill me."

"That's crazy."

"I'm not crazy!" If one more person accuses me of being crazy, I will go crazy. Okay, so I get into heated arguments with myself. I win more arguments than I lose. A lot of people can't put their right shoe on before their left. Big deal. That doesn't mean we're crazy.

I don't think the government is conspiring against me, I'm not stockpiling weapons in the basement, and I've never been abducted by aliens. I'm probably saner than the average Joe on the street.

"Calm down, Annie."

"Why? You don't believe me."

"Okay, I believe you, but you can relax. He'll never get away with it."

"So?" I responded in a huff. "I'll still be dead."

Luke sat back studying me in the muted light. I think he was trying to come up with a way to politely tell me I was nuts. I'm not. "Annie, level with me."

"About what?"

"About the abuse and the pills."

"I already told you ..."

Luke cut me off. "The charges have been dropped."

A strangled cry escaped before I could stop it. Mark tried to kill me and he walks? What ever happened to justice?

"Judge Swenson recommended counseling."

"He'll never go."

"Not for Mark, for you."

I turned to face Luke and pleaded my case. "I'm not depressed and I'm not suicidal. Can't you see what he's doing? Once he's convinced everyone that I'm off my rocker, he'll kill me and make it look like suicide."

"That's absurd."

"Is it?"

Luke sighed heavily. "Annie, you've been under a lot of stress lately."

"I'm so tired of hearing that! Stress has nothing to do with it. Mark wants to kill me!"

"Why?"

"I don't know! If I knew, I could do something about it."

"Document the abuse and get a restraining order."

"Mark wasn't abusive." I felt like I was beating my head against a wall.

"Okay, how do you explain the bruises on your neck?"

"He tried to strangle me!"

"And that's not abuse?"

"No! It wasn't abuse. It was attempted murder."

"Mark wasn't trying to kill you. Jed said you deliberately provoked him into losing his temper. There's evidence of abuse, but that's a long way from attempted murder. Unless you document it, and request a restraining order, there's nothing we can do."

Okay, so maybe Mark was verbally abusive, but up until he tried to kill me, he never laid a hand on me.

Liar!

Okay! Okay! Mark has a temper and sometimes it got the better of him. He slapped me around a couple of times, but when I threatened to leave him, he backed off. It has nothing to do with the here and now. Mark doesn't want to beat me into submission, he wants me *dead*. Unfortunately, Luke couldn't see it. I had to deal with Mark myself. "Have it your way, but if the medical examiner puts suicide on my death certificate, I'll come back and haunt you."

Luke's lips twitched. "Duly warned."

"You think it's funny!"

"No. No I don't. I wish you would level with me and I really think you should consider counseling. Until then, it would be better if you stayed with your dad."

Silence settled between us. I watched a lone car drive past the entrance and disappear into the night. Luke was right about one thing, I have been under a lot of stress lately. That doesn't make me suicidal, just human. Grammy used to say, if your life is easy, you're not living. At the time I didn't understand what she meant. I do now.

It was nice sitting here with the crickets and frogs serenading us. I see why the high-schoolers like to come out here and neck. It's isolated and sort of romantic. Not that I'm thinking any romantic thoughts right now. I may be separated from Mark, but we're still married. Besides, I'm with Luke. All romantic fantasies starring Luke were jettisoned the day Lynette married Bryce Sheridan. They were no longer appropriate.

He's not your brother anymore.

I wiggled around in the seat, and then cracked the window.

"Annie?"

Keep your panties on girl. He brought you out here to talk. Hot, sweaty sex is not on the agenda.

"It's stuffy in here. I just need a little fresh air."

Luke looked at me like I had lost my mind. Maybe I have. April's right around the corner. The days are warm, but it still drops to near freezing at night.

Desperate for a distraction I asked, "Have you talked to the sheriff? Has he agreed to an investigation?"

Luke sat back again. "No."

"No?"

"Relax Annie. You're not the only one pushing for answers."

"Who?"

"John LeBlanc. The money embezzled from the bank was insured, but the jewelry your mother took from the safe wasn't. He wants it back."

"Lynette's not a thief. She didn't embezzle that money, and she didn't break into John's safe."

"Did she leave any jewelry behind?" Luke turned and placed his arm across the back of the seat. My heart started going pitty-pat. Other than Mark, I don't have much experience with men. Mark's not much of a kisser. A couple of quick kisses and he was reaching for a condom. He didn't see any point in wasting time.

"Annie?"

I felt my face heat. At least the car was dark enough to hide it. "Sorry. I drifted for a minute."

Luke repeated the question. His fingers slid down and toyed with my hair.

Focus!

I wasn't about to tell him about the safety deposit box. Except for one antique broach, all the jewelry was modern anyway. None of Mr. LeBlanc's heirlooms ended up as part of Lynette's retirement fund. "I packed up mostly clothes and shoes. I didn't come across any jewelry." Luke's fingers had moved from my hair to the back of my neck.

"Speaking of which ..."

"I know. I know. I made copies of Lynette's journals. I'll give them to you when you drop me off." I leaned back enjoying the gentle caress. It was a new experience for me.

The fingers stilled.

Don't stop!

"Journals?" The hand slid away. I bemoaned the loss.

"Lynette always kept a journal. They date back to before she even married dad."

Luke straightened in the seat and reached for the ignition. "It's getting late. I need to get you home."

I slouched back in the seat, disgruntled. "Can we stop at Wal-Mart on the way back?"

"Why?"

"I need some batteries."

✳ ✳ ✳

"Doug promised to fix my door, but I don't think it will be high on his priority list." I took a big bite out of one of the hoagies I picked up on my way back from talking to Randy Lugie, my insurance agent. Luckily his office wasn't far from the Mountain. I was on foot and would be until the insurance money came through.

"Why? Doug's usually pretty good about helping you out." Tabby and I were sitting on the floor around the coffee table enjoying an early lunch. Louise was out visiting friends and wouldn't be back until dinner.

"Yeah well, that's before he decided I was suicidal."

"Annie, look at it from his point of view. You swallowed a handful of pills. When that didn't work, you deliberately provoked Mark into attacking you."

I set my sandwich down, my appetite gone. "Tabby."

"You scared him Annie. You scared all of us."

"Have I ever given up? Thrown in the towel before?"

"No, but you've never walked in on your husband screwing his secretary before either."

I stood and wandered around the living room finally coming to a stop in front of the window. I kept my back to Tabby. "No, but I walked in on my boyfriend in bed with my mother. I wanted to curl up and die that day, but I didn't. I'm not a quitter, Tabby." I turned and faced her. "It hurts to know you think I am."

"Annie, I don't …"

I cut her off. "I need to get going."

"Annie!"

"I'll call you in a few days." I left the apartment before she had a chance to stop me. I wanted to cry.

Oops. I can't do that. People cry when they're sad and sad is one step short of depressed. Once you're depressed, it's just a hop and a skip to suicidal. Before long you're six feet under and pushing up daisies.

Well, I don't like daisies. They make me sneeze.

My phone started ringing. I fished it out of my purse, glanced at the monitor, dropped it back in my purse, and kept on walking. I had several more stops to make. The bank was next on my list. I wanted to go back to First National Bank, but it was too far to walk. The only bank within easy walking distance of the Mountain was North Carolina Federal Savings and Loan, the bank where my mother used to work.

I pulled the big glass doors open and stepped into the lobby. I was carrying too much cash around. After the break-in on Saturday, I didn't dare leave it buried between my bras and panties.

The bank belongs to John LeBlanc, Sr., my mother's fifth and final husband. Actually I'm not sure if 'owning' is quite the right designation, but he has control of the big corner office. Most people just assume he owns the bank.

I slipped into line but kept my eyes on the floor. I took a step forward when the feet in front of me moved. Two more people and then it would be my turn. I needed to open a checking account eventually, but not here. For now all I wanted to do was stash some of the money in my savings account.

I've had an account here since I was a kid, but when Lynette left, I opened an account at First National Bank. When I married Mark, I closed those accounts. I didn't even think to close this one.

The hairs on the back of my neck started doing that tingling thing again. It was all I could do to keep from groaning. Nothing good ever came from it.

I shuffled forward. The prickly sensation was driving me crazy. Who's staring at me? Unable to resist, I rolled my head slowly to the side. My gaze came in contact with Johnny LeBlanc's. I abruptly dropped my eyes again.

I shuffled forward again. I ignored Johnny. Johnny, actually he goes by Jack now, but I still think of him as Johnny. Well anyway, he's John LeBlanc's son. That makes him Lynette's stepson and my stepbrother.

He didn't treat me like a sister.

I wised up before things went too far. Johnny wasn't interested in *me*. He was looking to add another notch to his bedpost. For a while there, his reputation rivaled Mark's. Johnny didn't take the rejection well. He's been antagonistic towards me ever since.

The woman in front of me finished and I hustled up to the counter. I made my deposit, took the receipt, and turned intent on getting the hell out of there, and ran smack dab into John LeBlanc.

"Oomph!"

I grabbed his arm to keep him from going down. "Sorry. I didn't see you."

John jerked his arm out of my grasp. "I want to talk to you."

I started backing away. "I'm sorry, but I don't have time. I have a million things to do today."

He grabbed my arm stopping my retreat. Everyone's been grabbing my arm lately and I'm getting tired of it. If they didn't leave my arms alone, I would never get rid of the bruises.

"Where's my jewelry? I want it back!"

"I don't have it." I glanced around discreetly. There were a dozen pairs of eyes riveted on us. John LeBlanc was 70 if he was a day. If he took a swing at me, I would have to be a man and take it.

"Why should I believe you? You're nothing but a liar and a sneak, just like your mother."

"My mother's not a ..." My words trailed off. What could I say? Lynette *was* a liar and a sneak.

John smirked. "Nothing to say to that, huh?" Have you ever seen a 70-year-old man smirk? It's not a pretty sight. What did my mother ever see in him?

Money.

I spoke slowly, enunciating each word. I didn't want any room for doubt. "My mother didn't embezzle that money, and she didn't steal your jewelry."

"She stole the money and I can prove it. The jewelry disappeared at the same time. It stands to reason she took that too."

"What proof?" I was 17 when my mother disappeared. Dad did a pretty good job of shielding me from most of the gossip. Unfortunately it was an all-or-nothing type of shield. I didn't hear the gossip, but I didn't hear the facts either. I never knew what they had on Lynette.

"Come with me." John spun on his heel and headed toward the offices off to the right. I followed him, albeit reluctantly. I couldn't pick and choose my truths. I had to uncover the good and the bad. I just didn't want to.

John's office was big and he had a desk the size of the Titanic right in the middle of it. He skirted it and opened one of the file cabinets running along the side wall. He pulled a file out and threw it on the desk.

I picked up the gauntlet, I mean the file, and paged through it as if I knew what I was looking for. I didn't. There were official documents, bank statements, and cash withdrawal slips. Where's the proof? It all looked like gobbledygook to me. "There's nothing here that points to Lynette."

John yanked the file out of my hand and rifled through it until he came to the cash withdrawal slips. He slid them out of the stack. "Look." He pointed to the signature at the bottom. "Your mother authorized these withdrawals without the client's signatures. She kept the withdrawals small and targeted accounts of people that wouldn't notice. It might have gone on indefinitely, but Maria Sanchez took over her mother's finances when they put her in a nursing home. Maria noticed the discrepancies and asked Johnny to look into it. He brought it to my attention."

"Was that before or after she disappeared?"

John dropped down at his desk with a sigh. "Maria came in late in the day. Johnny didn't bring it to my attention until the following morning. Lynette disappeared that night. I think she saw Maria come in and knew the game was up."

I couldn't hold his gaze. Lynette was a thief. Not only that, she preyed on the elderly and the infirm. It was a side of her that I had never seen before. I fingered the receipt in my hand stalling for time. I didn't know what to say.

I glanced at the signature again. Lynette O'Reilly was scrawled across the bottom of it, as plain as day.

Hold the presses!

I laid the receipt down on the desk and smoothed it out before studying the signature again. I didn't know if I should laugh or cry. "Mr. LeBlanc, my mother didn't steal that money. This isn't her signature."

"Say again?"

I took my index finger and stabbed the signature. "That's not my mother's signature. I'm positive. Lynette always made big loopy L's like Laverne did on the Laverne and Shirley show and the dot over the "i" in O'Reilly was never a dot. She made a little circle. Sometimes she even turned it into a smiley face."

I raised my head and met his gaze. "Lynette was framed."

John stood, leaned over his desk, and shook his finger in my face. "That's bullshit! The FBI checked the signature against her signature card on file here at the bank. It's hers."

I stood and glared back at him. "You're wrong! Lynette's not a thief! She didn't embezzle any money, and she didn't steal your jewelry. You had the *proof* all along!"

John's face flushed with anger and his eyes glittered. He reminded me of Roger Rabbit right after he downed a shot of whiskey. The only thing missing was the steam coming out his ears. "I want my jewelry!" He screamed at me in frustrated rage, and then fell back into his chair, huffing and puffing like a steam engine.

Uh oh.

"Dad!" Johnny ran into the room, shot an evil glare my direction, rounded the desk, and started opening and closing drawers as fast as he could. "Where's your nitroglycerine?"

My fingers inched forward, closed over one of the receipts, and slid it to the edged of the desk. It fluttered to the floor next to my purse.

Johnny opened the prescription bottle and waited until John slipped the little pill under his tongue before turning his ire on me. "I want you out of here! You're worse than your mother, stirring up trouble wherever you go."

"Hey, I didn't come barging in here. He invited me in."

"Leave and don't come back. If you step foot in this bank again, I'll call the police and have you arrested!"

"You can't do that! I have an account here."

"Close it."

"Fine!" I reached down, shoved the receipt in the pocket of my purse and stood. I wanted a copy of the signature. It wasn't proof of Lynette's guilt. It was proof of her innocence. Now all I had to do was *prove* it. Detecting wasn't as hard as it looked.

* * *

I left the bank with $263.27 more than I had when I went in. I wasn't happy about that. I didn't want to add my stash to the cash in the attic. That was Lynette's money. Yes, I took some of it, but that was in lieu of birthday and Christmas presents. As far as I know, Lynette didn't have a will so technically the money belongs to John LeBlanc now. He was her husband of record when she died.

I called Luke and left a message on his voice mail. He'll get back to me eventually. He's pretty good at ignoring my messages but gets pissed when I ignore his.

I'm not telling him about the signatures, at least not yet. He had a conniption when I gave him the copies of the journals. He wanted the originals, but I knew better than to give them to him. Unwelcome evidence has a nasty habit of disappearing out of evidence lockers. I'm not making that up. It's a chronic problem; at least it is in every detective story I've ever read.

The inspection on the Mazda should be done by now. As Luke hasn't called, I'm assuming I was right. I wanted him to call me so I could gloat. I started humming as I headed down the street. Mickey Spillane had nothing on me. One day on the job and I already had my first clue.

A couple more stops and I could head back to the Mountain. Walking toward Bradley's Drug Store, I dug into my purse and pulled out my ringing phone. I glanced at the monitor before dropping it back in my purse unanswered.

I walked past Ben Franklin, then turned and backtracked. Ben Franklin carries knickknacks and crafts, an assortment of other things from pots and pans to bath towels, and smelling salts. Until Doug fixed my door, which had better be soon, I was stuck at my dad's. I needed something to do.

I wandered up and down the aisles. I can knit and crochet, but afghans are winter projects and they take too long. I wanted to see some results.

I picked up a pack of large needles, some heavy duty thread, a sewing scissors, and several bath towels in dark green, burgundy, and beige. Happy with my selections, I headed toward the checkout counter. Grammy used to make braided rugs from old towels. I didn't have any old towels so I had to settle for new ones.

"... Mark wants to have her committed, but Tony will have none of that. Not that he has a right to voice an opinion, she's Mark's wife, not his." The sarcastic words drifted past my ears as I made my way toward the check out counter. My feet stumbled to a halt. I should have realized the peace and tranquility wouldn't last.

Gossip is an inevitable part of small town living. Cringe from it and it becomes a weapon. I lifted my chin and marched up to the counter. Mark had enough weapons in his arsenal. I wasn't giving him another one.

CHAPTER EIGHTEEN

"When?" I adjusted my phone so it was cradled between my shoulder and my ear leaving my hands free to cut another strip of toweling. The beige towels were already cut into three inch strips. The rug would be beige in the center with alternating rounds of dark green and burgundy.

"Sorry kid, I don't have time tonight." Doug responded totally unrepentant. I set my scissors down and turned my full attention to the conversation. Doug was stonewalling. I knew why. He didn't trust me. Left to my own devices, I might accidentally kill myself.

"Okay, when?" I put a little heat into the question.

"I'll stop by Lowes later this week and find out how much money we're talking and get back to you."

"Later this week! I can't wait that long."

"Why? What's the rush?"

"I want to go home!"

"Relax. I said I would get to it and I will."

"But not now."

"No."

"Doug, I'm not suicidal! I'm not going to swallow a bunch a pills and drift my way into eternity."

"I never said you were." He responded defensively.

"Mark lied."

"Probably."

"Probably? I can't believe you fell for his story!"

"Annie, calm down! I believe you. Hush now." I could hear the panic in his voice. It was disheartening. I'm not diving into the abyss,

175

not today, not ever. I'm not a diver. The one and only time I tried it, I ended up doing a belly-flop. It hurt like hell.

My shoulders drooped. Edna Telley and her cronies can believe whatever they want. I don't care, but Doug's my brother. No matter what the gossips threw at me, he always stood beside me. He always believed *me*.

"Annie?"

"I'm fine Doug, just depressed."

"Depressed?"

"Doug, you never doubted me before. You're my brother and I love you. If I was truly depressed and suicidal, don't you think I would talk to you about it?"

"Okay, okay! I'll fix the door, but you can't go home."

"Why?"

"Talk to Luke."

"I'm talking to you."

"Annie ..."

"Doug, what's going on?"

He sighed heavily. "Your brake line was cut."

"Who told you that?"

"Luke swung by Mark's office, made him come up with an alibi for Thursday. Word got out."

"Amy isn't much of an alibi. She can't even tell time."

"Mark's alibi is sound. There were a dozen people in and out of the office that day. I'll fix your door, but you've gotta promise to stay put. You're the only sister I've got. I don't want to lose you."

I closed the phone slowly and set it aside. It was after six and the Mountain was open for business. I was alone and would be all evening. Doug knew that, but he still wanted me to stay here instead of my apartment.

A warm fuzzy feeling sluiced through me. Doug wasn't lying. He trusts me. The contentment I felt earlier today settled back over me. I was warm, safe, and secure. It wouldn't last. I had to delve into the unknown and figure out why Mark wanted to kill me. My mother's killer was lurking in the shadows waiting to pounce. I don't know why he killed her or why I'm a threat to him, but for tonight, the peace would last. Humming, I went back to work.

* * *

I studied the long, thick braid before setting it aside and answering the door. Braiding was a mindless task and the rug rated low on the craft difficulty scale, but I didn't care. I hadn't made anything in a long time. I had forgotten just how therapeutic crafting could be. Practically floating, I pulled the door open.

My eyes widened into great big saucers and my heart jumped up in my throat. I guess that's good. That way if someone stabbed me in the chest, they would miss my heart by a mile. I might even survive the attack.

There was no one on the landing and the darkness pressed inward forcing its way into the apartment. With a strangled cry, I slammed the door shut again. A big hand stopped it six inches from the mark and pushed it open again.

I fell backwards stumbling over my feet. Regaining my balance I pressed my hand to my throat and glared at the intruder. "Why did you do that? You scared me to death!"

Miguel slammed the door shut and returned my glare. "You didn't bother to check and see who was out there before opening the door!"

"What good would it have done? You were hiding on the steps!"

"You're damn lucky it was me and not some ax murderer or rapist!"

"At least they wouldn't be yelling at me!"

Miguel's eyes widened. His jaw opened and closed, but no words came out. I've never seen him at a loss for words before. Perplexed by his actions, I backtracked over our argument.

I felt my face heat. I stared down at my feet rather than meet his gaze. I don't have very big feet, but they still don't fit in my mouth. I really hate when I try to shove them in anyway.

Miguel drew in a breath and released it slowly. "Annie, you didn't check to see who was out there before you opened the door. You know better than that."

I shuffled my feet but still didn't respond. It was a test and I scored a big, fat zero.

"What would you have done if it was Mark or your mother's killer lurking on the steps instead of me?"

"You made your point."

Miguel wasn't ready to let it go. "Well, what would you have done?"

"Mark knows better than to come here. If he gets within a hundred feet of me, dad will kill him and he knows it. He's seen dad's collection of knives." I turned away and walked back to the kitchen. I wanted the peace and contentment back. "As I don't know who killed my mother, I would have invited him in and served coffee and cookies."

I sat down and picked up the end of the braid and went back to work. "Why are you here? Did you draw the short straw and end up with suicide watch, or do you think I need a body guard?" Miguel prowled around the kitchen either too restless or too angry to sit down.

"Don't be so flippant. Your mother's dead. She was killed by someone local and if he perceives you as a threat, and apparently he does, he'll come after you. He has nothing to lose. If he's caught, he'll get the chair. It doesn't matter if he's killed once or if he's killed twice."

At least Miguel's words answered my question. I folded the raw edges in and then folded the strips in half, and started braiding again. It helped center my erratic thoughts. It would be easier to figure out who, if I understood why. Lynette was always stirring up trouble. Plenty of people cursed her for it, but no one ever tried to kill her. What was different this time?

"Annie, are you listening to me?"

"Yes. I understand the threat. I just don't know what to do about it."

"We need to read your mother's journals."

"I know." I knew I needed to read them, but I didn't want to read them with Miguel. I read enough the night I pulled them out of the attic. I didn't care if Miguel read them, and I didn't care if Luke read them. I just didn't want to be around when they did.

Miguel disappeared into the living room then reappeared with a folder in his hand. He moved the shoe box full of strips aside. I kept folding and braiding material.

"How do you want to do this?"

"I don't."

"Annie."

"Would you rather I lie to you?"

"No. The sooner we get started the sooner we finish." Miguel peeled off his jacket and hung it on the back of the chair. He sat down next to me, stretched out his legs, and picked up the folder. "Rather than work chronologically, I thought it best to start with the last journal and then go backwards."

I started to set the rug aside, but Miguel stopped me. "Keep working. I'll read."

December 22.

I hate this time of year, all the hustle and bustle. The greetings and good cheer are as phony as the "genuine" diamond earrings Ben gave Rita last Christmas. The poor girl wouldn't know a garnet from a ruby or a piece of glass from a diamond. Ben's tickled pink. Spend a few bucks and Rita will think he gave her the moon. She'll keep him happy and satisfied for at least a week or two. If he springs for the broach as well as the ring, I won't see him for a least a month.

He'll be back.

"Do you know who Rita and Ben are?"

I gripped the strips of material as if they were a lifeline anchoring me to the here and now. I didn't want to get sucked into Lynette's world where words like fidelity, love, and affection held no meaning. I would rather live without a diamond than accept a phony and call it real.

"Annie?"

"Rita runs a daycare on the east side of town. When I was little I used to go there after school. I think Ben's a real estate broker, but I'm not really sure."

"Your mother knew them for years."

"Yes."

"Did you know your mother was sleeping with him?"

I shook my head. "My mother had a lot of lovers that came and went and some that kept coming back. I didn't know Ben was one of them."

Miguel set the folder down. "I wish there was another way to do this. I know this is hard for you."

"Miguel, I knew my mother better than most. There's nothing in her journals that would surprise me. Keep reading."

Miguel picked up the folder, turned the page, and started reading again.

> *December 23.*
>
> *I do it every year. Every year I say it will be different, but it's not. Christmas is two days away and I still haven't bought Annie's gift.*
>
> *I don't know why I bother. She doesn't want anything from me. She doesn't even like admitting that she's my daughter. One mistake and she damns me to hell. Is that fair?*
>
> *Okay, so it was a big mistake. Annie was prancing around in those new shoes all giddy and excited. She was going to the prom. She didn't have a clue what that really meant, innocence turned to knowledge in the back seat of a Chevy. It's a right of passage. I didn't mean to deny her that right. I just didn't want her hurt by the bumbling efforts of an untutored boy.*
>
> *So I was wrong ...*

"Annie, do you want me to keep on reading?"

I shook my head. I didn't trust my voice.

"I'm sorry."

"Miguel, don't."

"You never let me say it before. Give me a chance to say it now."

"It's not necessary." My mother seduced my boyfriend, not out of jealousy, but because she wanted to tutor him in the finer points of lovemaking. What a noble sacrifice.

"I say it is. Your mother may have initiated it, but I was a willing participant. I knew it was wrong but ..."

"Was she a good teacher?"

"Jesus, Annie."

"Sorry."

Miguel closed the folder and dropped it on the table. "I don't care what the journal says; your mother's motives were not altruistic."

"Miguel, I'm not stupid. The journal entry is pure rationalization, an effort to assuage the guilt."

"You're wrong. Just before you walked in, your mother offered me a deal. Her silence came with a price."

"Blackmail." I slumped down in the chair. The mother I knew was a shallow, self-serving nymphomaniac. She bought condoms by the case and had the health department's phone number on speed dial. She kept her hair stylist and manicurist on retainer and drank her martini's with or without olives depending on her calorie count for the day. She adored money, but she was never very good at hanging onto it, or so I thought.

I closed my eyes and drew in a breath, held it, and then released it slowly. The Lynette I knew was an illusion. There was *Truth* and there were *Consequences*. Did I really want to know the real Lynette O'Reilly?

"Annie?"

"Would you have told me?"

"I would like to say yes, but I don't know. You were my best friend and my first love. I didn't want to lose you. If I told you, I would lose you, but if I didn't, the guilt would have eaten me alive. It didn't matter what I did, I was screwed."

"That was Lynette's forte."

"Annie, don't."

"Go away Miguel. I need to think."

Miguel stood. He touched his fingers to my cheek in a fleeting caress then quietly walked away.

CHAPTER NINETEEN

I'm sick. I think it's a malady caused by information overload. The synapses are firing, but the information isn't getting through. Until I'm functioning again, I'll just stay here and work on my rug.

I changed the design. I want an oval rug, not a circular one. The center is still beige but after three rounds, I started braiding with two beige strips and a burgundy one. One more round and I'll add a second burgundy. Once that's done, I'll start bringing the beige back in and then the beige will give way to green.

A detailed description of my rug probably isn't relevant, but I'm not ready to think about anything else.

Lynette slept with Miguel. I walked in on them so there's no room for doubt. Lynette wasn't embarrassed. She was pissed. I never understood that. I do now. Once I knew, she had nothing to hold over his head.

I thought I knew my mother, faults and all. I was wrong. If she was capable of sleeping with my boyfriend and then blackmailing him, she was capable of just about *anything*. It's the *anything* that has me floundering. If I continued to push for answers, *anything* could surface.

I'm not my mother. I've said it a million times and most of the time I believe it, but what if I'm wrong? What if I inherited more than my curly red hair and my love of shoes from her?

You did. Your mama liked sex and so do you.

Okay, so I like sex. What's not to like? It lowers stress, takes your mind off your troubles, and it gives you a good cardio workout. A condom is cheaper than an exercise bike and a whole lot more fun. To top that off, it works better than any number of sleeping pills.

I sighed heavily. I haven't had much exercise lately and I wasn't sleeping well either.

"Annie?"

"Hmm?" I glanced up. "What?"

"Are you coming down to the bar this evening?" It was after three. The Mountain would be opening in less than an hour. Dad would be heading down soon.

"I don't think so."

"Annie, what's the matter?"

I tried to muster a smile. I didn't like the worry in his eyes, but I couldn't quite manage it. "I'm fine, Dad. Just tired."

"I worry about you."

"I know and I'm sorry for it. Just give me another day. I'll be back to full steam tomorrow."

"Tabby stopped by last night. She said you're not returning her calls."

"She bought into Mark's story."

"Annie."

I hate one word rebukes. They pile on the guilt better than a 20-minute lecture. I know I overreacted, but I'm not ready to set it aside. I wasn't angry, I was hurt. I thought Tabby knew me better than that.

I glanced up at dad. He hadn't moved. He would stand there until I gave in and did what he wanted. "I'll call her tomorrow."

"Call her tonight."

"Yeah, sure."

He stood there for another minute before turning and heading for the stairs that led to the kitchen behind the bar. I watched him disappear through the door. With a shrug I went back to work.

* * *

With most illnesses, the first signs of recovery are felt through the stomach. I still wasn't ready to think, but I was hungry.

I prowled through the kitchen and came up empty. Dad usually ate breakfast here and then ate the rest of his meals downstairs. Unless I went down, I was stuck with scrambled eggs and toast.

It was time to face the world again. I tucked my cell phone in my pocket. I'm not sure why I bothered to take it. I switched it over to voicemail right after Miguel left two nights ago and haven't answered a single message. Tabby's called a million times. I guess I'm starting to feel human again. At least the guilt's creeping in. I need to call her.

Luke left a couple dozen messages. He even called dad when I didn't return his calls. I don't know what dad said to him, but he quit calling.

Not a word from Miguel.

I slipped down the stairs. Billy was in the kitchen adding the finishing touches on a couple of hamburger platters. My mouth watered. "Is one of those for me?"

Billy glanced up and his eyes lit. "Bout time you surfaced."

"What? Can't a girl take a day off?"

"Not if it's gonna put your dad in a mood. I've worked here for over 20 years with nary a complaint from the boss. Yesterday he threatens to fire me not once, but three times."

"Ouch."

"If you don't get those platters out front before the burgers are cold, I will fire you."

Billy winked at me, picked up the tray, and shouldered his way out the door.

Dad rolled his eyes. "I just can't get good help these days."

I burst out laughing. Billy's worked for dad since he opened the bar. Officially Billy is an employee, but I don't think the Mountain would be what it is today without their combined efforts. I know dad's considered making him a partner more than once.

"Are you ready to face the world again?"

I nodded.

He crossed the kitchen and wrapped his burly arms around me and squeezed me tight. "You scared me girl."

I closed my eyes and leaned my head against his chest as he rocked me back and forth. "I didn't mean to."

I felt him chuckle. "You never do."

"I'm hungry."

"Go out front and have a seat. I'll whip up something for you."

I pulled out of his arms. "Thanks Daddy." He knew I was thanking him for more than just the dinner. For two days he kept the world at bay giving me time to make some decisions and come up with a plan. He didn't ask. I think he was afraid I would tell him I wanted to hire a medium. Lynette had to know who killed her. With a medium, instead of searching for the killer, all I would have to do is ask her.

I grabbed a Corona out of the cooler and a slice of lime from the prep area. I shoved the lime down the neck of the bottle as I made my way to the end of the bar. It was Wednesday, hump day, so the bar was doing a brisk business. I knew a number of the patrons, some even qualified as friends, but I wasn't up to socializing just yet. I pulled dad's stool out, slid it down to the end of the bar so I wouldn't be in the way, and sat down.

Sipping my Corona, I watched the group of men in the corner. Most of them were from Harry's crew. They were relaxed and joking around, their jobs secure until they finished the mall.

There were a couple of solitary drinkers, a few tables with two or three people still dressed in their work clothes, and one table of college boys probably home on spring break.

"Here you go, baby." Dad set a mushroom and Swiss burger with fries and a pickle down in front of me.

"Thanks Daddy."

"Eat." He patted my shoulder, moved down the bar, and went back to work.

I bit into the burger and closed my eyes savoring the flavor. The mushrooms were fried crisp and the burger was medium well, just the way I like it.

"Good burger?"

My eyes popped open. Scotty sat down across from me. His trademark pencil stub was in its usual spot, behind his left ear, but the insolent grin that usually covered his face was gone.

"Hey Scotty. What can I get for you?" Scotty, actually his name is Andrew Samuel Scott, but not many people know that. Well anyway, he's the owner/editor of The Gazette, our local weekly paper. He was a friend of my mother's. A *friend*. Lynette had plenty of lovers and husbands, but there were few people she actually counted as friends. Scotty was one of them

"Are you working tonight?"

"No, but tell me what you want and I'll get it." He ignored my offer, signaled Billy, and then turned his attention back to me. "So, how's the investigation going?"

"What investigation?" I picked up a fry, dunked it the catsup, and folded it into my mouth.

"Don't play dumb. I know Luke's been over to talk to you. So …" He let his words trail off.

"So … what?"

"So do they have any leads?"

I sat back, disgusted. "The sheriff won't even admit Mama's dead."

"What do you think?"

"It doesn't matter what I think. Until her body surfaces, the sheriff won't get off his fat ass and investigate. I don't know who killed her or why. I'll probably never know, but I want her name cleared. She didn't embezzle that money …"

Scotty cut me off. "Are you sure? Do you have proof?" He was salivating like a dog on the scent. He got a whiff of a story, a stinky one.

"You didn't hear that."

Scotty wasn't put off. "What have you got? Where did you get it? Was it in your mother's journals?"

"What do you know about the journals?"

Scotty smirked. "Oops. Were the journals your little secret too?"

"Nope. I already handed them over to Luke."

Scotty paled. "I thought you said they weren't investigating."

I shrugged my shoulders and smirked just to annoy Scotty. "Luke said he would look into it. That doesn't mean he's investigating."

"What else did you hand over?"

"What more does he need? There must be at least a hundred motives for murder hidden between the pages."

"Was anything else hidden between the pages?"

"What?"

Scotty sat back as Billy set a draft in front of him. He picked up the beer and took a big gulp. He set his beer down and leaned forward, inviting confidence. "Annie, you know why the sheriff's not investigating. Your mother was trouble with a capital T. Most people, the sheriff included, don't care if she was murdered and then buried outside of town or if she headed for the moon. She's gone and that's all that matters."

"You're wrong. A lot of people were upset when she disappeared. She was the favorite topic of every gossip in town. Her late night visitors had to find a new outlet to relieve their sexual frustrations, and The Curly Do lost a regular customer."

"You make her sound like a frivolous nymphomaniac."

I cocked an eyebrow but didn't respond.

"Okay, she was a nymphomaniac, but she wasn't frivolous. She knew this town and its people better than most."

"So?"

"She knew their hopes and their dreams." His voice dropped to a whisper. "She was the keeper of the secrets. Don't let them die with her."

"What secrets?" A hand came down on Scotty's shoulder.

Scotty's head whipped around.

I glanced up and saw Luke. His eyes were hot. He told me to lay low and now Scotty was offering to help me stir things up.

Luke swiveled the chair around until Scotty was facing him. "You haven't returned my calls."

"Sorry about that, but I've been busy. The paper goes to the presses tomorrow." Scotty tried to ease back, but Luke had him boxed in, literally and figuratively.

"Let's talk now. You can tell me all about Lynette's little secrets."

"Luke, you've got it all wrong." Scotty plastered an innocent smile on his face and raised his hands palms out. "I was fishing, looking for a story."

"Fishing season doesn't open for another month. Come on." Luke shot me a look that said *you're next* before ushering Scotty over to a table in the corner.

I watched them out of the corner of my eye as I finished my burger and fries. I knew some of Lynette's secrets. She used an anti-wrinkle cream religiously and consulted with a doctor in Charleston regarding liposuction. Getting old terrified her. She was 36, not the 33 she claimed when she disappeared. Finding a gray hair hidden amongst the red nearly sent her into heart failure more than once. Oh, and she had a safety deposit box stuffed full of money and jewelry too.

I glanced over at the table in the corner. Scotty was sweating like a pig, but the *pig* was cool and controlled. It didn't bode well. Luke was in interrogation mode and I was next on his list.

Okay, so I didn't return his calls. There was no point. I already knew about the brakes, and Luke knows about my altercation with John LeBlanc. He stops by the Hess Express every morning on his way into work. Edna had to know the whole story within minutes of my leaving the bank. Why bother repeating the story when he already had *the facts*?

So? You ignored him. It was an insult, personally and professionally. If you think he'll take that lying down, you are a fool.

Personal! There's nothing personal between Luke and me!

Hah! You shared your bed with him three nights in a row.

I felt my face heat. I have an active imagination, but I *didn't* sleep with him.

No you didn't. You were too busy to sleep.

I'm innocent. So I let the man slip into my daydreams. There isn't a woman alive that hasn't daydreamed about hot, sweaty sex and forbidden fruit once in awhile. It's harmless.

Is it?

If people were expected to confess every single impure thought, priests would be stuck in the confessional from now until the second coming. As long as Luke doesn't know I was daydreaming about him, I haven't done anything wrong.

Luke's in interrogation mode.

I slipped off the stool, flipped up the walkthrough, and came out from behind the bar. I stopped and chatted with a few friends and acquaintances as I made my way toward the door. I'm a pretty level-headed thinker. I don't usually waste time daydreaming about sexy move stars, rock idols, or hunky detectives. I had to work off some of my excess energy before I *did* something stupid. I need my sleep.

A little hot sweaty sex and you'll be sleeping like a baby again.

I slipped out the door. A ten mile run might do it.

"Going somewhere?"

My head snapped up. Luke was lounging against the wall next to the door. Don't ask me how he got here; I don't have a clue. Last time I checked, he was in a heated argument with Scotty.

Maybe Scotty beamed him out here.

I rolled my eyes. Everyone knows that *Star Trek* technology is at least a hundred years away. Besides, if Scotty could beam Luke out of the Mountain, he would beam him a couple of light years away, somewhere like Planet Druidia. Scotty prefers to ask questions rather than answer them.

"It's not like you to run from an argument."

I kicked my foot out. "What kind of shoes do I have on?"

Luke's lips twitched. "Sneakers."

"Not sneakers, running shoes and I put them on *before* I came down, and *before* I saw you."

"They look like sneakers to me."

"I wasn't sneaking out!"

Luke grinned.

"Oh shut up!" Flustered, I spun around and headed down the street. I've never known a man that could tell the difference between sneakers and running shoes. It was disconcerting.

Luke fell in step beside me.

"Go away."

"No."

"I don't want to talk to you."

"Tough. We need to talk."

"Why?"

"Your brakes were tampered with."

"I know, but why do I need to talk to you about it? You're not with the Police Department. You're with the Sheriff's Department."

"Someone's trying to silence you. I think you know who killed your mother and why. You just don't realize it yet."

My feet stumbled to a halt. "Are you investigating now? Did the sheriff give you the go ahead?"

"No, but if someone is trying to silence you …" Luke let his words trail off.

"I understand."

"Good."

"Without a body, you can't investigate, but if the guy manages to kill me, then you'll have a body so the sheriff will have to investigate. As he doesn't want to investigate, he sent you to protect me."

"That's ludicrous."

"You can tell the sheriff thanks, but no thanks. I don't need protection and I don't need help nailing my mother's murderer." With that said, I sprinted forward.

"Annie!"

I weaved around a trashcan and darted into the alley. I was wearing sneakers and not running shoes, but Luke was wearing boots. I had the advantage.

The jerk! Did he really believe I bought into his story? I wasn't born yesterday and I don't need protection. The protection is just a cover anyway. The sheriff wants to know how *my* investigation is going.

Forget that.

I didn't feel like running anymore, but I wanted Luke off my tail. I cut across Lexington and veered off in the direction of the park. Turning the corner, I sprinted down to the middle of the block and slipped into the alley. Pressed up against the building, I waited.

I knew the boots would slow Luke down but damn, what's taking him so long? He must be out of shape.

He's not out of shape. There isn't an ounce of fat on that man.

Shut up! I'm not listening to you anymore. A conscience is supposed to keep me out of trouble, not spur me on.

No more daydreams?

No.

Are you sure?

Why did I feel like crying?

I watched Luke's Explorer drive by and turn on the next block. I drew in a breath, held it, and released it slowly. Investigate? What a joke. I wasn't investigating. I was hiding. I straightened my shoulders and marched back toward the Mountain. It was time to do what I felt was right regardless of the consequences.

Luke's Explorer was sitting in the parking lot when I got back. I ignored him. I stepped into the bar, glanced around and spotted Larry, the owner of our local equivalent of Rent-a-Wreck. I knew what I had to do.

CHAPTER TWENTY

It's time to take back control of my life. I'm 27-years-old, not 16. I crept out of the bedroom before eight, careful not to make a sound. I was reclaiming my independence, but I didn't see any point in spoiling dad's illusions. As far as he was concerned, we would be roomies until all ties to Mark were severed, and Lynette's murderer was behind bars.

Forget that. I'm not timid and I will not be intimidated. As long as I stay here, hiding behind my father, I'm controlled by circumstances. Whenever my luck turns sour, I blame it on fate. In truth, fate may start the ball rolling, but how we respond to the situation determines our luck.

We learn from our mistakes. I learned the definition of discretion at the age of six. Telling your current step-dad about your mother's afternoon visitors was a definite no-no. At the ripe old age of 13, I realized that girls with braces shouldn't kiss boys with braces. Now, at 27, I've learned the hardest lesson of all. If I value my life, if I want to live instead of simply exist, I need to stand up and fight back.

I scribbled a note and left it on the counter. I slung my purse over my shoulder and slipped out the door.

I walked out into the parking lot and glanced around. I spotted the ancient Honda Civic parked at the far end of the lot under the street light. That had to be it. Four-hundred dollars doesn't buy much class. It would run. Larry's a top notch mechanic even if he's a shyster when it comes to business. I needed wheels and Larry was the only game in town.

The door creaked when I opened it. I fished around under the mat, located the key, and a copy of the rental agreement. It was a Xeroxed copy of the napkin we wrote on last night.

I was renting the car for a hundred a week for two weeks. The other two-hundred bought Larry's silence. I slid behind the wheel and inserted the key. The engine coughed and sputtered before finally catching. I buckled my seatbelt and eased out of the parking lot.

I stopped by Grammy's on the way out of town. My door was fixed, but Doug still had the key. He said he would give it to me when I gave him the money for the repairs. I don't know why he's being such a prick. I already promised to stay at dad's until this was resolved. I guess he thought I would sneak out and end up doing something stupid.

Doesn't matter. I have a spare key.

I'm not going back on my word. I have a very strong aversion to dying. I picked up my mail and rifled through it. Once I moved into the apartment, I turned in a change of address. They started forwarding my mail last week. The stack of bills didn't surprise me. Visa, Discover, Belk ... I stopped when I flipped a bill from State Farm Insurance to the top of the pile. The Mazda's insured through Nationwide. Why am I getting a bill from State Farm?

Shrugging, I shoved the stack in my purse. I watered my plants, crawled up into the attic for the envelope of money, and hit the road. I wanted to be in Raleigh before ten.

I stopped by the law office of Winston, Martin, and Goldstein first. I plunked down a 1,000-dollar retainer and made an appointment for next Wednesday. I crossed that off my list and moved on to the next. I made a copy of the withdrawal slip appropriated from John LeBlanc's file and headed for the bank.

Last week I made copies of my mother's journals and stashed the originals in a safety deposit box in my name. As Miguel kept my copies, I had to either make *another* set or take the originals.

With a sigh, I pulled them out of the box and stuffed them down in a Bi-Lo bag. I'll make another copy and then put them back. I had to keep them safe. They're the only lead I have.

True, but that's not why you're guarding them.

The journals are my mother's thoughts, not mine.

So? Pick out a pen name, rent a post office box, and send a few stories to Playboy. Your financial worries would be behind you.

The journals are too explicit for *Playboy.*

All the better.

I rolled my eyes. I can't do that. If Father Nolen got wind of it, I would be on my knees forever.

Use a pen name.

I rolled my eyes again. My conscience is just one more example of my luck. A conscience is supposed to keep a body on the right track, not offer inappropriate alternatives to your financial woes.

Blocking my conscience, I put what was left of my mother's emergency fund in the safety deposit box. Right or wrong, I'm keeping it. A few months back I read a book called *Slow Burn* by Julie Garwood. The main character, Kate, inherited 85 million dollars from an uncle. He was a nasty old man and built his fortune on the misfortune of others. The money was tainted. Rather than keep it, she gave it all away. I would like to say I'm just as altruistic, but I'm not. I don't know where the money came from and I don't care. Well, I do, but I'm keeping it anyway. Once I'm back on my financial feet, I'll decide what to do with the rest of it.

And you have the gall to blame me!

I copied the journals, swung back by the bank, and stashed them back in the safety deposit box. Okay, so keeping the money's wrong, but so is claiming authorship on someone else's work, to say nothing of publishing it.

I had one more stop to make before heading home. I pulled into the parking lot in front of Albert's Pawn Shop and slid out of the car.

I wandered around the shop. Albert had TV's, CD players, VCR's, boom boxes, and computers. The prices were high considering the stuff was used. I would do better going to Wal-Mart, but Albert might be a little more amenable if I bought something.

I carried the little 12-inch TV up to the counter relieved that my arms didn't protest the abuse too much. The bruises were fading and the stitches were scheduled to come out tomorrow. God willing, I'll be working tomorrow night.

Well anyway, I set the TV on the counter before shifting over to look at the jewelry. The pendant was still there.

It's my mother's. I'm almost positive.

"Can I help you little lady? How about some genuine fake emerald earrings? They're a pretty green, just like your eyes." The man behind the counter gave me a smile. It was a 'trust me' smile. The kind you would expect from the devil posing as an elevator operator.

I suppressed the shiver and tapped on the glass display case above the pendant. "I would like to take a closer look at that pendant right there."

"Are you sure? It's kind of old for you. How about a locket? You can put your boyfriend's picture in it."

"No, I would like to see the pendant. It reminds me of the one my mother used to have."

"Did she lose it?" Albert unlocked the display case and slid the pendant out of its resting place."

"No, it was stolen."

Albert jerked the pendant out of my reach. "This ain't no hot goods. Don't you go bringing the cops in here. I run an honest business."

I smiled in an effort to ease his suspicions, all the while kicking myself for riling him up. "I'm sorry. I didn't mean to imply that. Mama lost her pendant over ten years ago. I saw the pendant here the other day and thought I would take another look. Daddy's taking her on a cruise for their anniversary, and I thought the pendant and the matching earrings would make a nice bon voyage gift."

"All right then." Albert handed the pendant over in a huff. "I don't have any earrings to match."

I studied the pendant closely. The silver was tarnished in places and some of the detail had worn down, but the emeralds were as brilliant as ever. I let the heavy chain run through my fingers.

Little bits of dirt flaked off in my hand.

"Hey, are you okay?" Albert reached over and plucked the pendant out of my hands.

I put both my hands on the counter top and tried to regain my equilibrium, but I wasn't having much luck. Mama's murderer must have taken the pendant off her skeleton when he dug her up earlier this spring. What kind of cold-blooded bastard would do that?

"Well, what do you think? It would make a pretty gift for your mama."

I drew in a breath and tried to gather my scattered thoughts. "Yes it would, but mama's pendant came with matching earrings. I can't give her one without the other."

"I don't have the earrings."

"What about the guy that brought it in? Do you think he still has the earrings? Maybe I could call him and see."

Albert's eyes narrowed. "Transactions are confidential."

"Do you think you could …"

"No."

"Please."

"Do you want the pendant or not?"

"Not without the earrings."

"Leave your name and number. If the guy comes in, I'll ask him about the earrings."

My heart skipped a beat. "Do you know who brought in the pendant?"

"Forget it. I'm not giving you his name."

"Fine." I paid for the little TV and carried it out to the car. I glanced back over my shoulder. Albert had already moved beyond our exchange. He was on the phone wheeling and dealing.

The facts tumbled through my mind, coming together and then separating into a discordant mess. The more I thought about it, the faster they tumbled. I pulled into the parking lot next to the Mountain and stumbled out of the Honda. I waited for the dizziness to dissipate before gathering up my purse and my fortitude.

Luke was waiting for me.

He climbed out of his Explorer and slammed the door. The excessive percussion clued me in to his mood. He was pissed at me, *again.*

Luke stopped ten feet in front of me. His hands hung loose at his side, but his stance gave him away. I wouldn't get past him until I told him what he wanted to know. "Where have you been?"

"I went to Raleigh."

"Can you verify that?"

I scowled at him. "I don't have to answer to you." I spun on my heels and headed across the parking lot. Arrogant jerk! I don't owe him any explanations. Okay, so someone was trying to kill me. I'm taking reasonable precautions. It's not even dark yet.

Damn it! I had to tell him about the pendant. I spun back around. It would be a whole lot easier to work with him if he didn't deliberately try to rile me up.

The thunder boomed. I glanced up, surprised. Where did the storm come from? The sun was setting, but the sky was clear.

I hit the ground hard.

* * *

"Annie! Answer me!"

What happened? Winded, I couldn't seem to get my addled brain to function. Why was I was sandwiched between a 180-pound detective, and the unforgiving cement.

"Annie!" Luke was swearing a blue streak. He slid off of me. I rolled over and started to sit up, still dazed. Luke shoved me back down again. "Stay down! He might shoot again."

"What?"

"Did he get you? Are you hurt?"

The world snapped back into focus. It wasn't thunder. "Oh my God! Someone was shooting at me!"

"Be quiet and keep down." Luke whispered before tugging on my arm. We eased forward coming to a stop between Luke's Explorer and an ancient Chevy pickup.

"Stay here." Luke dropped my arm and belly-crawled to the end of the pickup. He had his gun in his hand.

I turned around and crawled after Luke. Two sets of eyes were better than one. "Do you see him?" I whispered as I came up beside him.

"Get back!" Luke hissed in response. "He might try again."

"Okay." I eased back and hunkered down next to the Explorer. I offered and that's what counts.

I heard the sirens off in the distance.

"Annie, were you hit?" Luke didn't look at me, but kept scanning the parking lot and the buildings behind it, looking for the assassin.

"I'm not sure. I don't think so." Someone was *really* trying to kill me. Until now I never really bought into the idea. Well, except for Mark, but he's into sleeping pills and peanut butter.

I curled up into a little ball and rocked back and forth. Time passed in a blur. Police officers and deputies were crawling all over the place. I ignored them as they ignored me. I just sat there between the Explorer and the pickup, rocking quietly as I contemplated the mysteries of the universe. Did time really slow in a black hole? How do they know? It's not like they can fly up there and check it out. If the center of the earth is really liquid, why don't we sink?

"Annie!" I was snatched up and wrapped in a bear hug.

I relaxed into my father's embrace. I *needed* a hug. "Daddy!"

"You scared me to death!"

"I'm okay." He looked older tonight. I guess having a daughter who's jinxed can do that to a man.

"How long will it take you to pack?" Daddy's words were muffled. He was talking into my hair.

"Why?"

"I'm sending you to New York. You can stay with Uncle Guido."

I wiggled and squirmed in his arms until he eased his grip. The minute my feet touched the ground, I pulled out of his grasp. "No way! I'm not moving to New York."

"Just 'till Luke catches the bastard."

"How can he catch him when he won't even admit Mama's dead?"

"I don't give a rat's ass if they nail him for that. He shot at *you*. That's what matters. I'm not losing you! You're going to New York."

"No."

Luke grabbed my arm and started pulling me toward the Mountain. Dad trailed behind us muttering under his breath.

"Slow down!"

Luke came to an abrupt stop. "You're hurt!"

"No, just bruised, *again*."

Luke started walking again. "Sorry, but I wanted you out of the line of fire."

"She'll be safe in New York. If the bastard follows her, my Uncle Guido and his buddies will take care of him."

I ignored dad and responded to Luke's comment. "I thought it was thunder."

"The sky's clear."

"I know."

Silence descended when we stepping into the bar. My feet stumbled to a halt.

"Keep your chin up." Luke whispered as he nudged me forward.

I tried that. It doesn't work.

I ignored the stares and the comments but winced when someone punched in Bruce Springstein's *Born to Run* on the juke box. *This gun's for hire …*

I struggled with the tears as we escaped into the kitchen and headed up the stairs to the apartment. I don't know how or why, but the gossips will find a way to blame me for the shooting. That's just the way it is.

Would Luke blame me too?

Who was shooting at me? Was it Mark? That didn't seem likely. He has a collection of guns, but it's too easy to trace the bullets back to the weapon. He wouldn't risk it. Maybe Luke is right and my mother's assassin is after me. I don't know why. I'm not a threat to him. I don't even know who he is.

Okay, so maybe I shouldn't have slipped out this morning. Had I known there would be a gunman waiting for me when I got back, not even a two-for-one shoe sale at Belks would have enticed me into leaving the relative safety of dad's apartment.

I set my purse on the counter before dropping down at the table. "Ask your questions."

"What kind of trouble did you stir up in Raleigh?"

"What?"

"You stepped on someone's toes. Why else would there be a gunman waiting for you when you got back?"

I waved Luke's indignation away. "That's my luck."

"Nobody's luck is that bad."

"Hah! I was born on the Ides of March and baptized on April Fools Day. I have thirteen freckles across the bridge of my nose and fell in love with a black cat when I was ten. I had a lucky rabbit's foot once, but it end up in the fan belt on the dryer. I don't know how it got there, but Grammy almost lost the house that day. My perpetual bad luck worried her to no end. She even gave me a tourmaline pendant to ward it off. I broke out in a rash from it."

I drew in a breath and continued my diatribe. "When I bought my first car, I clipped a shamrock *and* a St Christopher's metal on the key ring. I lost my keys two days later." I glanced over at Luke. "Do I need to continue?"

"Okay, so your life gives every known deity in the universe a little comic relief. What's your point?"

"I don't have to step on toes to bring the sky down on my head. I've been jinxed since the day I was born."

"Okay, what were you doing in Raleigh?"

"I went to see a lawyer."

"Why?"

"The only lawyer here in town represents Mark."

"What time was your appointment?"

"I didn't have an appointment. I stopped by this morning, paid the retainer, and made an appointment for next week."

"What else did you do? Can you verify your whereabouts?"

"Why?"

"Rosetti's house was broken into today. He's pointing the finger at you."

"Mark's house?"

"Yes. It was ransacked. The perp was looking for something."

"It wasn't me."

"What was he looking for?"

"How should I know?"

"Annie, it was the same MO. He searched your apartment and came up empty. Now he searched the house. If he didn't find what he was looking for, he'll try here next. What did your mother leave behind?"

"Her journals."

Luke studied me through hooded eyes. "What else?"

I shrugged. "Sixty-two pairs of shoes."

"Annie! I know you're trying to protect your mother's reputation, but someone's trying to kill you. Level with me."

I leaned forward, put my elbows on the table, and buried my face in my hands. "I'm not protecting Lynette's reputation. She didn't have a reputation worth protecting."

"What did you do today besides talk to a lawyer?"

"I tracked down a lead."

"Do you have a death wish or what?" Luke responded. Profound frustration colored his voice.

I ignored the outburst. I had to get this out. "My mother was killed and then buried. Is it safe to assume she was buried fully clothed?"

"Yes, why?"

"When he dug her back up, all he would have found would have been bones, right?"

Luke's eyes narrowed. "Why?"

"When Lynette married John LeBlanc, he gave her a pendant. She loved it. Most of the time she wore it under her blouse, but she never took it off."

"What are you getting at?"

"I saw the pendant a couple of weeks ago at a pawn shop in Raleigh. I went back today for a closer look." My voice cracked. Killing my mother was bad enough. He didn't have to rob her makeshift grave while he was at it.

I raised my eyes and met Luke's gaze. "There was dirt caught in some of the links on the chain. He must have found it when he dug up her body earlier this spring. He took it, and he pawned it."

"You didn't step on his toes, you stomped on his foot! Annie, what were you thinking?"

"I want him caught."

"I understand that, but you should have told me."

"I didn't want you to get in trouble. The sheriff told you not to investigate."

"Annie …" Luke closed his eyes for a moment. I think he was starting to wish the shooter hadn't missed. "What other fuses have you lit?"

I glared at him, indignant. "I haven't lit any fuses. I'm investigating in a logical and orderly manner."

"Right."

My scowl deepened. I don't have much experience when it comes to investigating, but I've turned up some clues. That should count for something.

"What about John LeBlanc?"

"Oh, I guess you heard about that." Luke didn't respond. He just sat there staring at me with hooded eyes waiting for me to crack. I'm not a nut and I had every intention of telling him about the signatures. He doesn't have to weasel it out of me.

"Annie."

"Lynette didn't embezzle that money. The signature on the withdrawal slips wasn't Lynette's."

"Are you sure?"

"Yes. I think someone killed her and then set her up to take the blame."

"Don't make an assumption. Stick with the facts."

"But …"

The signature and the pendant are facts. They can be verified. Motive is harder to pin down."

A warm fuzzy feeling sluiced through me. Luke didn't discount my efforts. I'm a contributing member of his investigational team. "Tomorrow I'll talk to some of the employees at …"

Luke cut me off. "No!"

"Why not?"

"You *are not* investigating."

"But …"

"Your brake line was cut, your apartment broken into, and now someone tried to shoot you. If you even think about going out alone, *I'll* shoot you."

CHAPTER TWENTY-ONE

"The only thing missing is the orange jumpsuit." I was under house arrest. If I even thought about leaving the apartment without an escort, dad swore he'd chain me to the bathroom sink.

"Stop complaining and get in the truck." Dad had deliveries coming in this morning so he couldn't take me over to the clinic to get my stitches removed. Rather than let me go alone, he called Miguel.

I climbed into the truck and slammed the door. "I'm not complaining and I'm not objecting to the escort service."

Miguel grinned. "Escort service?"

I felt my face heat. "Just shut up and drive."

"Relax Annie. I'm not going to let anything happen to you."

I know that, but it's not the assassin that's bothering me this morning. For two weeks I've managed to avoid thinking about potential scarring. I couldn't put it off much longer. It shouldn't bother me. I'm alive and that's what counts. I keep telling myself that, but it's not helping. My mother was vain, and deep down, I guess I am too.

I watched Dr. Cantrell pop the stitches one-by-one. The scars were *bright* red. When she was stitching me up, she compared my arm to a 100-year-old Raggedy Ann doll. I don't see that. What I see looks more like a road map, a map with lots of roads that crisscross and loop around. It didn't take much on an imagination to add a river or two and a couple of lakes.

"Annie, they'll fade."

Why did I let Mark talk me into leaving my purse in the car? I knew better. Despondent, I listened to Dr. Cantrell's instructions before heading back out to the lobby.

Miguel stood when he spotted me. He took my hand and walked with me out into the parking lot. "Annie, a few scars doesn't change who you are. You're not that shallow."

"How do you know?"

"I knew your mother and she set the standard."

I didn't know how to respond to that. I climbed into the truck, buckled my seatbelt, and waited for Miguel to return me to prison. I didn't want to go back. My rug was almost finished and I didn't have a single library book to read. I couldn't even look forward to breaking the monotony with work. I was banned from the Mountain during working hours.

Miguel slid behind the wheel but didn't start the truck. "Do you want to go back?"

"No, but if I'm not back within the hour, dad will call in the National Guard. The shooting sort of wigged him out."

"You scared him Annie. You scared all of us."

"Why is he trying to kill me?"

"I don't know, babe. Maybe the answers are in the journals."

"Maybe, but I have my doubts. I think …" My words trailed off when I saw Amy exiting Dr. Steinman's office, the town's only OB/GYN doctor. All of the doctors in town have offices in the same professional building. Dr. Steinman's office is on the same side of the building as Dr. Cantrell's.

Normally Amy's presence wouldn't catch my attention. I run into her periodically, but she ignores me and I ignore her. The confrontation at Bi-Lo was the one notable exception.

Miguel followed my line of sight. "Interesting."

We watched Amy exit the office, walk three doors down, and go into Palmetto Land Radiology.

"It doesn't prove anything. Maybe she was getting her yearly pap."

"Do you believe that?"

"No. Mark told his grandmother that there would be a little Rosetti for her to cuddle and spoil by this time next year. I thought it was wishful thinking on his part. I guess I was wrong."

"Is he still trying to talk you into coming back?"

"Yes."

"I wonder if Harry knows Amy is pregnant." Miguel contemplated quietly.

"I doubt it. When Harry finds out, he'll kill Mark."

Miguel shook his head. "No he won't. What Amy wants, Amy gets, and Amy wants Mark."

"Mark can't marry her. He's still married to me."

Miguel started the truck and shifted into gear. "Forget it for now. We have more pressing issues to deal with."

"What?"

"We need to go through the journals."

"Don't you have work to do?"

"I set my own hours."

I wrinkled my nose at him.

"So, does Mark know you're seeing a lawyer next Thursday?"

"How do you know?"

"I found your name in Winston, Martin, and Goldstein's scheduling program."

"That's an invasion of privacy."

Miguel shrugged.

"What other interesting little tidbit did you stumble across while you were tiptoeing through cyberspace?"

"I don't tiptoe. I waltz in, get what I need, and slip out again. If I don't want them to know I've been there, they don't. That's why I get paid the big bucks."

I shifted in my seat turning toward him. "Can you access Mark's bank accounts?"

"Why? Are you planning on hosing him in the divorce?"

"Don't be ridiculous. Mark and I were only married for two years."

"That didn't stop your mother."

"Miguel!"

"I know. You're not your mother. So why do you want a look at Mark's finances?"

"I'm looking for a motive."

"For what?"

"Murder."

"Annie …"

"Will you shut up and listen to me for a change." I gave him a detailed rendition of the altercation alongside the road, a play-by-play of the incident on Sunday, and repeated my conversation with Jay. Miguel was frowning by the time my words wound down, but he didn't say anything.

"Mark wants to kill me and until I figure out why, no one's going to believe me. Luke thinks Mark's abusive, but he doesn't see it as any more than that. Doug and Tabby are both convinced I'm suicidal."

"You're not suicidal. You're a fighter. It's not in your nature to give up."

"What about Mark?"

"Mark didn't cut your brake line, and I don't think he was the shooter."

"Mark doesn't want to kill me outright. He wants me to die in an accident. The night of his grandmother's party, Mark talked me into leaving my purse in the car, he ordered the dessert, and he shoved the spoonful of peanuts into my mouth. He knew I would go into anaphylactic shock, and without my EpiPens there wasn't a damn thing I could do about it."

"If it was intentional, he planned it well. You can't prove he knew it was peanuts and not pralines on top of the ice cream."

"What do I do now?"

"As long as you're staying at your dad's, Mark can't get to you."

"I'm not staying there forever."

"You are for now. Call your dad and tell him you're spending the day with me."

"Why? The journals are not going to tell us who killed my mother."

"Do you have a better idea?"

"No, but I don't want to read them. They're my mother's private thoughts. They were not meant to be shared."

"Okay, then tell me what you found in the safety deposit box."

"How did you know?" I whispered. I spent a lot of sleepless nights wondering and worrying about the money found in the safety deposit box. Need and greed kept me quiet, but that didn't ease the guilt. The money wasn't mine.

"The billing's done via computer."

"I had to do it. Mark used the Mazda for collateral on another loan, and he was behind on the payments. They were getting ready to turn the paperwork over to a collection agency."

"You went looking for money."

"No, I went looking for jewelry. Lynette collected jewelry. It was her retirement fund." I closed my eyes and let the guilt wash over me. "I pawned some of the jewelry. I didn't know what else to do."

✳ ✳ ✳

We spent the afternoon reading my mother's sexual fantasies. At least I think they were fantasies. Some of the things she described didn't seem possible.

Miguel maintained a professional detachment throughout the afternoon. I tried to, but I was embarrassed on my mother's behalf. The journals were her personal thoughts, not meant to be shared. I'm assuming she would be embarrassed if she knew we were reading them, but with Lynette, one never knew.

"Do you have a key to the outside door of your dad's apartment?" I snapped back to attention as we pulled into the parking lot next to the Mountain. We read through three of the journals before calling it quits.

"Annie?"

"Yes, but it's in my jewelry box along with the rest of my spare keys. I need to let dad know I'm back anyway."

"Call him. He can let you in the back."

It was Luke, not dad that opened the back door. Security wasn't this tight at Alcatraz. Annoyed, I turned to Miguel. "Are you turning over the watch or are you coming in?"

Miguel's lips twitched. "Get inside."

I undid the seatbelt. "I'm sorry we didn't find the answers you were looking for."

"The answers are not in the journals."

I closed my eyes for a moment, praying that I would get my temper under control before I did something stupid, like strangle Miguel. "Why did we spend six hours reading through my mother's sexual fantasies if you didn't think we would find the answers?"

"I thought you would crack within an hour."

"What do you mean?" I hissed in response.

"What else did you find in the safety deposit box?"

Money.

There were two envelopes in the safety deposit box.

Oh God! How could I have been so stupid! I've been so worried about the money that I completely forgot about the other envelope. That had to be it.

"Annie?"

"What?" I asked innocently.

"Fine. When you're ready to level with me, give me a call. Until then, enjoy your father's hospitality."

"That's not funny!"

"It wasn't meant to be."

I climbed out of the truck and slammed the door behind me.

Luke stepped back and let me storm past him. "Did Manning annoy you?" I could hear the smug satisfaction in his voice. I didn't understand it, but I heard it. Were all men morons?

"Miguel doesn't annoy me anymore than you do." I turned around and glared at him. "Why are you here?"

"The Raleigh PD talked to Albert today."

My hostility evaporated. "What did he say? Did he tell them who pawned the pendant? Did they get a look at the signature? Do you think a handwriting expert can tell if the signature on the withdrawal slips and the pawn slip were written by the same person?"

"Annie! Slow down!"

"I'm sorry, but we're so close. I want him behind bars and then I'm going to spit in his eye."

"Annie!"

"Sorry." I closed my mouth, but I was hopping up and down in my excitement.

"They got the pendant and the pawn slip, but he denies calling anyone regarding the earrings."

"Who pawned the pendant?"

"Black Jack."

My shoulders drooped.

"I'm sorry, Annie."

"What about phone records?"

"Detective Kavanagh said it would be a waste of time. The only phone in Albert's name is the land line, but they saw two cell phones in Albert's office."

"Oh. So what do we do now?"

"You're going to butt out."

"But …"

"Someone's already shot at you. They may try again."

"But …"

"Trust me, Annie."

My eyes narrowed. Luke had a blank expression on his face much like that of a gambler holding a royal flush. "What?"

The blank expression shifted to innocence. Like I'm going to believe Luke's innocent. He was holding out on me and I didn't like it one bit. I kicked him in the shin. "Spill it buster!"

"Ow!" Luke stumbled back, regained his footing, and then bent down to rub his shin. His expression was thunderous. I don't know why; I'm wearing sneakers. If the assassin started shooting at me and I needed to run for cover, I wanted traction.

"You kicked me!"

"You're holding out on me!"

"This is a police matter and I've already told you more than I should."

"So?"

"So, I want you out of the line of fire."

I rolled my eyes. "I'm not in the line of fire. You make it sound like I go looking for trouble."

"You do. Maybe your dad has the right idea. New York is pretty this time of year."

I took a hasty step back.

"Your apartment's been broken into, your brake line cut, and then you were a moving target in an obstacle course. You're not safe here."

"Did he leave fingerprints at the house?" I knew better, but I wanted to deflect the conversation away from one-way tickets to New York.

Luke's scowl deepened.

"What?"

"I understand the shooting, but why did he break into your apartment? What was he looking for?" Luke eyes narrowed to those annoying little slits, the ones that tell me he's running out of patience. That's kind of scary as he doesn't have a lot of patience to start with. "Your brake line was cut before you started stirring up trouble."

I bit my lip and tried to look innocent.

"How many people are trying to kill you?"

CHAPTER TWENTY-TWO

Two.

There were two people trying to kill me. I dropped the rag and the scrub brush on the floor in front of me before dropping to my knees. I knew Mark was trying to kill me, but I couldn't prove it, and I could prove the assassin was gunning for me, but I couldn't identify him.

Grabbing the scrub brush, I started scrubbing ten years worth of wax buildup off the kitchen floor. I vacuumed, dusted, washed clothes, ironed dad's shirts, and scrubbed the bathroom. I didn't know what I would do once I finished the floor.

Sneak out.

I called Tabby, but I got her voicemail. I left a message. She'll get back to me eventually. I even tried Doug, but he said he was busy. It's just as well. He's still mad at me. So I didn't tell him I had a spare key to the apartment; he didn't ask.

I called Miguel. He asked about the safety deposit box *again*. When I refused to tell him anything, he hung up on me.

I could call Luke, but he's scaring me again. He's slipping into my daydreams again. The only way I'll get him out of my bed and my head was to call an exorcist. I looked in the yellow pages, but there wasn't one listed. I need to keep my distance until I can figure out what to do about it.

My cell phone rang. I dropped the rag and sprinted across the room. I've been in solitary confinement since Thursday night. The phone was my lifeline, unfortunately this is the first time it's come to life in two days. I flipped it open and glanced at the monitor. *Tabby to the rescue.* "Hi, Tabby."

"I got your message. What's up?"

"I'm going crazy. Come over. We can play cards or something."

"Ah …"

"What?"

"I have a date."

"You had a date Thursday night."

"It was postponed to tonight."

"Oh. Why?"

"Family emergency."

"Tabby, you're evading. Who is this guy?"

"I would rather not say."

"He's married!"

"He is not!"

"Okay, so why all the secrecy?"

"I'm not being secretive, just cautious. I really like this guy, but he's a little out of my league. I don't want to jinx it."

"Do I know him?"

"Annie!"

"Okay. Sorry, but I've been in solitary for two days and three nights. I'm starving."

"Your dad's not feeding you!"

"Oh, dad brings some food up before happy hour starts, but he's still mad at me. He grunts every now and then, but he's not *talking* to me."

Tabby chuckled. "You're a closet gossip."

It was my turn to be indignant.

"Okay. I've got a few minutes. Hmm, let me see …"

Tabby spent the next ten minutes filling me in on all the latest gossip. It was nice to know that I wasn't the only one being dissected and discussed. "Give me more."

"Okay! Okay! Let me we think … Oh, John LeBlanc was rushed to the hospital Thursday night. He had a stroke or a heart attack or both. Jack found him passed out on the floor and called 911."

"Jack? When did you start calling Johnny, Jack?"

Tabby huffed out a breath. "Annie, we're not kids anymore. How would you like it if everyone still called you Orphan Annie?"

"Your point."

"Okay then."

Tabby was prickly tonight. Usually when she starts gossiping, she spits out dirt so fast I can't take it all in. Not tonight. The mystery man must have usurped the need to gossip. That's not a good sign.

Tabby hasn't dated anyone seriously in six months. She didn't have a little itch to scratch, she was covered with hives. Mystery man better be carrying protection.

The mystery man would remain a mystery until Tabby saw fit to tell me. I don't have the right to complain. I didn't tell her about Mark for two whole weeks.

I switched the conversation back to the topic at hand. "Will Mr. LeBlanc recover?"

"I ... Oh! He's here!" Tabby said in a whispered rush. "I'll talk to you later."

"Use protection."

"Annie!"

Laughing, I hung up the phone. Glancing around the apartment, my smile dropped. Sighing heavily, I headed back to the kitchen and the half washed floor. I dropped down to my knees and finished the job.

I was back in solitary.

The floor vibrated. It reminded me of what I was missing. It was Saturday night and the band dad booked for tonight used volume to disguise the fact that they couldn't carry a tune. They always pulled in a crowd so dad usually booked them every six weeks or so.

I wanted to go downstairs, put on an apron, and go to work. Actually, work was optional. I wanted out of the apartment, period.

No go. If dad caught me sneaking out, he would shackle me and dump me on the next plane heading for New York. Even if I could get around him, I know my luck. If the gunman wasn't waiting for me, the Honda I rented from Larry would blow up in my face.

Take your dad's truck. As long as you're back by midnight, he'll never know.

Uncle Guido's wife refers to their guest room as the rose room for a reason. If there were yellow roses on the walls and all over the bedspread I wouldn't mind so much. Well, yes I would, but that's beside the point. I can't live in a room covered with pink roses. I would be stark raving mad within a week.

Sneak out.

I wish I could. Luke said to give it time, but it's been three days. Sherlock Holmes would have the case wrapped up by now.

Cinderella snuck out. She took a chance and ended up with a prince. Why should Tabby have all the fun?

I'm fresh out of glass slippers. Besides, I'm not looking for a man. I'm looking for a distraction.

Fine. Spend the rest of your life washing floors and scrubbing toilets.

Statistically speaking, I rarely win an argument with myself. I didn't want to sneak out, but if I didn't find something to occupy my mind and my time, damn the consequences, I would.

I snatched up the phone the second it rang. I didn't care who it was.

"Hello."

Click.

I glared at the phone before dropping it back in the cradle. It was dad's phone anyway. My gaze shifted to the door. I jerked my head back. I'm *not* sneaking out!

I paced back and forth.

I spotted my purse sitting on the sofa and snatched it up. I could go through my mail. That would keep me busy for five minutes or so.

And then you can sneak out.

I set the envelopes on the table and dropped down on a chair in front of them. Drawing in a deep breath, I ripped open the Belk bill. Glancing at the balance due, I cringed. I had to get out of prison and back to work soon. If my Belk card was canceled for lack of payment, someone would die.

The Visa bill was next. It wasn't any better than the Belk bill. The Discover Card wasn't so bad.

So?

So I'm in trouble. Sighing heavily, I reached for the last envelope. It was from State Farm, but I don't have any insurance through State Farm. It had to be an advertisement, a ploy to get me to switch insurance companies.

I'm not switching. Randy's always treated me square, but reading the flyer would kill another three or four minutes. I tore open the envelope.

What …

I stared at the bill dumfounded, and then started scanning the document. I reached the bottom line, figuratively, not literally. Bile rose in my throat.

I shoved away from the table and dropped my head between my knees. I was looking for a motive, but I hadn't really counted on finding one. Deep down I was still hoping I was wrong.

I wasn't. How did Mark manage to take out a $500,000 life insurance policy on me without my knowledge?

I sat up slowly. I had to call Luke. Miguel would find out eventually, but I wanted Mark in jail before then. Miguel *would* kill him.

That's not necessarily a bad thing. The police would suspect him, but they would never be able to prove it. Unfortunately, Miguel wouldn't feel the least bit guilty, so he wouldn't go to confession. I don't want him damned to hell just because I married a murdering bastard.

I snatched up the phone but set it back down again. I've been scrubbing and cleaning all day. I didn't need to look in the mirror to know I wasn't at my best. It would be better to shower and change first.

Why? You've got a jumbo pack of batteries.

My toys are back at my apartment. I jumped out of the chair and paced back and forth. What was I thinking? I'm not interested in Luke *that* way. We're friends, sort of.

Liar.

I'm not lying! Besides, if I set my sights on Luke, two weeks from now I would find out he was a cross dresser. That's how my luck goes.

Who knows? He might be cute in a mini skirt and stilettos.

I rolled my eyes, picked up the phone, and called Luke. He's not a cross dresser. He's a manly man with broad shoulders and narrow hips. If he saw me like this, maybe he would stop sending out signals.

You are lusting after him.

Maybe a little, but I'm not going to act on it. "Luke?"

"Annie, I'm in the middle of something. Can I call you back?"

"Can you come over? I need to show you something."

"Yeah, sure. I'll see you in about an hour."

I hung up and headed for the shower. Fate wouldn't give me an hour if she didn't want me to use it. I dropped my clothes in a pile on the floor and crawled into the shower.

You're making a mistake.

I'm not going to jump him.

Yeah, right!

A tingle ran across the back of my neck. I wiggled my shoulders. The tingle dissipated but resurfaced two seconds later. Scowling, I grabbed the shampoo and went to work. I know Luke is trouble. I don't need *The Sight* to see that. When it comes to men, I just don't know how to pick them. I thought Mark was to die for.

Apparently he thought so too.

I gritted my teeth. It was a philosophical statement. I didn't need a response. Stepping out of the shower, I grabbed a towel. Even if I considered dating Luke, the tingling running across my shoulders would give me pause. Nothing good ever comes of it.

I wiggled my shoulders again.

Grumbling, I wrapped a towel around me, opened the bathroom door, and froze. Mark was leaning against the wall waiting for me.

I swallowed hard. Mark had the advantage. I was wet, naked, and wrapped in a skimpy towel. Oh, the gun in his hand factored in as well.

Mark let his eyes roam over my scantily clad body and grinned. "When I married you, I knew I would have to maintain the illusion of a loving husband with a lusty appetite. It was the only part of the plan Amy had a problem with."

The blood leached from my face. "Amy?"

"She hates your guts. The thought of spitting on your grave is the only reason she agreed to the plan. If she knew how much fun I had screwing you, she would claw my eyes out."

"You told her I was sexually dysfunctional." I don't know why that pissed me off more than the fact that Mark had a gun on me, but it did.

Mark's grin widened. "I had to. I love her, but she can be a vindictive bitch. I didn't want her ire aimed at me."

"Why are you doing this? Why do you want to kill me?"

Mark shrugged, but the gun didn't waver. "You know why. I saw the bill lying on the table."

"Why risk it? The Rosetti money is legendary."

"The Rosetti money *is* a legend. At least it is now. My dear ol' dad gambled most of it away. I couldn't ask Amy to marry me until I refilled the coffers. It's a good plan. At least it was." Mark's grin turned into a scowl. "I set up a dozen accidents in the last two years, but your damned Irish luck kept getting in the way. Only you would go into anaphylactic shock with two EMS guys sitting in the booth behind you."

"You took my EpiPens!"

"I didn't take them. I just put them back in your old purse." He shrugged his shoulders. "If you had died, it would have been attributed to your carelessness."

"You cut my brake line!"

"No, I didn't. Harry did that."

"Harry?"

"He thought I was trying to win you back. I almost killed him when I found out. An accident would have been brushed off as another example of your lousy luck, but cutting the brake line was attempted murder. Between Miguel, Luke, and your father, I couldn't get near you."

I tightened my grip on the towel. I really didn't want to go to the hereafter bare ass naked. I wouldn't be able to look Saint Peter in the eye. "If you're going to kill me and make it look like suicide, you better let me get dressed."

"Nah, that's not necessary now. You're mother's murderer is gunning for you. He'll take the blame."

Do something!

What?

Drop the towel.

I tightened my grip. I didn't want to die, but I wasn't sure if I could live with myself if I followed that train of thought. I shuffled my feet nervously.

Mark glanced at my bare legs. His tongue slid out moistening his bottom lip. "I'll miss you. You're definitely Lynette O'Reilly's daughter. I couldn't keep my hands off of you."

"I'm not my mother!"

"No, you're better. One look at you and an 80-year-old man's pecker would stand at attention."

"Mark, don't."

"What? Compare you to your mother or kill you? Damn, I wish I thought to bring the handcuffs. I wouldn't mind one last ride for ol' time's sake."

"You would be leaving evidence behind."

"I've got a condom in my wallet."

I knew it!

Mark stepped back and gestured toward the living room with the gun. "Come on. Maybe we can improvise."

I stepped forward. I didn't know what else to do. My heart was beating like a timpani and panic sweat was adding a sheen to the water droplets clinging to my skin.

Sitting down on the sofa, I tucked the towel around me securely, pulled the towel off my hair, and started balling it up in my hands. *Hail Mary, Mother of God, hear my plea …* Whatever the consequences, I wasn't going down, on my back or otherwise, without a fight.

Mark fumbled with his belt buckle one handed. His face was lit with an unholy glean. "I can bind your hands with the belt."

I didn't respond. Once Mark decided on something, there was no talking him out of it. He enjoyed the bondage games. The more I fought him, the better he liked it.

Pulling his belt free of the loops, Mark's lecherous grin faltered. He was out of hands. "Stand up."

I glared up at him mutinously. If he wanted me off the sofa, he had to drop the belt or the gun.

Wrong.

With the flick of his wrist, the tip of the belt kissed my arm. "That's a warning. The next one will peel skin."

"Does Amy know you like to play rough?"

The belt snapped again. "Stand up!"

I bit my tongue to keep from screaming. My arm burned like hell's fire. I don't know what scared me more, the gun or the belt. Did I want to die fast or slow? Swallowing hard, I stood.

I nearly sagged in relief when I spotted Luke slipping through the door coming from the bar. Some prayers were answered.

"Turn around and put your hands behind your back."

I don't think so. I flung the towel clutched in my hands at Mark's face and dove for the floor as Luke shot up from his crouched position.

A gun fired.

I rolled to my feet mildly surprised that I could. I spun around prepared to fight for my life.

Terror grabbed hold of my heart and squeezed. Luke was down and his face was covered with blood. He can't die! He saved my life, twice. I haven't had a chance to return the favor!

Now would be as good a time as any.

I stepped forward intent on my mission, but my feet tangled in the towel that used to be wrapped around me. With a cry, I stumbled forward.

Mark was on his knees, but he still had the gun in his hand. He was swinging it around wildly. Hearing my voice the gun swung back toward me. "Bitch!"

Oomph!

The gun fired again.

CHAPTER TWENTY-THREE

"Come on Annie, it's just a flesh wound. Open your eyes." I recognized the voice. It was Greg Derogatis, the EMT tech that saved my life when I went into anaphylactic shock while having lunch at the Copper Kettle.

Open my eyes, why? The moment the darkness lost its grip on me, the memories flooded in. Fear, relief, and grief were all bidding for top billing. "Luke?"

"Luke's fine."

I opened my eyes and met Greg's gaze. "His face was covered with blood."

"I'm fine Annie. It's just a nose bleed." Luke moved into my line of sight.

Relief washed over me. He was talking through a wad of tissues, but he was alive. Luke didn't die protecting me. "Mark?"

"Mark's on his way to the hospital. From there he'll be fitted with an orange jumpsuit and taken to the county jail."

"Harry cut my brake line and Amy …"

Luke cut me off. "We'll straighten it out later." He reached over and tucked the towel a little more securely over my right breast before stepping back.

The gurney slid into position beside me. "Wait! I can walk."

I tried to sit up, but Greg put his hand on my shoulder holding me down. "You're going to the hospital. You're bleeding from holes you shouldn't have."

"Holes?"

"You were shot, twice."

The pain I managed to ignore up until that point forced its way into my consciousness. A dull ache radiated from my left arm and a hot white pain radiated from my left side.

I've been shot!

With a strangled cry, I slid back down into the darkness.

＊ ＊ ＊

Flesh wounds hurt like the devil even if they don't garner much sympathy. I've been shot, twice. Surely that deserves more sympathy than a broken nose. It wasn't my fault Luke tripped over the towel and hit his nose on the corner of the end table. If I hadn't thrown the towel, Mark's aim would have been dead on.

Ouch, bad choice of words.

Dr. Cantrell sewed up the gashes caused by the bullets and released me. Dad took me back to his apartment, locked the outside door and pocketed the key. He disconnected the house phone and confiscated my cell phone. That was two days ago. If Ryan Adkins, the Chief of Police didn't need a statement from me, I would still be in solitary.

The chief turned off the tape recorder and stood. "Once your statement is typed up, you'll need to swing by and sign it."

I nodded. When I came in to give my statement, I thought I would be dealing with Luke, not the chief of police *and* the sheriff. I don't know why the sheriff is here. He didn't say anything. He just sat back and listened. It was unnerving.

The chief smiled down at me. "Annie, it's over."

"What about the shooting in the parking lot? Mark has an alibi."

"Amy's fingerprints are all over Mark's 22 and it's been fired recently."

"It wasn't Amy. My mother's …"

The sheriff cut me off. "Let it go, Annie."

"My mother didn't embezzle that money. She was set up and I can prove it."

The sheriff glanced over at the chief to see how he would respond to my declaration.

The chief raised his hands, palms out. "Annie, even if I had the manpower to investigate, what good would it do? The statute of limitations has come and gone. It's too late."

"My mother was murdered!"

"Can you prove it?" The sheriff asked. It was more of a smirk than a question.

I turned my attention away from the chief and glared at the sheriff. "She was murdered and you know it. You just don't want to investigate because you're afraid the whole town will find out how many times you snuck in her back door."

"I'm out of here." The chief gathered up his tape recorder and fled.

The smirk dropped off the sheriff's face. "You start spreading lies about me and I'll have you arrested for slander."

I sat back. Apparently Luke didn't tell him about the journals. But then, how could he? He wasn't supposed to investigate.

I pushed away from the table and stood. "If you're finished with me, I would like to go home now."

The sheriff eyed me suspiciously. "Don't do anything stupid."

"Stupid? Do you think Lynette was stupid?"

"No, but she sure could stir up trouble."

I gave the sheriff a cheeky grin. "Like mother like daughter." With that, I spun on my heels, and stormed out.

* * *

"When are you moving back to your apartment?" Tabby asked before she shoved my head under the faucet to rinse the chemicals off my hair. My hair is fire engine red. I use a rinse to tone it down. That's one of *my* secrets.

My mother's secrets are hidden in the attic of a hundred-year-old building, and the man that killed her is still at large. Frowning, I sat up and let Tabby wrap a towel around my head. I wanted my mother's killer caught, but I didn't want to spill all of Lynette's dirty little secrets in the process. I didn't know what to do.

"I don't know. Amy wasn't the shooter."

"Both the chief of police and the sheriff claim she was, and Harry admitted to cutting your brake line."

I picked up a comb and headed back out to the living room, sat down, and yanked the towel off my head. The sheriff was trying to put the blame on Mark and Amy in the hopes of putting an end to my search for Lynette's killer. I'm starting to think that maybe he was the killer. In any event, he doesn't want the bastard caught. Whatever happened to justice?

Tabby pulled the comb out of my hand and started working it though my hair. "What does Luke have to say about it?"

"I don't know. I haven't seen him."

"That's probably for the best. His nose looks like an overgrown turnip and he has two black eyes. Needless to say, he's not in a very good mood."

"It's not my fault!" Well, yes it was. Luke saved my life, *again*. At least we're even on the other score. Unfortunately Luke wasn't the only one that saw me bare ass naked Saturday night. If discretion is the better part of valor, Greg Derogatis, the EMT tech, is in the wrong profession. The whole town knows I have a birthmark on my right hip now.

The comb caught in a tangle. My head snapped back when Tabby ruthlessly pulled through it. "Ow!"

"Sorry." She caught another tangle.

"Ow!" Turning, I snatched the comb out of her hand and glared at her. "What's with you?"

"Your hair's too long and too thick. Let me cut it for you."

"No. I like my hair long."

"Your mother wore her hair long with curls going every which way."

"So? What's your point?"

Tabby shrugged. "You get mad when people compare you to your mother, but you dress like her, and you wear your hair the way she did. You even use the same shade of lipstick. You're the famous Lynette O'Reilly's daughter. God help anyone that forgets that."

My jaw dropped. In all the years that Tabby and I have been friends, she never compared me to my mother. I snapped my mouth shut, slid off the sofa, and stepped away from her. "I thought we were friends."

"We are. I didn't mean it the way it sounded. I just thought …"

I turned my head away, blinking rapidly.

"Annie, please." Tabby's cell phone rang. Now if my cell phone rang while I was trying to explain to my best friend why the insults I just dished out were not insults, I would have let the call go to voice mail. Tabby didn't. She fished her phone out, glanced at the monitor, and put it to her ear as she turned away. "I can't talk right now. I'll call you right back."

"You have plans for tonight."

Tabby slid the phone back into her purse. She didn't meet my gaze. "Yes, later. Annie, I didn't mean to insult you."

Yes she did, but the words were not hers. If anyone was acting like Lynette, it was Tabby. Secret lovers and hushed phone calls were Lynette's forte. I walked over to the door and opened it for her. "I wouldn't want you to keep your mystery man waiting."

Tabby's head snapped up. The ground shifted and a ravine wider than the Grand Canyon opened between us. There was no spanning the distance.

With her shoulders back and her chin up, Tabby walked past me and out the door. She had the phone at her ear before she reached the bottom step. "Sorry about that ..."

I closed the door quietly, turned, and caught my reflection in the mirror above the buffet. I stared at the image until the fear and the grief brought me to my knees.

* * *

"Annie?" Miguel unlocked the door, stepped into the apartment, and locked the door behind him. He came into the living room stopping two feet in front of me.

Grief is a crippling emotion. It leaves you hollowed out and incapable of functioning at a normal level. It's like a virus. The doctor can give you something for it, but ultimately it just has to run its course. I wasn't ready to talk to Miguel or anyone else for that matter. "Why did you go get the key from dad? If I wanted company, I would have answered the door."

I was sitting on the floor with socks from dad's sock basket scattered around me. Washing clothes, Dad invariably ended up with mismatched socks. He threw them in a basket figuring the mates would show up in the next wash. They usually did, but by then he forgot about the socks he put in the basket the week before. If I managed to pair all of them, dad wouldn't have to buy socks for at least ten years.

Pairing socks was easier than thinking.

I glanced up at Miguel. My tongue slipped out and moistened my bottom lip. Miguel was wearing a tight black tee-shirt, jeans, and boots. How can anyone look rough and tumbled and smooth and elegant at the same time? It's not fair! How's a girl supposed to keep her libido in check around a man like that?

I swallowed hard. What's wrong with me? Two minutes ago I was sitting here daydreaming about Luke, and now I'm contemplating a tumble with Miguel.

You're a nymphomaniac, just like your mother. Go ahead and jump him. You can claim temporary insanity due to genetic predisposition.

Maybe I should have taken a biology class in high school. At least then I would understand how this genetics thing works.

I pulled my attention away from the fit of Miguel's jeans and focused on the problem at hand. It was easier to think about a murderer lurking in our fair town than my growing lust for *two* different men.

I drew in a deep breath, and released it slowly. Okay. The sheriff refuses to admit my mother was murdered. If I want the investigation to move forward, I have to push the sheriff into investigating or investigate on my own.

I don't believe for a minute that Luke's satisfied with the sheriff's decree. Amy wasn't the shooter and he knows it. Luke's handling it the only way he can. He told dad to keep me in solitary.

I glanced up at Miguel again. The shooting doesn't bother him. Well, it did, but it doesn't. He thinks the shooting was an impulse. The shooter thought I had evidence that would lead to him. I don't and now the whole town, killer included, knows it. If he lies low, he's home free.

There's only one venue of investigation left. If I wanted the killer caught, Lynette's secrets had to come to light.

"I stopped by your apartment, watered your plants, and picked up your mail."

"Thanks." I spotted a rogue black sock and snatched it up. "Just dump it on the table."

"Annie, you need to go through your mail."

"Why?" I couldn't pay my bills until I opened a checking account. I couldn't open a checking account until I had my own money. Until dad let me go back to work, I had $3.62 to my name.

"What if there's something important in there?"

I reached up and snatched the envelopes out of Miguel's hand. "Reading other people's mail is illegal."

"I know. That's why you're going to read it to me." He turned away and disappeared into the kitchen.

I glanced at the envelope on top. It was the insurance check for the Mazda. I wasn't broke anymore. Maybe going through my mail wasn't such a bad idea after all. I shuffled through the rest of the envelopes pausing over the one from Benjamin Griggs, Attorney at Law. That had to be the envelope that caught Miguel's attention. Ben is Mark's lawyer, but that doesn't mean much. He's the only lawyer in town. Anyone with a problem goes to Ben.

I pulled out the letter and started reading.

"What is it?" Miguel set the glasses of tea down on the coffee table with a thump and reached for the letter.

I shook my head clutching the letter to my chest as the tears welled up. "Johnny LeBlanc is asking the court to declare my mother dead."

"Johnny?"

"He's acting on his father's behalf." John LeBlanc's in the hospital. Tabby was right. He had a heart attack the same night the gunman came after me. He's been comatose ever since.

Miguel sighed heavily. "Annie, your mother is dead. You had to know this would happen eventually."

"What about the apartment building? It's in both our names. Miguel, it's all I've got. What if he insists on selling it?"

"The apartment building isn't an issue right now, the safety deposit box is. It's time to level with me."

I threw a balled up pair of socks at him.

"You can't hide its existence or the fact that you've been in it. Whatever was in the box belongs to John LeBlanc."

"John, not Johnny."

"Same difference. If Johnny finds out you took something of value out of the safety deposit box, he'll raise holy hell."

My lips compressed. First the sheriff refuses to admit my mother is dead and now Johnny wants to take the money and run. Well they can't have it both ways. Once my mother's killer confesses, I'll be more than happy to stand by and let the judge sign her death certificate, but not until then.

How are you going to get him to confess? You don't even know who he is.

I'll set him up and hope he takes the bait. Once I spring the trap, I'll have him.

You don't have a trap.

I'm working on it.

An idea took root. I weighed the pros and cons, scratched it, and started casting for another. Johnny's actions pissed me off, but I'm glad he did it. I needed a swift kick in the ass. I was sitting here on my duff while my mother's murderer was running around scot-free.

"Annie," I heard the warning in Miguel's voice. He knew I was up to something, but I couldn't tell him. He'd shoot a hundred holes in my plan and then call it off.

What plan?

I ignored the question and glanced up at Miguel. "What?"

Miguel's eyes narrowed. "What are you …"

His phone rang. Swearing, Miguel yanked the phone out of his pocket and disappeared into the kitchen.

I was thankful for the reprieve. I folded the letter and tucked it in between the rest of the mail, put the stack on the table, and sat down. I tried investigating on my own. It didn't work. Instead of exposing Lynette's killer, the bastard started shooting at me.

Grimacing, I rubbed my side. The shooter didn't shoot me, Mark did and it hurt like the devil. Whatever my plan, I wanted to stay out of the line of fire.

Miguel will help you.

No! Miguel would, but what if he got hurt? He doesn't even carry a gun.

Luke?

Okay, Luke has a gun, but if he starts snooping around again, the sheriff will fire him. If he loses his job, he'll have to move to find work. I would never see him again.

Miguel closed his phone and came over to the table. He put both his hands flat on the tabletop and leaned over so we were eye-to-eye. "I have to go, but this conversation is not over."

"Yeah, sure."

"Don't do anything stupid."

My eyes narrowed. I'm not stupid.

He leaned forward and touched his lips to mine. "I don't want anything to happen to you."

CHAPTER TWENTY-FOUR

Maybe I am a nymphomaniac. One minute I'm daydreaming about Luke and in a blink of an eye, Miguel has taken his place. Only one man can have the lead role in my fantasies and daydreams. I just don't know which one to choose.

Stand them up, side-by-side and compare their attributes.

I can't do that! Besides, I haven't seen Luke's attributes since he was 16, and I've never seen Miguel's.

I wasn't talking about their physical attributes.

I'm losing it.

I closed my eyes and drew in a deep breath, held it, and released it slowly. The daydreaming is just a ploy to keep my conscience from shooting holes in my plan. I know it's risky, but once I walk out that door, there's no turning back.

Is it worth it?

Yes. I don't want to spend the rest of my life looking over my shoulder. I picked up my backpack and headed down to the bar. Miguel would be back. It would be better if I was long gone by then.

"Daddy, I'm going home."

"What! Why? What's the rush?" I timed it well. A delivery truck was backed up to the back door, and dad was counting off cases of beer as they were hauled in. He didn't have time to argue with me.

"Mark's in jail. So is Amy."

"Harry made bail."

"Harry won't come near me. He acted on impulse. His daughter was pregnant with a married man's child. Harry knew that once the gossips got wind of it, they would rip Amy to shreds. She had to get married before that happened, but Amy couldn't get married until they got rid of me."

"I can't believe you're defending him!"

I rolled my eyes. Harry's not the issue. Dad knows it, and so do I.

"Get your butt back upstairs."

"I love you Daddy." I backed up a step, turned, and walked out.

* * *

I miss my Mazda, but I'm starting to like the Honda. It doesn't use much gas and it's as nondescript as they come. With my hair shoved up under my hat, I drove through town in relative obscurity. It's raining out. That helped.

I made a to-do list. I'm back to tackling one problem at a time. Choosing between Miguel and Luke didn't even make the list. That was one problem I was creating out of nothing. They both offered *friendship*. If I wasn't so frustrated, I would have seen that. Celibacy sucks. I don't know how the Virgin Mary handled it.

Well anyway, I have to deal with the envelope of newspaper clippings and pictures first. I was so worried about the money that I completely forgot its existence. *What was he looking for?* Both Luke and Miguel have asked me that question a hundred times. I thought it was the journals, I was wrong. He was looking for Lynette's Pandora's Box.

I glanced around warily before pulling the Honda to the curb two blocks over and three blocks down from Grammy's. I left my backpack in the car, flipped up the collar on my jacket, pulled my hat down low, and stepped out of the car.

Heading away from Grammy's, I walked up two blocks, circled around and came at it from the opposite direction. It probably wasn't necessary, but the rain was light and after being cooped up in dad's apartment for days, walking was liberating.

I entered the apartment building from the back and ran smack dab into my neighbor Sam.

"Good, you're here. My faucet's leaking again. The constant dripping is driving me nuts."

"I'll let Doug know."

"Say, what." Sam shouted in response.

Sam assumes that if he can't hear you, then you can't hear him. I can't imagine a leaking faucet bothering him. He would never hear it over the blare of the TV. "I'll get Doug on it."

Sam scowled in response. "You don't have to shout at me, girl."

"Sorry."

"What?"

I resisted the urge to roll my eyes and patted his arm. "I'll make sure it's fixed in the next day or two."

"The faucet can wait. My sister needs me."

"What?"

"My sister!" Sam was shouting again.

"Not *who*, what?"

"I told her, but she wouldn't listen to me. Nope, she had to put wax on the kitchen floor."

I didn't have a clue what he was talking about, but I shook my head in understanding. It would save time.

"The floor was slick as spit. She's lucky she didn't break her hip. A sprained ankle's nothing. Why I remember when …"

"Sam!"

"What!"

"I'll get to the faucet, I promise."

"I don't care about the faucet! Haven't you been listening to me?"

"Yes, but you might want to tell me again."

"I'm heading to Charlotte. I need you to look after Cooper for me."

Great, just great. Now I had to add feeding and watering the *Black Bastard from Hell* to my to-do list. I swear that cat is the devil incarnate. "Don't worry. I'll make sure he's taken care of." A ride in the dryer might settle him down.

"You know he starts tearing up the furniture when he gets lonely. Maybe you can take him over to your apartment."

Not in this lifetime.

"But Sam, if I took him to my place, he'll think you abandoned him. He'll quit eating and waste away to nothing. It will take years for him to forgive you."

"Girl, I'm 84. I don't have years."

"There has to be another way."

Sam sighed heavily. "I would ask you to stay at my place, but those cats of yours are spoiled. I don't want Cooper picking up any of their bad habits."

I bit back the retort. Palmer and Mascara are not spoiled. Well, they are, but they don't shred metal in a fit of temper. "Mascara and Palmer are still at my dad's. They can stay there until you get back."

"Are you sure you don't mind?"

"It will be inconvenient, but I'll manage." I responded soberly. It was all I could do to keep from jumping up and down and shouting halleluiah. My prayers were answered.

Sam didn't give me a chance to change my mind. "I'll be back in a couple of weeks." He handed me the key and headed for the door without a backward glance.

* * *

I was tired of getting cussed at, so I turned my phone off. I'm not an irresponsible little fool. I don't have a death wish, and I'm not an idiot. How am I supposed to get any work done if I spend the whole evening defending my actions? Jeez!

I gave the *Black Bastard from Hell*, a ball full of catnip. He's stumbling around somewhere, higher than a kite. I didn't want to deal with him any more than I wanted to deal with the phone calls. I know what I'm doing.

Maybe.

I went through Pandora's Box. A few weeks ago, Clyde McDuffy told me that if the Sheriff's Department ever figured out who killed Lynette, rather than arresting him, they should give him a metal. He did the town a favor and should be honored for it, not prosecuted. I'm starting to think maybe Clyde was right.

I made a hasty sign of the cross before slumping back on the sofa. I don't know why I held onto the hope that the money came from a legitimate source. I knew better.

Blackmail.

At least she was an equal opportunity blackmailer.

So she blackmailed the poor and the wealthy alike. I hardly consider that an attribute.

I had a list of Lynette's blackmail victims, at least the ones I could figure out, but I didn't know what to do with it. The blackmail ended with Lynette's death.

Did it?

Okay, she had a partner. There were enough notes and messages tucked in with the evidence to substantiate that. It was an uneasy partnership. Lynette called him an ass more than once.

Was he the one tearing up my apartment? Was he looking for the evidence in the hopes of resuming the blackmail?

I can't let that happen. Whatever their sins, the people my mother blackmailed have paid enough. God doesn't expect us to repent over and over again for the same sin. If we are repentant, we're forgiven. I'm willing to bet the people on Lynette's blackmail list truly regret their indiscretions. At least that's the assumption I'm working under.

I could destroy the evidence, but if it were me, I would always wonder if it would surface again. With a heavy sigh, I added stamps and envelopes to my shopping list.

I knew where the money came from, but I still didn't know who killed my mother. The assassin ended the blackmail, but he also ended a life. If he gets away with it, what's to stop him from killing again? He has to be brought to justice.

How?

I looked at the blackmail list again. The collection dates were as random as the amounts, the lowest being five dollars a week and the highest 500 dollars a month. The majority came in around 25 dollars a week. Who would risk the chair for that?

Lynette's partner is innocent. Well, he's not innocent, but he didn't murder my mother. She had the evidence tucked away and out of his reach. His free ride stopped the day Lynette disappeared.

Face it. The murderer is not on the blackmail list.

No he's not and I don't have a single clue to point me in the right direction. He's out there. Given the opportunity, Luke would figure it out. When he starts asking questions, he's relentless.

He'll lose his job.

I'm not going to let that happen. I need to twist the sheriff's arm until he agrees to let Luke investigate.

How? You're not strong enough.

I stood and stretched before crossing over to Sam's desk. Muscle? I may not have it, but I know where to get it. It's an election year. What better muscle than the voting public?

I sat down in front of Sam's ancient typewriter and fiddled with the buttons. I knew he had it. Sam has strong opinions and is not afraid to voice them. He was even on the city counsel for awhile. Since retiring, he kept his hand on the pulse of the town, and made his opinion known through letters to the editor. We could count on a scathing commentary at least once a month.

I fiddled with the buttons again, not really sure where to begin.

Are you sure you want to do this?

I don't have a choice.

Finding your mother's murderer won't bring her back.

I know that, and if our positions were reversed, Lynette would move on without a backward glance.

I'm not my mother.

Drawing in a breath, I started typing.

Dear Editor,

*When I was alive, I never bought into the idea of ghosts and spirits walking the earth. When you were **dead**, you were **dead**. Imagine my surprise when I woke up **dead**, trapped on this side of the abyss.*

*My name is Lynette O'Reilly, at least it used to be. I'm **dead** now so names don't really matter. I'm six feet under and pushing up daisies. At least my body is. I would like to move on to the next* *world, but I can't. There's a limit to how much unfinished business you're allowed to leave behind.*

I want my name cleared and my murderer caught. That's not an unreasonable request. I'm counting on the good people of this town to help me. If I don't get the help I need, I'll be forced to haunt this town through all of eternity. I really don't want to do that. I took a lot of secrets to the grave with me, and I'm afraid some of them might slip out.

I really don't care who used to stay in room number seven at the Motel 6 in Raleigh, every third Wednesday of the month. Who she was meeting was her business, not mine.

Okay, so the Shady Inn has thirteen rooms instead of twelve. No one ever rents the little room around back. Why would they? It's too easy to monitor from the K-Mart parking lot.

What went on behind closed doors is personal and private. I would like to keep it that way. Help me bury the past so I can move on.

Forever yours,

Lynette

I pulled the letter from the typewriter and scanned it. It's the best I could do. Folding the letter, I slipped it into an envelope and addressed it.

Don't do it! The letter will stir up more trouble than a cat at the Westminster Dog Show.

Whatever the consequences, I was dropping it in the mail in the morning.

* * *

I crept out of the apartment before dawn. I left food in Cooper's bowl and then tiptoed around the cat, careful not to wake him. Mark was a bear when he woke up with a hangover. Cooper wouldn't be much better.

I made good time. I was in Raleigh standing in line in front of the bank when they opened.

I handed my key to Ashley, the pert little bank teller. "I need to get into my safety deposit box."

"Come on." Ashley snatched the key out of my hand, spun on her heel, and marched into the vault. I kept my mouth shut. Ashley had a severe case of PMS. It was either that, or she was pissed because there were customers lined up all the way back to the doors.

She glanced at her watch, scribbled the time on the index card, dropped the pen, and turned to find the safety deposit box. "Sign the card."

Yes ma'am.

Ashley pulled out the box and shoved it into my arms. "Let me know when you're done." She hustled out of the vault and back to her station. "Next!"

I glanced at the signature card lying on top of the file cabinet and then back at Ashley. Last time I was here, she re-filed the card before returning to her station.

My gaze shifted back to the signature card. As my mother's courier, I was in and out of the safety deposit box at least once a month. When one signature card filled up, they started a new one.

The signature card slid off the top of the file cabinet and found its way into my pocket. Smiling grimly, I dropped the jewelry I hadn't pawned into the safety deposit box.

As far as Johnny was concerned, the envelope of money never existed. My mother would never have saved for the future. If there was money left over after paying her bills, she bought a new pair of shoes.

CHAPTER TWENTY-FIVE

My mother married and divorced a bunch of times, but I never knew when she actually filed for divorce, or how long it took. As far as I knew, she kept her lawyer on retainer and he started the paperwork the minute she said I do.

Mr. Goldstein, the lawyer I chose to handle *my* divorce seemed like a nice man, and he was willing to answer my questions.

"How long will it take?" In truth, it really doesn't matter how long it takes to obtain the divorce. Once I've changed my name back to Annie Natali, I'm keeping it.

You're going to live in sin!

No!

Are you going to donate your stilettos to charity and take a vow of chastity?

I'm keeping my shoes!

You can't have it both ways.

"That depends. If the divorce is not contested, it will take a year, maybe a little less, but if it's contested ..." Mr. Goldstein let his words trail off.

"Contested!"

"Divorce isn't always the answer. Have you considered going to a marriage counselor?"

"What!"

"The judge will be more amenable to the divorce if he knows you tried to salvage your marriage."

"Forget it. Mark tried to kill me. There isn't a marriage counselor on the face of the earth that could talk me into giving him a second chance."

"Are you sure?"

"Yes!" If I didn't know better, I would swear there wasn't a drop of Irish blood in my veins. How did I end up with the dumbest lawyer in all of North Carolina?

"Fine. I'll need a list of your husband's assets. It may take a court order to get them, but once I know his net worth, I'll know what to ask for in the settlement."

"Mr. Goldstein …"

I was hoarse by the time I left the office. I want my clothes, the rest of my shoes, my jewelry, my antique butter churn, and my books. That's it. Mr. Goldstein didn't believe me. In some respects he was like the warriors of old. If he couldn't go for the throat, there was no point in fighting. He was pouting like a baby when I left the office.

I barely slid into the seat of the Honda when my phone started ringing. I pulled it out of my purse and glanced at the monitor. I glanced around warily before answering the phone. Miguel was on the phone and he knew *exactly* when I left the building. "Where are you?"

"Two rows back from you."

I let my head drop down on the steering wheel. "Your faith in me is touching."

"I have faith in *you*. It's your mother's legacy that has me worried."

"My mother's legacy?"

"Who was she blackmailing?"

"How did you know?"

"She tried to blackmail me. It stands to reason I wasn't the only one. Hang up the phone and come back here and talk to me."

"Will you make me go back to dad's?"

"No."

"Promise?"

"Get your butt back here."

I closed the phone slowly and dropped it back in my purse before sliding back out of the car. I walked back to Miguel's truck. He's not Irish. He doesn't have *The Sight*. So how did he know I would be in Raleigh today? "Were you following me?"

He ignored my question and asked one of his own. "Where is it?"

"What?"

"The evidence. Did you get it out of the safety deposit box?"

I sighed. I know Miguel can walk and chew gum at the same time. I've seen him do it. His single minded determination is really getting on my nerves. The blackmail's an issue, but it's not the only issue. "No. I had it. I just didn't realize I had it."

"What are you going to do with it?"

"Why?"

"Answer me!"

Damn him! Miguel thinks I'm going to pick up where my mother left off. "I'm not my mother!"

"I never said you were." Miguel's demeanor switched from interrogation mode to solicitous.

"Hah! I thought you knew *me*. You know what my mother was capable of, what she did, and now you're assuming I'm just like her."

"Well what do you expect me to think? You didn't want to go through the journals, you didn't admit to getting into the safety deposit box until you were cornered, and you never admitted to having the evidence."

I grabbed the door knob and stumbled out of the truck. "See if I ever daydream about you again!"

"Annie!"

I picked up the pace. The ass-hole jerk was out of the truck and coming after me. Why did I let down my guard? I knew better. Men are toads. Okay, so some of them act like a prince every now and then, but they can't maintain the facade for long. Once a toad, always a toad.

A hand clamped down on my arm stopping my flight. I swung around and kicked him in the shin. "Let go of me!"

"No." He jerked me up against his chest and clamped his mouth down on mine. It wasn't a friendly kiss. It was the kind of kiss that has both parties looking for the closest horizontal surface. I couldn't fight him. I was too busy fighting my libido. I've dreamed of being kissed like this, but instead of making me feel loved, it was humiliating.

Miguel released my mouth and rained little kisses across my face. "Annie, I'm sorry."

I jerked my arms free of his grasp and backed up a step as I tried to regain my equilibrium.

Miguel stepped forward reaching for me again.

I took a hasty step back. "Don't touch me!"

He let his arms drop to his sides.

"I handled it wrong. I'm sorry."

"Handled?" Miguel wanted the evidence, not me. Why didn't he just tear out my heart and stomp on it?

I don't solve problems by hopping in bed with the enemy or seal a bargain with a quick fuck. I don't blackmail friends and neighbors. Well, technically Lynette didn't blackmail any friends, just neighbors, but that's not the point.

I focused on the traffic as it came to an abrupt stop on the four lane road behind us. The cars vibrated with impatience as they waited for the light to turn green. The waves of energy hung in the air above and around them. Miguel's like that, leashed energy and barely contained impatience.

I kept my gaze on the stop light rather than look at Miguel. I can deal with the impatience, but if I saw regret, anger, or even pity in his expression, I don't know what I would do, maybe kill him.

"Annie, let me help."

My gaze shifted from the stoplight to Miguel. I couldn't read his thoughts. I only have *The Sight* when I don't want it.

At least there's no pity in his eyes.

True.

I started walking across the parking lot without a word. Miguel fell in step beside me. We waited at the stoplight like polite strangers. I crossed the street and veered into a stationary store. It was the first in the row of little stores lining the street. Miguel followed without a word.

I made my way down the aisle, picking up stationary, pens, pencils, etc. as I went. I added each new find to the growing pile in Miguel's arms.

"Annie ..."

"Hush. You said you wanted to help." I tucked another box of envelopes under Miguel's chin, turned, and headed for the checkout counter.

I stopped six feet short of the cash register and waved Miguel forward. "I'm broke."

Miguel hesitated.

I raised an eyebrow.

With an imperceptible shrug, he stepped up to the counter, and dropped the bundle.

I inched back a step and glanced through the glass front door.

Miguel glanced back at me.

I smiled benignly.

When the light turned green, I started counting. I stuck a *Please Lord, let this work*, between every third number or so. Just as the light turned yellow, I sprinted out the door and across the street.

"Annie!" Luck was with me. I was across the street and half way across the parking lot before Miguel managed to get his debit card back from the lady and follow me. There were four lanes of heavy traffic between us now. I was safe.

I didn't stop to think. I'll have plenty of time to cry and rail against fate later. I crawled into the Honda and shot out of the parking lot. I drove like a madman daring a cop to pull me over. Just let him try and give me a ticket! I felt like killing someone and it didn't have to be Miguel.

The anger carried me through the afternoon. I don't know if it was the kiss or the fact that Miguel didn't trust me that angered me more.

Anger?

Okay, I'm not angry, I'm hurt. I shouldn't be. Daddy knows me better than most and he still gets me mixed up with Lynette. Maybe Tabby's right. I could dye my hair black and start dressing in fatigues. Lynette wouldn't be caught dead in fatigues.

Neither would you.

True.

I waited until it was dark before heading for home. Miguel didn't call, but that doesn't mean he won't try to pick up my trail again. I blew up a balloon, taped it to the passenger seat, and plopped a cap on top of it.

You're starting to feel guilty.

Maybe.

It was an awesome kiss.

So? My life is a fairy tale and fairy tales are rife with tragedy, betrayal, human sacrifice, and lost love. Who would want to be a part of that? I don't even want to be a part of it and it's my life.

I slowed down and signaled when I reached exit 210. I followed the signs to The Sweetwater Tavern, pulled into the parking lot, killed the engine, and just sat there. I needed work. The Mountain is the only game *in* town. The Sweetwater Tavern is ten miles out of town. There are no other businesses, not even a gas station out here, but from what I've heard, the tavern stays busy.

It was worth a shot.

"Hey there, little lady. What can I get for you? A Coke, maybe?" The bartender leaned on the bar and grinned at me.

I smiled in response to his veiled request for ID. I slid onto a barstool and opened my purse to comply. "How about an application?"

The bartender looked to be in his fifties and he had an easy smile. He was hefty, but he had some muscle under the layer of padding. That's important. There were times when Billy, my dad's bartender, was all that stood between me and an amorous customer.

His smile dropped. "You're not even old enough to drink."

I set my driver's license on the bar. "I'm 27 and I've bartended for years."

"Where?" He didn't even glance at the ID, but kept his gaze focused on me.

"The Mountain."

His eyebrows shot up. "You worked for Tony?"

I grimaced. "Sort of, but because of recent events, I've been temporarily banned from the Mountain."

The bartender glanced down at my driver's license. "So you're the famous Annie Natali."

I rolled my eyes. "Does it matter?"

"Nope." He slapped an application on the bar. "One of my girls just turned in her notice. Be here next Thursday at six. I won't need you before then."

Relief washed through me. "Thanks, I really appreciate it."

I parked the Honda behind the elementary school ten blocks from the apartment, and crept through the shadows toward home. I left the application in the car. It wouldn't take long to fill out, and I had a week to do it.

I slipped off the sidewalk and into the trees that defined the property line between Grammy's and the house next door house. I peeked around the old oak noting the fact that Miguel's truck was in his driveway. He didn't even try to pick up my tail. I should be pleased.

It added to my feeling of isolation.

With a quiet sigh, I unlocked Sam's door, flipped on the light, and sucked in a breath. The bag of stationary was sitting on top of the coffee table.

✳ ✳ ✳

The weekend was quiet. The letters with the blackmail evidence were ready to go in the mail. I wrote a short letter of apology and tucked it in with the pictures before sealing the envelopes. It was an atonement of sorts.

I know I'm not responsible for my mother's actions. It was her life and her choices that landed her in purgatory, but if a little atonement on my part will help her along the way, I'm all for it. I would rather not meet up with her there. I might say something that would land me on the escalator going down rather than up.

With that done, I had nothing to do. I made loop after loop around the living room. I had to get out of the apartment. I was wearing a path in Sam's carpet. My phone rang and I dove for it. I wanted to talk to Tabby, but I didn't know how to repair the dent in our friendship.

I need to talk to someone. I needed help straightening out my confusing thoughts and dreams. Miguel doesn't trust me and I don't trust him. I've managed to keep him out of my daydreams, but I woke up wrapped in his arms three mornings in a row. My libido has a mind of its own. I don't know how to make it behave. It would have been a whole lot easier if Miguel gave me a wet, sloppy kiss instead of a kiss to die for.

I glanced at the monitor hoping it was Tabby, but I knew in my heart it wouldn't be. She turned her back on a lifelong friend in favor of hot sweaty sex.

I hope it works out for her. It might. Now if it was me, the man of my dreams would turn out to be a modern day Romeo. Instead of a life of love, we'd get our wires crossed and both end up dead.

I hesitated before pushing the receive button. Dad was on the line and I wasn't in the mood for another lecture.

You might as well talk to him. He'll keep calling until you do.

"Hi Daddy."

"Are you ready to come home?"

"Are you ready to let me go back to work?"

"No. There's no future for you here. I want you to go back to school. You would make a fine accountant."

"You want me to be an accountant." That's a new one. The other day he suggested mortuary school.

"Okay, maybe not accounting. How about nursing? Have you considered journalism? Oh, I know. You spend hours and hours at the library. You could be a librarian."

"I can't afford to go to school."

"I'll help. There are some fine schools in Alaska."

"I'm not moving to Alaska, at least not until my mother's killer is behind bars."

"Let it go baby."

"I can't."

"Why?"

"Justice."

"Forget it. The price is too high."

I made another couple hundred loops around the living room after dad hung up. I wouldn't mind going to school, but I don't want to move to Alaska. I would have to wear boots *all* the time. What kind of a fashion statement is that?

I made another loop around the apartment. Enough! I was getting dizzy. I dumped the envelopes into a Bi-Lo bag and picked up my purse. If Fate wants to kick me in the ass again, it won't matter where I'm hiding. She'll find me.

CHAPTER TWENTY-SIX

I made it back to the apartment unscathed, but I had one close call. When I was leaving Wal-Mart, I saw Luke's Explorer coming from the other direction. He spotted me. Luckily, the median was between us and he couldn't get to me. I think there was steam coming out his ears.

I drove around in circles for an hour before heading back to the apartment building. I really, really, really didn't want to deal with Luke right now.

I set the bags of groceries on the counter and glanced around warily. Everything was in its place, but something didn't feel right. I shrugged the unease away and started putting the groceries in the refrigerator.

My cell phone rang again. It was Luke. I didn't need *The Sight* to know that. He called four times since spotting me. I didn't want to talk to him. I would turn off my phone, but I sort of promised dad I wouldn't do that.

Resigned, I closed the refrigerator and reached for my phone.

"What the hell do you think you're doing?"

"Hello to you too."

"You're supposed to be hiding, not gallivanting about town."

"I wasn't gallivanting. I went to Wal-Mart. Besides, why do I need to hide? Amy is in jail."

"Amy didn't shoot at you."

"The sheriff says she did."

"Annie, move back in with your dad."

"No. Moving in with dad would just delay the inevitable. I can't hide forever."

"Give me time."

"Time for what? The sheriff is already pissed at you. I don't want you putting your job on the line for me."

"My job is not on the line."

"Oh, so you volunteered to man the speed trap out on Highway 78 for twelve hours a day for the rest of your life."

"Who told you about that?"

"Does it matter? I'm not moving back in with dad, and if my gallivanting across town makes my mother's assassin nervous, you'd better be ready to intercept him."

"You're deliberately antagonizing him!"

"No, but I'm through with hiding."

"Okay, where are you?"

"I can't tell you."

"You said you were through with hiding."

"I am."

"Then where are you?"

"I can't tell you!"

"If you're anything like your mother, I understand why someone killed her."

I sucked in a breath.

"Tell me where you are. *Now!*"

I closed the phone and threw it aside. I'm not my mother. Lynette would disregard personal safety and pursue the killer with the tenacity of termites tackling the Empire State Building. I may be pursuing a killer, but I'm not disregarding personal safety. Besides, Lynette wouldn't bring him to justice; she would offer him a deal and seal it between the sheets.

I pulled the vegetables back out of the refrigerator, made a salad, and settled down in front of the TV to eat. I glanced around for Cooper, but didn't see him. Once he realized that I was the keeper of the catnip, he hadn't strayed too far from my side. He still hisses and spits, but at least he's trying. That's more than I can say for Luke and Miguel. Men are toads.

With a shrug, I finished my salad and dumped the bowl in the sink. A tingle slid across my shoulders. I glanced around warily. With the TV muted, the only sound to break the silence was the incessant dripping of the water from the leaky faucet.

The refrigerator kicked in. With a heart-wrenching howl, Cooper bolted out of his favorite hiding space, between the refrigerator and the wall, streaked across the room, and clawed his way up into my arms.

I wrapped my arms around him and tried to soothe him as I extracted his claws from my chest. Who would have thought *The Black Bastard from Hell* was a wimp. "Poor baby." I crooned as I carried him into the living room. "You've heard that refrigerator kick in a thousand times. Why did it scare you now?"

"That cat's a menace. Someone ought to take him out and shoot him. Put him out of his misery."

I tightened my grip on Cooper and turned around slowly. A million little clues fell into place. My mother's blackmail partner was an ASS, Andrew Samuel Scott, aka Scotty. Not picking up on that made me look like an *ass*.

I continued to pet Cooper as if I didn't have a care in the world.

"Where is it?"

"What?" I asked innocently.

Scotty looked injured, frustrated, and irritated all at the same time. "You know damn well what I'm talking about."

I let Cooper slide to the floor. He wasn't happy about it, but Scotty had a gun pointed in the general vicinity of my chest. Cooper was right in the line of fire. If Scotty shot Cooper instead of me, Sam would kill me.

I don't think Scotty will shoot me, at least not on purpose. His hands were shaking worse than a washing machine with an unbalanced load. Scotty's a bigger wimp than Cooper.

It's not working.

Okay, Scotty's a wimp but he still has a gun on me. I'm scared, *really* scared. I know what Scotty wants, but I mailed them earlier this evening. I can't break into the post office and get them back. That would be a federal crime. Caught, I would be in jail until the second coming, maybe even the third.

"How did you find me?"

Scotty shrugged. "It doesn't matter."

"Yes it does!" If Scotty could find me then maybe a Knight in Shining Armor would too.

One Knight is mad at you and the other one doesn't know where you're hiding.

A girl can always hope.

"Sam's typewriter is a dead giveaway."

"Oh."

"Enough chatter. I want the evidence."

"What makes you think I have it?"

Scotty rolled his eyes. "You wrote the letter. Besides, after Lynette left, I searched your apartment a dozen times figuring she gave it to you for safekeeping. You didn't have it, so I assumed she took it with her. She talked about moving to New York, but I thought she would wait until you finished school."

"You thought she left?"

"Scotty shrugged. "Someone broke into my house, took *my* copy of the evidence, and *my* share of the money. It had to be Lynette. Nobody else knew about it."

Scotty gestured with the shaky gun. "Lynette took the money. I'm pretty sure of that, but I know you have the other envelope and I want it."

"Why?"

It was Scotty's turn to roll his eyes. "What do you think? I want to retire before I'm 120. The blackmail business is a great part time job. The hours are flexible and the pay's good."

I inched toward the sofa. "When did you and Lynette go into business? What prompted it?"

"What difference does it make?"

"I'm curious, so shoot me."

Scotty's eyes widened.

Oops. I held my hands out in front of me. "I didn't mean that."

"Give me the envelope!"

Desperate, I grabbed the TV remote and hit the volume button. A blood curdling scream reverberated through the room. I had it on the History Channel and they were doing a docudrama on Vlad the Impaler.

A shot went wild.

I dropped to the floor.

Cooper shot out from behind me with a howl.

Scratch hiss, spit, meowww ... Cooper clawed his way up Scotty's leg and kept on going. Scotty's arms swung wildly. His scream rivaled the one on TV. He crashed into the TV and went down.

The TV cut off mid-scream.

I popped up off the floor. The sudden silence scared me more than the screaming did. Scotty was flat on his back with Cooper crouched on his chest. They were nose-to-nose.

Cooper hissed.

Scotty whimpered.

The door crashed against the wall and Miguel did a dive roll into the room. He landed on his feet, and swung around assuming a fighter's stance. He wasn't wearing armor, but he was impressive, even if he was a bit tardy.

"Annie?" Miguel kicked the gun out of Scotty's reach.

With a cry, I crossed the room and fell into his arms. "He wants the evidence."

Miguel pulled me close. "He was in cahoots with Lynette."

"Yes."

"Did he kill her?"

"No."

"Damn."

✳ ✳ ✳

Scotty was charged with breaking and entering, possession of an unregistered gun, and carrying a concealed weapon. It wasn't much, but it was the best the chief could do.

I told the chief everything. He's not happy with me. The evidence that would have put Scotty away for the next fifty years disappeared into the black void of incoming and outgoing mail.

Word got out. By the time Scotty made bail, there was a mob of angry people picketing in front of the Law Enforcement Building. Scotty slipped out the back and beat feet. The bail bondsman lost his bet on that one. He won't be back.

I picked up Mascara and Palmer and moved back into my apartment yesterday. Cooper's here. He's still hissing and spitting, but as long as I don't turn the volume up on the TV, he's trying to get along.

"Scotty didn't publish my letter."

"You're damn lucky he didn't. Scotty's not the only one that would have been gunning for you." Luke wandered around my apartment as he talked. I wasn't sure why he was here, but then I don't know why Miguel stopped by earlier either. If I didn't know better, I would think they were still trying to protect me.

That's sweet, but really not necessary.

"Drop it Luke. I told you I wouldn't yank the tiger's tail anymore. My mother's sitting on a beach perfecting her tan and drinking pina coladas with little umbrellas in them." When dad went in for his regular check up yesterday, Dr. Cantrall had to increase the dosage on his blood pressure medicine. Luke's riding a cruiser again, and spending most of his time out on Highway 78.

Miguel fried two computers trying to hack into the FBI archives in an attempt to retrieve the write up on the embezzlement investigation. My determination to get to the truth is hurting the people I care about. It's not worth it.

"I heard you had lunch with Mary Jo Mitchell yesterday."

Mary Jo worked at Carolina Savings and Loan alongside my mother, and she was one of the 25-dollar contributors to my mother's retirement fund. "So? I've known Mary Jo for years. We bumped into each other and decided to have lunch."

Luke turned around and studied me. The sheriff made a big mistake busting him back down to a beat cop. He could read people. I sent a prayer winging upward. I didn't want anyone else hurt because I was too stubborn to give up. I *officially* quit. He's off the hook.

Luke nodded. "There's a pre-summer shoe sale at Nordstrum's today. Why don't you check it out?"

"Why are you telling me about that?"

Luke shrugged. "I miss the carefree, fun loving girl that had a different pair of shoes for every occasion."

I eyed him suspiciously. "Do you have a shoe fetish?"

"No, but I love your feet." He sat down on the loveseat next to me, picked up my foot, and slid my sneaker off. He ran his thumb along the arch. "I can't see them when you wear boots and sneakers."

I sucked in a breath when he pulled off my sock and started massaging my foot. I leaned back on the arm of the love seat and closed my eyes with a sigh. If Luke wanted to massage my feet, who am I to deny him? That is, as long as he doesn't venture past the knees ...

"When are you going back to work?"

Tomorrow night.

"Dad's giving new meaning to the word stubborn. He won't let me come back to work until I agree to go to school in the fall. Yesterday he gave me some brochures advertising a school up in Maine. The day before that, he wanted to pack me off to the University of North Dakota."

"He cares about you." My other sneaker and sock hit the floor.

"I know that, but my home is here. I'm not leaving."

"Good."

"Would it bother you if I did?"

Luke dug his thumb into my arch. Lightning shot up my leg and settled low in my belly. "What do you think?"

I think I'm in trouble.

CHAPTER TWENTY-SEVEN

The man lunged to his feet. "She's not!"

His drinking buddy rocked back on his chair with a grin. "Face it man, she's seeing Joe Danielson every time you take a rig to Richmond."

I set the tray of beers on the table and smiled, all the while praying that the inevitable fight wouldn't break out until I was out of striking range. "Here you go gentlemen, one Budweiser and one Coors. Can I get you anything from the grill tonight?"

"Nah, we're good." The man gave me a quick smile, took a quick swig of beer, and then took a swing at his drinking buddy. "You lying bastard!"

I took a hasty step back. *Oh shit!*

He missed by a mile. The momentum of the swing swung him around nearly toppling him as he tripped over his own feet.

I scrambled back to the relative safety of the bar. The Sweetwater Tavern was nothing like the Mountain. Oh sure, the Mountain had its fair share of fights, but after one fight, Dad banned the participants for a month. Most contained the rage until they were out in the parking lot.

Frank, the bartender, gestured toward the table with a grin. "Don't worry about him. Clyde's too drunk to cause any permanent damage."

I picked up a book on genetics when I was in Raleigh last week. From what I've read so far, I should have brown eyes instead of green and there's a good chance that if I have children, they'll be cursed with red hair. The lack of manners, belching at the table, scratching their balls in public, and the love of a good fight, are all recessive traits, but the dominate gene is on the leg of the Y chromosome that got lost in the shuffle. Men are toads. It's genetic and there's not a damn thing we can do about it.

I dropped the tray on the bar and leaned against it giving my feet a ten-second break. "Is it always this busy?"

Frank shrugged. "We attract a different crowd than the Mountain. We get the drunks that aren't ready to admit they're drunks. They need a drink, but they don't want to be seen out drinking every night, so they come out here."

"The married men meet their girlfriends here, unhappy housewives rendezvous with their lovers, and the professionals can come out here to relax without worrying about their reputations. We're only ten miles out of town, but it's a different world. Most of what goes on here doesn't get repeated."

I eased up on a stool. "My mother used to hang out here." It was more of a statement than a question. I just knew.

Frank shrugged. "She was a classy lady."

She was a slut.

"We didn't see much of her after she married that banker."

"When did you see her last?"

"She was here the night she disappeared."

"Was she with anyone?"

"No. She was alone." Frank picked up the bar rag and swiped it across the surface in front of me. "Your break's over."

I switched to autopilot. I served the drinks, smiled, and chatted with the patrons without conscious thought. I was thinking about my mother, trying to piece together her movements that fateful night ten years ago. Who murdered her and why?

Figure out who embezzled the money and you'll have your murderer.

Sighing heavily, I made my way through the throng of tables with another tray full of beer. I know who worked for the bank at that time, but I didn't know who had access to what, and without that, I was stuck.

I picked up another loaded tray from the bar and started weaving my way through the crowd again.

The double doors swung open. A couple came through the door both dressed in black and wrapped in each other's arms.

The woman giggled. "Do they have a roulette wheel here?"

"Nope, but they have a poker game going in the back room every Saturday night." The man responded as he led the woman toward an empty table.

I pulled up short. It wasn't just another couple of patrons. It was Tabby and Johnny LeBlanc.

"Poker, as in five card draw? I thought your game of choice was black jack."

Black Jack!

The tray slid from my fingers and crashed to the floor.

Johnny swung around and froze. Our eyes met.

"Annie! Are you all right?" Tabby stepped forward.

"You!"

Johnny grabbed Tabby's arm and jerked her back to his side. An insolent grin spread across his face. "Be careful what you say Annie." The light reflected off the knife in his hand as he moved his arm up and wrapped it around Tabby.

What now Sherlock?

I don't know! *Detecting for Dummies* doesn't cover hostage negations.

"Come on Tabby, let's get out of here."

I rolled my eyes back and crumpled to the floor. I never had to fake a faint before, but I did a fair job of it.

"Annie!" Tabby broke away from Johnny and rushed toward me.

Johnny bolted for the door. I pushed up from the floor, sprinted across the room, and launched myself at him. "You bastard!"

Johnny grunted when I slammed into him, but he kept his footing as we stumbled through the door. I wrapped my legs around his waist and started pummeling him with my fists.

"Stupid bitch! Get the hell off of me!" He grabbed my legs and started prying them loose.

"You killed her!" My fist connected with his jaw. His head snapped back. Pain radiated up my arm.

"Fuck!"

"Where is she? Where did you bury her?" I dug my fingernails in and raked them across his cheek.

"Ow! Fucking bitch! You've got nothing on me." Johnny hissed as he grabbed me by my waist and threw me against the building. My head bounced once, twice ...

* * *

"Annie! Open your eyes!"

Groaning, I rolled into a fetal position holding my stomach as I coughed. "Did you get him?"

"Who?"

"Johnny." I opened my eyes and met Luke's gaze. "He killed my mother."

"I know." Luke whispered as he helped me into a sitting position.

I glanced up and saw Johnny and Tabby standing together with their arms wrapped around each other. "What ..."

Luke pulled out the handcuffs. "You have the right to remain silent ..."

"You're arresting me!" I shrieked.

"Anything you say can, and will be used against you." Luke stepped behind me, pulled my arms behind my back, and slapped the handcuffs on my wrists.

"If you cannot afford an attorney, one will be appointed for you." Luke continued to chant the Miranda rights as he pulled me to my feet.

"I had to do something." I choked quietly as the tears dribbled down my face. "He was holding a knife on Tabby."

"Hush." Luke put his hand on my head and pushed me down into the back seat of the cruiser.

* * *

"This is so wrong." I mumbled under my breath as I made another loop around the holding cell. Johnny killed my mother. So maybe I can't quite prove it, I know he did it. Make him take a polygraph test, interrogate him.

Where the hell is Luke? He dumped me in the cruiser, told the deputy to haul me in, but didn't tell him, *or me*, what the charges were. I haven't been booked and until I'm booked, bail can't be set, and until bail is set I'm stuck here.

I slept most of the night on the little cot in the corner. I think Johnny knocked some screws lose when he slammed me against the wall. Once I woke up, I commenced pacing. My head hurt and I was dizzy.

Eating was out of the question. That greasy mess they called breakfast could be construed as cruel and unusual punishment.

Think about something else.

Why am I here?

You attacked Johnny LeBlanc without provocation.

He killed my mother!

Prove it.

I can't. I made another loop around the holding cell.

Okay. In every TV show and in every book I've ever read, the suspect always has a right to make a phone call. I didn't press the issue when I was hauled in. I was in no hurry to call Daddy. He's going to plotz over this.

I have a right to a phone call, *a phone call*, as in one. I had to make it count. It took another three loops around the holding cell before I came up with a plan. I glanced at the clock behind the desk. The timing couldn't be better.

"Hey you." I beckoned to the officer sitting at the desk. It was the same rookie that had answered my 911 call when Mark staged the suicide attempt. I don't know if that's to my advantage or not. He's stuck here babysitting the holding cell rather than cruising the streets.

"What do you want?"

I gave him an innocent smile. "I would like to make a phone call."

Officer Rookie shook his head.

"I want to call my lawyer. That's my right and you know it."

He shook his head again. "You have a right to a phone call once you've been booked."

"Okay, book me."

"I can't do that."

"If you're not willing to charge me, you better let me go."

Officer Rookie paled. "I can't do that."

"Okay, let me make a phone call and I won't press the issue."

"Let me call Luke."

"Let *me* call Luke."

"Damn it lady! You're going to get me in trouble again."

"Let me call my lawyer and I'll leave your name out of the lawsuit."

"Lawsuit?" Officer Rookie squeaked. The rest of the blood leached from his face. That would be a handy trick to know for Halloween.

"The phone. Now." I held out my hand and put as much authority in my voice as I could.

Officer Rookie acquiesced. He set the phone down on the floor outside the holding cell and shoved the receiver through the bars. "Here."

I sat down on the floor Indian style, tugged on the cord so that the phone was aligned with the bars, and dialed The Curly Do. "Hi Sherri, is Tabby there?"

Officer Rookie's head shot up and his eyes narrowed.

"Hey Annie. She's up to her elbows in black dye right now. Can you call back later?"

"Can you relay a message for me?"

"Sure, no problem."

"Tell her Johnny LeBlanc murdered my mother. I have the proof and once I get out of here, I'm turning it over to the sheriff."

Sherri sucked in a breath. "Johnny LeBlanc murdered your mother!"

"Shit!" Officer Rookie dove for the phone. I jerked it into the holding cell.

"He had a gazillion gambling debts and the mob was threatening to kneecap him. He embezzled the money and framed Lynette."

"You're kidding!"

"He screwed up when he dug up the body and moved it. I know where . . ."

The phone went dead.

I set the receiver back down in the cradle and slid the phone back between the bars. "Thank you."

Officer Rookie snatched up the phone and carried it over to the desk. "What should I do? Update my resume or plan my funeral?"

I turned my back on him and walked over to the cot in the corner. With a quiet sigh, I curled up on the cot and let the weariness overtake me. It was out of my hands now.

CHAPTER TWENTY-EIGHT

"Annie, wake up."

"What?" Groaning, I sat up, shoved my hair out of my face, and stared up at Luke.

Luke took my arm and pulled me to my feet. "Let me take you home."

I glanced around the holding cell dazed, and then *poof!* The world snapped back into focus. I jerked my arm free of Luke's grasp and scowled at him. "You arrested me!"

"I locked you up, but I didn't arrest you." Luke shrugged unrepentant.

I stepped back and crossed my arms over my chest. "You might as well book me. I'm not going back to dad's."

"No need. The sheriff's booking Johnny as we speak."

"You believe me!"

"Johnny was on top of our suspect list ever since you turned up the pendant at Albert's Pawn Shop, but we didn't have enough evidence to make an arrest. We needed the body." Luke took my arm and led me out of the holding cell.

"Okay, so I figured it out, but you still don't have the body."

Luke's smile bloomed. "We do now. When you called The Curly Do and told Sherri you knew where the body was hidden ..."

"He panicked."

"Yep."

"You haven't been sitting in a cruiser out on Highway 78!"

"Nope. I've been following Johnny LeBlanc."

I pulled out of Luke's grasp again. "The sheriff's been in on the investigation right from the beginning."

Luke nodded soberly. "He knew you would figure it out eventually and once you did, you would stir up a ruckus."

"You used me."

"Yes."

"He shot at me!"

Luke's lips compressed. "We didn't think he would go after you."

We cleared the door and stepped out into the parking lot beside the Law Enforcement Building. I pulled my arm out of Luke's grasp *again*, and stepped away from him. "Was it was all an act?"

"Not all of it." He responded softly.

I shook my head, turned, and walked away.

* * *

I typed in the last of the numbers, hit save, and closed down the program on my laptop. Dad and I compromised. I'm currently enrolled in an accounting class at the community college. I haven't decided what to do about my future, but *I'm not moving to Alaska.* I'm thinking about opening a business of my own, but I haven't told dad that yet. I don't want to upset him. I haven't had time to update my CPR certification.

Last time I talked to dad, he called me a traitor. I refused to quit work at The Sweetwater Tavern and come back to the Mountain. What can I say? The tips are better.

Cooper wove around my feet before jumping up on the loveseat beside me. Sam came back from Charlotte, stayed long enough to pack up his apartment, and headed back. He felt he had to. Left to her own devices, his sister would kill herself within a month. In truth, I think it was the hot tub and the plasma TV, not concern for his sister that had Sam packing and running. As I ruined Cooper, Sam didn't feel the least bit guilty leaving him behind.

Mark's lawyer argued and got a change of venue. The trial is set for sometime this fall. I try not to think about it. Amy turned States Evidence, but she will still be doing some time.

I don't know what will happen to Harry. He's been charged with attempted murder, but sentiment is on his side. He tried to kill me, but he was trying to protect his daughter. His intent was honorable even if his actions were not. Go figure.

I heard a quiet knock on the patio door, a little click, and the slide of glass on metal. "You left the patio door unlocked again."

I shrugged totally unrepentant. "Why are you here?"

Miguel headed straight for the refrigerator. He doesn't come to see me, he comes for my tea. "Tabby called. She asked me to relay a message."

"I don't want to hear it."

"Annie, you've been best friends since kindergarten. Don't turn your back on that."

"I'm not ready to talk to her."

"What about Luke?"

"What about him?" I know. Miguel's arguing on Luke's behalf, but Miguel and I settled on friendship. Deep down I think we both knew that my mother would always come between us.

"Luke did what he had to do."

"He lied to me."

"He knew you wouldn't give up until your mother's murderer was behind bars. He opened the playing field to you. I don't think they would have nailed Johnny without your help."

The sheriff irked me more than Luke did. He knew I didn't trust him, and he used that distrust to his advantage. I thought I was better at reading people than that.

Miguel drained his glass of tea and headed for the patio door. "Lock up behind me."

The sun was setting before I moved from my spot on the loveseat. It was easier to study than to think about those last few days in March. My mother's dead. She was murdered ten years ago. When I think about it, there's more regret than grief, and then all I'm left with is the guilt. Father Nolan told me not to fret about it. That I would come to terms with my feelings eventually. I hope he's right.

Restless, I moved out to the garden and sat down on the bench. I pulled my knees up and wrapped my arms around them. The loneliness crept in. Maybe that's why Lynette kept looking for Prince Charming. She was lonely.

Prince Charming is out there.

Is he?

You don't have to kiss a room full of toad to find him, just open your eyes.

"Annie?"

My head snapped up, I spotted Luke, and struggled to suppress the smile. I didn't want him to think I was happy to see him.

You are.

Am I?

"I brought a peace offering." Luke held up a pair of lime green flip flops. They were covered with pink flowers and sparkly yellow butterflies. It was a charming gesture.

Prince Charming?

Maybe.

CPSIA information can be obtained at www.ICGtesting.com
Printed in the USA
LVOW06s1808260214

375274LV00003B/801/P

9 781596 635586